Books by *April Alisa Marquette*:

Fiction

~The Cohort Trilogy
Absolution
Progression
Iniquities

~The Cohorts, Generation Next
Improbable

~The Sea Isles Series - A Trilogy
Exodus
Affinity
TBA

Turnabout

~A Tranquility Tale
Rebuke

---------------------------- * ----------------------------

Non-Fiction

Co-Authored with Jessica Janna

~The Relinquish & Reap Series
Seedling
Sowing
Yielding
TBA

Ask for them … at your local Barnes & Noble, or Books-A-Million bookstore

Absolution

To be pronounced clear of guilt or blame;

To be pardoned …

The Cohort Trilogy

Book I

by

April Alisa Marquette

April Rain Publications

Absolution
© Copyright 2011 by April Alisa Marquette
Cover Design by April A. Marquette
Photograph: iStockphoto/mocker_bat

ISBN 978-0-9837206-0-7

Printed in the United States of America

Visit the author at www.aprilalisamarquette.net
Library of Congress Catalog Card No.: On File

Publisher's note:

The novel *Absolution* is a work of fiction – for adults, only.

My husband, my precious gift, you've given me wings

My family, you are the very best parts of me

My friends, you're priceless, each and every one

Bind up the broken hearted...comfort all that mourn,
Give unto them beauty for ashes, the oil of joy for mourning,
the garment of praise for heaviness...

Isaiah 61:1, 2, 3

Chapter 1

$\mathcal{T}$HE year? 2000-something... Beau rang the doorbell, again, because he couldn't stand around all night. Just as he turned away, she appeared. Finally!

From behind her half-open door, she hurriedly said, "Hey. Come in, before I catch cold." Backing up, she turned and on bare feet, she rushed away. She called over her shoulder as she went, "Lock that—thanks!"

Obliging, Beau snatched off his leather bike jacket. When he'd hung it on a wooden peg in the foyer, he passed living room, dining room, and kitchen. Trekking down the hallway from which Kismet Staar had disappeared, he stopped at each doorway asking, "You in there?"

"Diddley..."

Hearing his nickname, Beau pivoted to enter the candlelit, jasmine-scented bathroom. Now he knew why it had taken her so long to let him in. She'd been taking a bath. Mindful not to allow Kismet Staar's cozy heat to escape, Beau re-closed the door.

Nearly invisible in her bubble-filled tub the woman relaxed. With her eyes closed and her head on a bath pillow she spoke. "Cousin of mine, weren't you supposed to be here, an hour ago?"

"I was," Beau replied, annoyed that she wasn't ready. "But I guess you got in that tub because you started *thinking*, for me, again." Like her three bedroom ranch house on the border of Queens and Long Island was super easy to get to. He'd had to take the train, for crying out loud, and a semi-slow moving bus. Then he'd had to walk over, a few more blocks.

"Well," Kismet Staar replied, "there was that time, or two, when you didn't show."

Leaning quickly over, Beau splashed water into his first cousin's face. Funny, she no longer looked serene as she sputtered, "Hey! Quit that."

Yeah, her hair; "Look Kiss;" Beau dried his hand on a nearby towel. "Get out of there. I'm ready to go."

Well I'm not, Kismet Staar thought as she simply stared. "Diddley, you'll just have to wait." She finally stated, "Like *I* waited for you."

Beau felt his lips thin into a tight line because just some times his cousin got on his nerves. Yes, with her meditation and prayer routine, or whatever she was calling it these days.

Yeah, yeah, Beau knew it was necessary to cleanse the self of impure thoughts and toxic emotions. He was also aware that during her designated evening hour, Kismet Staar abhorred interruptions; she wouldn't even answer her telephone. However, on this particular evening she was going to have to cut all the who-do short. This Beau mused, because he was hungry, and he had something he wanted to discuss.

Therefore, he used Kismet Staar's nickname, "Kiss..." He hated that she appeared entirely too relaxed beneath that blanket of bubbles. "Get up," he ordered. "Let's be out." Loudly he clapped, "Chop-chop girl!"

Kismet Staar opened her eyes, and realized that just some times her cousin got on her nerves. He knew how important her evening time was, and yet he'd insisted that she accompany him to dinner. Then he'd had the gall to not show up on time!

Yet, to keep the peace, with a sigh, she reached for her towel; her cousin stood. Turning away, he said he'd get them both a drink.

Grateful for a few moments alone, Kismet Staar wrapped her body. She recalled, while shaking her head, that she had actually believed that her time had reverted to being her own. Well, so much for that. She snuffed out each jasmine-scented candle.

Entering the cozy Afro centric motif bedroom with its warm neutrals and dried flower arrangements, Beau placed two coasters and glasses on Kismet Staar's mahogany chest of drawers. Seating himself, he asked if he'd mentioned his new friend.

"No," his cousin replied, glad that she'd quickly pulled on her undies while the tall buff brown man had been in her kitchen. "You hung up too fast," she admitted. "I thought perhaps somebody said something, and that was why you had to go."

"Puh-lease," Beauregard DeVeaux scoffed behind a sip of white cranberry juice. He *wished* somebody on some job would approach him, ever, about being on the phone. He would verbally let that person have it, because as an actor he had to stay connected, and he wasn't about to use up his cell phone minutes if there was a landline. He'd further lambaste said person because speaking with his agent was a must, one of his top priorities, and just having somebody *look* like they wanted to say something would make him angry.

Heck, slaving away in an office building was one thing, but unlike those whose career it was, Beau would only do so until the big time beckoned. Then bye-bye per diem, and hello big bucks per movie!

"I didn't mention anything?" he asked while adjusting the comfy boudoir chair's mudcloth-covered pillow.

"Not a thing." Kismet Staar smoothed her short stylish hair. She took a quick sip of juice, dabbed on scent and viewed her just-beginning-to-brown biscuit colored, five foot four frame in her cheval mirror. Shoot! Even in the loose fitting chambray shirt, she couldn't hide the curves that caused some to refer to her as 'the healthy sista.' She had even heard others say she was built, or stacked, like a *brick house*.

With a sigh she grabbed a silk scarf and wondered, again, who told the Commodores to sing that song anyway? Didn't Lionel Richie know women preferred ethereal, feminine descriptions?

Comfortably seated in the bedroom chair, Beau eyed his cousin's cuffed black slacks and her high heeled ankle boots. It seemed she could always manage to look chic without trying; even now, in the hard to dress for period between waning winter and oncoming spring.

Beau wondered if it was the freshwater pearl lariat at her neck and the same dangling at her ears. Did those things display her style? Or was it her simple, silver, right-hand band ring? Beau mentally waved; perhaps style was just something Kismet Staar had been born with.

Forgetting style, his mind drifted back to "Those law firm folk, I remember now—" They'd wanted him to work on another batch of hearing packets. "That was why I had to go," he said, "but I wanted to tell you about my new friend. He is the shi—" Beau caught himself. "My new friend's the shi-iz-nit."

"Okay," Kismet Staar smiled, knowing that her cousin was attempting to quit it with the foul language. With her tailored black car coat and purse slung over an arm, she entered her hallway, and motioned for Beau to follow and get his jacket.

Outside, in the light of the lantern beside her front door she locked up, as she asked, "So…where'd you meet this 'friend?'"

"At the Regency Publisher's charity event," Beau announced. "He and I were checking each other out."

Oh, at the lavish party they'd attended a few weeks back. Kismet Staar remembered, because her longtime sister friend Veronica Marie Brown had invited them. Veronica, Ronni's employer had thrown the gala. "So this person works in Ronni's office?" Kismet Staar asked, hoping not, lest there be trouble.

"He freelances," Beau admitted, "but I don't think he's met Ronni."

Noting the quickly approaching night, Kismet Staar seriously doubted that. She and Ronni had worked in the over twenty-story building on Third Avenue, for different companies for nearly four years, and it seemed there wasn't a soul there that Ronni hadn't met. Kismet Staar took the short slate path through green grass. Liking that it had been mowed for the first time that year she called out, "Beau." In the driveway, she unlocked her car door. "Take it slow, okay? Just hang out with your new friend—*become* friends, first, alright?"

The man's jaw clenched, and he growled, "Don't mother me, Kiss. You know I hate it." He also hated, but he did not say, that she always seemed to think the worst. For once, why couldn't she—four years his senior—give him the benefit of the doubt? Why did she always have to think he was going to dive headfirst into a relationship, to wind up hurt? Despite the fact that that's what usually happened ...

In the old car that had been a gift from her and Beau's recently deceased grandmother, Kismet Staar backed onto her tree-lined street.

Fastening his seatbelt, Beau spoke. "Kiss, understand one thing. I did not ask you to dinner so you could lecture me."

"Gotcha," the elder cousin nodded, vowing to keep her counsel. "So tell me Diddley," she suggested too brightly, "about your new friend."

Having slipped into a blue funk, Beau didn't know if he wanted to. Heck, as he stared out into the on coming dark, he didn't know if he wanted dinner anymore either.

"Come on Diddley, what's your guy's name, where'd he go to school? Where does he live?"

Beau's lips twisted wryly as a thought struck. Since Mama wanted to know so much, he'd hit her with the big ticket. "I think 'my friend' is bi," he sardonically quipped.

Bi-sexual. Kismet Staar managed not to sigh, and she spoke because just that fast she'd forgotten her vow to keep counsel. "Diddley, in your *same sex* relationships you encounter enough hurdles. If you get involved with someone who is into males *and* females you'll only add other dimensions of worry," and drama.

Now Beau felt all-out agitated, because he'd pondered the same thing.

Thirty-one, Kismet Staar Moore tried another angle when her cousin remained silent. "Diddley, have you mentioned this to Val, or Ronni?"

"I did not," he snapped, very nearly wanting to get out of the moving car, because what did his two female roommates have to do with anything? Sure, he lived with them in Astoria, New York, in a big pre-war apartment that they referred to as The Cohort Quarters—The Quarters for short. However, he didn't tell the two women he roomed with the myriad details of his life! Shoot, if they knew this latest, they'd probably feel like their onetime college dorm mate Kismet Staar felt. Ronni and Valeria [Val-er-REE-ah] would be against him seeing a bisexual man.

"Beauregard DeVeaux," Kismet Staar called because her cousin had not answered. "Bo-regard De-Vo, what did the girls say?"

He stared out of the window. "They've said nothing, yet."

Kismet Staar chuckled, because that meant Beau had said nothing, yet, not to them. When he did though, Val would be pragmatic. She would admonish Beau to look before he leapt, but Ronni would say, Beau was crazy.

Kismet Staar parallel parked across from the intended eatery. Again, she recalled why she'd chosen to live alone in Elmont, New York. Carefully she'd selected her tidy, three-bedroom ranch with its beautiful shrubbery and two and a half baths. For her it was perfect. With a remodeled kitchen, it was picturesque and set back, among trees, on a cul-de-sac. In Queens, it was also quiet and peaceful, whereas in Beau and his roommates' abode something was always brewing.

Removing her key from the ignition, Kismet Staar sang out, "We're he-ere. You ready to eat?"

Beau kept his eyes closed, and wished he'd never suggested this fake evening out, even as he churlishly announced, "I'm no longer hungry."

"Okay." Kismet Staar laughed and pushed on her door, "but I heard your stomach growling all the way over here."

Chapter 2

IN in mid-Manhattan, Kismet Staar met her girlfriend at a gourmet eat-in deli.

"Hey, Kiss." Fast-talking Ronni Brown piped up as she seated herself across from her old college dorm mate. "Girl, your cousin is a trip— without the luggage, and I'm thinking you should have a talk with him."

Kismet Staar wondered what Beau had done now.

"He hasn't done anything, yet," the all female Ronni stated, as though she'd read the other woman's mind. "However…"

Oh Lord, Kismet Staar thought, she also hoped that whatever Ronni would tell her would not have a thing to do with the charity gala, or with the man that Beau had met there.

"Kiss," Ronni began, not beating around the bush, "Diddley met somebody at the Regency party a few weeks back, and now things aren't working out—at least not like boyfriend hoped. He's moping." Quickly Ronni, who appeared to be ever on the prowl, visibly scanned the eatery, for men. "So you know, between him and my sulky other roommate, I'm going nuckin' futs."

Kismet Staar chuckled. "Maybe Diddley's having a bad few days."

Ronni leaned forward. "This sound like a bad day to you, Kiss? Yo' cousin had a call back, that he didn't go to."

Kismet Staar's eyes widened, because that wasn't like Beau. Not when his philosophy was: one never knew where their big 'break' lurked. So something was wrong, Kismet Staar cogitated, because desperate to become a star, Beau would never just blow off a second audition.

Ronni noted her friend's creased brow. "Now," she triumphantly crowed, "ya see why I said speak with yo' cuzin; no potential boyfriend is more important than making money. Not even one as fine as Vaughn."

So that was the 'friend's' name, huh? Well so much for having told Diddley to go slow, Kismet Staar mused, because from what Ronni had just implied, it appeared her first cousin had not.

"Just talk to him," Ronni suggested, "so that he, Val, and I, can keep paying the Cohort Quarter's high rent. Oh, and another thing; tell Beau to get with a sista, one who'll blow his mind. If you know what I mean."

Kismet Staar understood, but when, she wondered, would Veronica Marie Brown understand? Beau was homosexual, plain and simple. Yes, Kismet Staar mentally admitted, both she and her mother Nell, who'd raised Beau, had prayed diligently for him, because he had been through so much, but he was what he was. So they loved him and let him be. As Beau's friend, Ronni needed to do the same.

"Brownie look," Kismet Staar began, for the umpteenth time. "You, Val, and Beau have been in that apartment for near 'bout three years. You should know, my cousin is not going to change; now about this seemingly missed audition, I will speak with him."

Ronni shrugged. "Okay."

Kismet Staar leaned forward. Purposefully, she blocked out the buzz of other patrons' conversations as she said, "Tell me something Brownie. You know this guy?"

"Who? Oh. Diddley's jump-off—Vaughn." Ronni cocked her head and her short, naturally wavy hair caught light. "I've seen him around the office. We've said hey. He was at the Gala. You saw him."

She had? Kismet Staar scrolled through her memory bank as she looked away from the mouthy spirited Ronni Brown who was also five foot four. On this day Kismet Staar didn't envy, as she often did, the fact that Ronni appeared taller because Ronni was thinner. Kismet Staar did recall though, that Ronni was a woman who got what she wanted, and intuitive, Kismet Staar knew her friend wanted the questionable Vaughn.

Kismet Staar shook her head, because why would she think such a thing? Maybe it was because Diddley [Beau] had said he thought Vaughn was bisexual.

With her eyes blurring, Kismet Staar had a vision. Seeing things was 'a gift' or so she had been told. The 'gift' of seeing visions she'd inherited from her mother. Lasting only seconds long, the visions Kismet Staar had never mentioned to her girlfriends. She'd never said that although unclear, they often came true. Therefore, while she trusted what she saw, she also experienced trepidation.

"Kiss, I know that look," Ronni announced poking around in her shrimp salad. "It means you've got questions. And I've got answers."

A nearly indiscernible nerve in Kismet Staar's jaw jumped as she decided to play along.

Noticing the slight tick, the light-skinned Ronni Brown shrugged and spoke, almost too sweetly. "Kiss, whatever you want to know I'll tell you; you won't even have to ask."

Kismet Staar hated that her old college dorm mate could read her so well, but she really did want info. For Beau's sake, she told herself. Therefore, with her jaw tightly clenched, she nodded.

Theatrically, Ronni took a deep breath.

Oh cut the drama, Kismet Staar thought as the other woman began.

"This is the condensed version, Kiss. Vaughn is tall, tan, blond, and built. He is one fine white man. He works in your and my office building, as a freelancer, and he has a ton of admirers. He's a graphic arts designer—or something, and he likes both sexes."

Ronni dusted one hand with the other. "See? Painless."

Kismet Staar looked pinched. "How do you know?"

"Know what?"

Kismet Staar remained silent, and Ronni winked, before she stated that it seemed Vaughn had had a tryst with a co-worker of hers, male. "It didn't end well. There was yelling and crying, in the office. Oh, but a little birdie told me that our Vaughn is *also* into women."

Our Vaughn? Kismet Staar watched a balding man exit the eatery, and for the umpteenth time she wondered *why*? Why would Beau get involved with somebody who wanted every body, it seemed?

Smirking because her friend's jaw was clenched, Ronni announced that 'Beau's friend' had gotten heated, next to *her* at the Gala...

Ronni Marie Brown, all butter-yellow skin, raven blue-black hair and tight fitting clothes, had been at the Regency Publishers Charity gala. Standing in a group, the center of attention, as she so loved to be, she'd seen a man, tall and tan, inch closer.

Not acknowledging the blond freelancer, Ronni had effortlessly finished her tale, to revel in the ensuing chuckles. Then in her snug-fitting, glittering, midnight blue gown with its daringly low back, Ronni extricated herself from the publisher's guests and affiliates alike. Aware that the eyes of the freelancer followed her, she cast a knowing grin, before she sashayed off, to be effervescent in a different circle...

Seated in the gourmet eatery, and having told the scaled-down version, Ronni had omitted that at the gala, she'd left the grand ballroom. Away from the lavish buffet with its meticulously carved ice sculptures, twinkling overhead lights, live band, and the clink-clink of spirit-filled glasses, Ronni had met the freelancer. In a quiet upstairs corner, they'd worked on 'graphics' of their own.

Believing Ronni and the freelancer had only made eyes at each other, Kismet Staar spoke. "Brownie, maybe the man just thought you looked fab." Curvaceous Kismet Staar sure hoped that was the case, because her cousin Beau believed the so-called freelancer had only had eyes for *him* on gala night.

A Production Division Head for Regency Publishers, Ronni waved. "I did look fabulous girl, but I know what I know; that man was fiendin' for me."

Kismet Staar frowned. "You're sure," she slowly began, "that Vaughn," Beau's Vaughn she wanted to say, "gave *you* the eye?"

"Do robins fly?" Ronni rhetorically asked. She also hugged to herself the fact that Vaughn had given her much more than 'the eye.' Leaning forward she said, "Kiss, I'm going to let you in on a little secret." Ronni revealed that at a one point during the evening, "There were fireworks, and heat, emanating from that man, so much so for me, until I felt like I was standing near Moses' burning bush."

"That's sacrilegious," Kismet Staar winced. Glancing at her watch she looked back up at her friend, and realized something. Although Ronni Brown was considered many things, she was *not* a liar. Kismet Staar sighed and knew intuitively that Ronni had screwed the man. Dang! it looked like her cousin had found himself another fine mess.

Pushing her food aside, Kismet Staar felt the need to pray. She also hoped that one day her cousin would find himself attracted to someone who would be good for him. She hoped and prayed the same thing for her sister friend whom she inconspicuously took a good look at.

She saw, and not for the first time either, that although attractive, Ronni exuded a type of hardness. Kismet Staar recognized it, but immediately recoiled from the knowledge, because she had seen Ronni's hardness before...on *whores*, and on her *aunt*, Beau's mother.

Ronni's type of rigidity implied that she'd been mistreated, that she'd led a tumultuous life. Her confrontational mask was worn to stave off further pain and disillusionment. This façade was projected to make people think she didn't care, about what they thought or said about her, when the truth was: she did care; a bit more than she let on.

Replenishing her lipstick and clicking her makeup compact shut, Ronni spoke. "Kiss, you didn't thank me thank me for answering all your 'unasked' questions."

"Girl you owed me, for picking you up last week."

Ronni eyed the remains of her salad. "Don't be a sourpuss, Kiss. Oh, and quit worr'in over your cousin because if I suspect correctly, that playa Vaughn will have forgotten Diddley in a week."

That was not what Kismet Staar wanted to hear, or was it? She really didn't know. All she knew was that she wished Beau's 'new friend' lived clean across the country. She also wished she was on her way home instead of back to work. Yet, rising, she said, "Brownie, quit batting them store-bought eyelashes and let's go."

Outside, in the spring sunshine, Kismet Staar adjusted her shades. She also recalled something said. "Brownie, you really think that man is a player?"

"I do." Ronni nodded, "but he's nothing to worry about."

Yeah right, just like her brother Clifford, a bona fide skirt-chaser was nothing to worry about, although he beat his wife, and ran women for sport.

Wow. Ronni realized she hadn't thought about Clifford Jr. in years; although he was the reason she could readily spot a Romeo...

Trying to shake thoughts of her family, Ronni told herself that Cliff Jr. was not to be blamed. He'd garnered his woman-chasing ways from their father, Big Cliff. That wild man had run the streets for as far back as Ronni could remember, freakin' and frequenting hired honies under the clandestine cloak of darkness.

As Ronni and her friend walked through hot, colorful, bustling Manhattan, she shook her head because heck if she wanted to think about her family. They weren't worth thinking about. Ronni simply wanted to forget that she and Clifford Jr. had not been allowed to have friends, parties, or sleepovers; Big Cliff had forbid it. He'd mistakenly believed if he kept his family from interacting with others, even the people at church, then his family would never get wind of *his* misdeeds.

Stopping at a corner to wait for traffic, Ronni saw her mother's face, and she furiously attempted to push the woman from mind.

Once curvaceous and beautiful, Ronni's mother Minerva had become a skinny and shapeless mouse, under the heavy hands of her husband. As a result, Ronni had counted the days until she could leave home. She'd wanted to get away from her mother's weak attempts at pretending all was fine.

Despite not wanting to, Ronni recalled more; when she'd finally left home, she'd believed she would become her own woman. Unlike Minerva who had answered to Big Cliff, Ronni had thought she would answer to no one.

As she and Kismet Staar resumed walking, Ronni tried not to recall that away at college, she'd lost her virginity, the first week. She had shed all inhibitions, just like her brother Cliff Jr. had, a few years prior. Then, she, Ronni Marie Brown, had been called wild, skanky, and a stunt. She'd wound up with sexually transmitted diseases. After her second abortion she'd received distressing news... Still Ronni chose to believe that she, like her wayward brother, had simply been making up for lost time. She chose to believe she and Cliff Jr. had only enjoyed the simple freedoms that others their age had always taken for granted.

In the sunshine, Ronni blinked back into the present. Focusing on the couple walking before her and Kismet Staar, she wanted to forget the past. Therefore, she reminded herself that she had calmed down, some, since receiving her degree from Clark-Atlanta University.

However, when her family remained on her mind, Ronni mentioned Beau, in an attempt to shove the fam out. "You know Kiss," she began, "it wouldn't hurt Diddley to become more settled..."

Kismet Staar agreed, as she thought the woman beside her could do with some of the same, herself.

Chapter 3

$\mathcal{I}$N the hallway at the Cohort Quarters, Ronni passed Beau, who muttered, "Whorelina."

Stopping, Ronni eyed him, and said she just *knew* he was not speaking to her!

Walking back to where his roommate stood, Beau shrugged. "Well, you and I *are* the only ones in this hallway..."

"Look, if you got something," Ronni spat, "bring it, or let me get back to what I was doing." Angrily she pushed past Beau, hoping he wouldn't follow her into the kitchen.

Blast! He'd followed. Not about to acknowledge his presence, Ronni pulled slinky under-things from the apartment's small washer. Turning, with laundry basket on her hip, she headed back to the bathroom. There, on padded scented hangers, she busied herself, hanging her slinkies. She also mumbled that she would throw Beau out of The Quarters if he messed with her...

As *she* comfortably lay in the living room, Valeria René shook her head, because her roommates were forever at it. And for shame because whenever they fought, Ronni always threatened Beau with the streets, just because her name was on the lease.

Yet, Valeria René ruminated, whenever *she* and Ronni quarreled, the street threat was never issued. There were a number of reasons for that, one of them being that Valeria René's room was larger than Beau's. Therefore, she paid a larger portion of the rent. Also, if she left the lovely Cohort Quarters, it would be glaringly obvious because most of the furnishings were hers.

Although she wanted to peacefully drift, Valeria René recalled that nearly three years prior she'd agreed to move in. Easily she'd fell into the role of homemaker...maybe because Ronni was usually out, and about; most likely prowling the circuit for men.

Valeria René also recalled that at the historically black college that she, Kismet Staar, and Ronni had attended, their roles had been the same.

Back then Valeria René had constantly picked up after Ronni, her dorm mate, and often Kismet Staar had asked, 'Val why do you do it?' Then, like now, Valeria René admitted she didn't mind.

Half listening to her roommates' bickering, she told herself to forget them, to simply enjoy the hazy Saturday afternoon, as back in the large black and white tiled bathroom, the pigeonholed Ronni hissed.

"Get out of here Beau!" Wasn't it obvious she was busy?

"See?" he said moments later, "if you'd kept your hands to yourself, we wouldn't be beside this tub struggling. Like you, ninety five pounds, soaking wet, could make me go anywhere."

"I weigh more than ninety-five pounds," Ronni huffed, yet struggling.

Clearly stronger, Beau nearly laughed, and knew that effortlessly he could have ended their silly fray.

Aware of it also, Ronni didn't care that her strength was no match for Beau's. Struggling, she huffed that he should get his hands off her.

"Oh, so that's how it is, now, huh?" This Beau inquired, "Because any other time you beg me to put my hands on you, any and everywhere."

Hating that it was true, the diminutive butter-yellow Ronni became stalwart in her struggle. Subsequently she felt doubly incensed when Beau only appeared amused.

Suddenly she screamed, and didn't know how she and he had tumbled over! They weren't exactly in the tub, but only because thinking quickly, Beau braced a hand against the wall. However, Ronni could feel herself slipping. So what though. This she thought as she continued to struggle because she wanted up, and her face, beet-red, said so.

"Yo, hol' up," Beau commanded and reminded her that he could remove his hand.

Knowing she would fall face-first into the porcelain tub, Ronni settled down, somewhat.

Then straightening, Beau pulled himself and his roommate up. He also told her, as she snatched her shirt from where it had creased above her breasts, that he was tired of the games. "I'm sick of wrestling with you for the attention of people who drop by here to see *me*."

Emphatically he also told Ronni, "Get your own men." Beeyotch.

Dismissing Beau, butter-yellow went back to hanging her 'unmentionables' on the shower rod. Yet well aware that her roommate had been speaking of the prior evening's incident in particular, Ronni closed her eyes. She didn't want to think about it, because truly, she hadn't meant to become excited. It just seemed to happen, whenever Beau entertained.

Unbidden, the scene mentally unfurled... The evening before, Ronni climbed the train station stairs, glad that the workweek was done. On the street, she shielded her eyes from the waning sun's rays and just thought she could make out Beau, half a block away. He stood before their building, and it appeared...he was speaking with *Vaughn*.

Like a heat-seeking missile then, on stilettoes, Ronni purposefully sidestepped furiously pedaling children whose animated squeals filled the air. Swatting a flickering firefly, she didn't even notice the neighborhood elderly.

Seated in the manicured courtyard, the aged saw all that Ronni did not. Taking in the late-spring evening, they watched passing cars, stroller moms, and dog walkers. They saw sinewy youths in the park across the street, as the youths pounded the b-ball court. There were joggers on the path, and the elderly also eyed Ronni.

Shapely and stunning, with her short glossy 'do, her bazooms jiggled, her pencil skirt clung, over legs that were bare, and on the sidewalk, her high heels clicked as she picked up the pace.

With a groan, Beau noted her rapid approach. Then he watched her dismiss him, to shamelessly flirt with Vaughn Gruskin, the man who had come to see him. Gently however, Beau attempted to inch his roommate along. He asked hadn't she things to do? Especially when she made sure Vaughn noticed she wore no bra. Disgusted, Beau felt like strangling her. He also felt like asking who went to work looking like a hooker, because he could not have known that while sitting on the train, Ronni had discreetly removed her brassiere.

Sensing that Beau was upset, but not caring, Ronni angled herself between her roommate and his guest, to invite Beau's guest up to The Quarters—where she might have the man, again. She imagined sinking her slick sheath down on his upright, rock hard cock... Mmm.

Politely however, Vaughn declined, like he really didn't know Ronni, and then she had to insist.

Beau diplomatically ended the madness. Letting Vaughn off the hook, he also rescued his roommate from the depths of near begging.

Grudgingly then, Ronni flounced up the lobby's wide marble staircase, a worn but well maintained affair, while below, Beau saw his guest off. Angrily afterward, Beau turned, to pound up the three wide flights of stairs to the shared apartment.

In the Cohort Quarters Ronni had disappeared, along with what Beau wanted to drink. Therefore, he pounded right back down.

On his way to Carlos' corner bodega, Beau became sidetracked, and wound up watching an older gent and a young hipster match wits in a game of chess. By the time it dawned on him to get his drink and go home, he felt somewhat calmer.

He noticed it was twilight, his favorite time of day. With the quiet and the cool beckoning, he crossed the street. Entering the park, he fingered the dog tags that ever dangled from the silver chain about his neck.

As he slowly strolled, Beau watched people who played after-work tennis, under bright stadium lights. Walking on, he noticed couples, in less lighted areas, giggling and demonstrating spring fever. Then a small dog trotted before a jogger, and Beau stepped aside, allow both to pass.

At the end of his walk, he crossed the street. Still fingering his dog tags, he wondered, again, how best to approach Ronni about her loathsome behavior, because this time he couldn't let it go. He had to say something; but how to do so, he wondered, without sparking a fight?

In the Cohort Quarters' bathroom, Beau shook his head, because last night Ronni had stayed holed up in her room. Therefore his and her struggle, only moments prior, proved that while park-walking the prior evening, he hadn't thought long or hard enough.

Well, so much for that, Beau mused as he bent and splashed his face. When he rose from the basin, in the mirror, his eyes locked on Ronni's, and slowly he spoke, his voice deadly low. "You and I won't ever go through yesterday again. Understand?"

Ronni knew she had been wrong, but Beau wasn't her daddy. Big Cliff was dead. Probably. Therefore, she saucily stated, "Don't nobody want your kinky lil blond boyfriend."

Beau's voice remained steady as his eyes held hers. "I'm telling you Ronni, nix the games." He turned then, about to exit the bathroom. With the mouthy little yellow woman behind him, both saw their roommate Valeria René. Blocking the doorway, *she* shook her head, before she pivoted away.

Plaintively Ronni moaned, "Shaking her head; didn't nobody ask her a thing."

Feeling sheepish as well, Beau agreed, because he nor Ronni had solicited Val's opinion.

Chapter 4

$\mathcal{T}$HE next afternoon, in the Cohort Quarters living room Valeria René Thompson lay on her purple velvet chaise longue and Beau sat across from her, on the floor. Sorting various personal documents, he placed them in specific piles.

Looking up, he eyed the purple velvet sofa that matched the chaise on which Valeria René lay. Both pieces were hers, and held an array of silk throw pillows, made by her mother, Chitra. In the manner that the older woman had been taught, while growing up in India, Chitra had intricately woven gold thread throughout each pillow.

In the Cohort Quarters living room there was also an ivory sofa that belonged to Ronni. The sheer, ivory window treatments were Valeria René's, as were all the lamps, but the big screen T.V. and the various stereo components belonged to Beau.

Sunlight streamed into The Quarters through Valeria René's sheer ivory panels and on this particular spring afternoon, the living room seemed alive, with mysticism. Perhaps, it was the way the hand-carved works of art appeared, sheathed in golden light, or maybe it was the African music that softly played in the background. Valeria René really did not know, but looking around, she suddenly remembered an expedition that she had taken, with Beau.

Together they'd traveled to India her mother's homeland. They'd visited the seaport Bombay. The two roommates and others had also sojourned to the Sudan, which in times of old had been called Nubia, in Northeast Africa. In both places she and Beau had purchased exquisite objects d'art. Made of soapstone or semi-precious jewels, some of their acquisitions they'd housed in Beau's tall brass and mirrored corner curio. Other treasures in wood or tusk that had not fit in the cabinet, they displayed on end tables, or from their very own carved pedestals.

Turning her head, Valeria René looked at Ronni's ivory sofa. Then she eyed the hardwood before it, where Beau had placed an off-white flokati wool rug. It was on this that he sat, as she mentioned last night.

"See Val, there you're wrong. Ronni and I weren't fighting over 'someone neither of us really knows' as you put it. We were at odds over the principle of the thing, and over the fact that Ronni's go no respect."

"That may be," Valeria René nodded, because she had seen her female roommate in action, a few times; "but I want to understand. Do you feel Ronni is trying to holla, at Vaughn, or could she simply be trying to work your nerves, again?"

Beau squinted and feigned interest in a document.

"Diddley..." Valeria René called; her voice soft, as always. "I know you heard me. Answer, or tell me why you two fought."

Beau looked at the feline being stretched comfortably on her chaise. With an arm thrown across her eyes, she appeared calm and poised, as usual. So very unlike him, Beau thought as he pushed up from the floor.

From the kitchen he called, "Val, do you ever want the wondering and the hoping to be over?"

"Huh?" She *wondered* had her roommate hadn't changed the subject, just that fast. She truly *hoped* not.

Beau returned popping the top on a beverage can. "Val, have you ever just wanted to be in love?"

"Oh. Yes," she replied, "and I'd like stop wondering with whom I'll be in love. I'd also like to stop hoping for the day when I'll meet him."

Beau gulped from his can. "I want that too, with the reckless abandon of a teenager thrown in. I also want the high that used to come from being so into another person, but I don't want Ronni around my person...because she doesn't know how to act."

Valeria René, an optician, languidly repositioned herself, and her wine-colored slip dress cascaded about her small frame. "Okay," she nodded, before she divulged, "I think being in love is cool, but that reckless teenaged feeling? Not for me. Probably because I'm older, and because of experiences I've had."

"Well, *I* don't see myself as too old for the zing-n-ping of love," Beau remarked while eyeing the products of Valeria René's green thumb.

"I don't see myself as too old either," she explained, "but now that I've lived, for approximately three decades, quite naturally I'm cautious about zing-n-ping's flip side."

"See Val, you think I'm on a stimuli seeking expedition, but I'm not. Like you," Beau stated, "I want to examine commitment, a together life, with somebody, but I'm not willing to settle for just anything. I want all the accoutrements."

Valeria René smiled, and noted the floor, patterned by the sun's rays. "So you're ready for monogamy, that big 'you for me' and vice-versa thing, huh?"

"I am." Beau placed his beverage can on the floor. "I just didn't quite know it, until a moment ago."

Valeria René slid her legs over the chaise. Sitting upright, with both elbows on her knees, Beau knew she was thinking.

Looking at her, he wondered. Why wasn't *she* in a relationship? She was heterosexual. It was so much easier for them. Well, maybe she didn't want a relationship. Or maybe, Beau thought, she was too picky, because little Val was definitely attractive. Lord knew she got looks everywhere she went.

Milk chocolate in color, she had long, big, fluffy, natural curls that she often tried to straighten. Her eyes were almond shaped, and some color, gray, green-flecked, or like liquid honey, it depended on her mood. She was thin, too much so for a sista, but in Hollywood, or even Bollywood, she would have been perfect, because she was top-heavy, God's gift. She even had a picture perfect doll-face, with her African-American father's snub nose, and lush lips.

So, Beau decided, it was Ms. Vee Reenay's choice not to be in a relationship. Yes, because she also possessed an incredible inner beauty that most people found magnetic.

She sighed, and Beau averted his eyes. "Penny for your thoughts."

"I was just thinking, about my family, Diddley."

"What about them?"

"Well, you know we lived in St. Albans," New York, not far from where Beau grew up. "You know my brother Horace Jr. was killed, four days before he was nineteen, and that left me, four younger sisters, and my parents, of course."

Valeria René sighed. "Diddley that was the worst time, for all of us..."

"I can only imagine," Beau said, as he wondered how Horace Jr.'s death tied into what he and she had been discussing. Yet he listened as his roommate told of how she'd had to grow up fast, to care for her younger sisters. She divulged that for two years following her brother's death, her mother existed in a semi-catatonic state.

On the third anniversary of Horace Jr.'s death however, Chitra Thompson returned from the cemetery, to slowly begin to emerge from her grief-induced cocoon.

"My mother had seen my brother," Valeria René voiced. Over the African rhythms in the background, she further stated, in a faraway voice, that Horace Jr. had visited on that chill, gray morning, "At his gravesite, Junie backed away from MaMa... Junie told my mother," Valeria René whispered, "that she had to stop calling to him, in the wee morning and in the late of night."

Beau looked up then, envisioning Horace Jr. whom he had seen in photos. He imagined the young man beseeching his mother to let him go.

Horace Jr. entreated his mother to understand, he wasn't unhappy where he was. "But," Valeria René revealed, "Junie said he sorrowed for my mother's grief; still, he announced, it had been too long."

Beau noted that his roommate almost whispered.

"Junie said he could no longer watch MaMa," not like he had, because it was time. "He had to go on, if my Ma would allow him to."

Beau was intrigued, even though he wondered why would his roommate tell him such things, and seemingly on a whim.

With a sigh, Valeria René released the reverie as softly she acknowledged, "You're probably wondering what that was all about."

Beau looked sheepish. "To listen costs me nothing."

The curly locked one smiled, because her roommate had been sweet, when he could have caused her to regret sharing one of the major events of her life. "I know the timing, and my telling, seem inappropriate, but to tie everything together," she stated, "I wanted to share. I felt that need when you mentioned the type of relationship you wanted. I realized a committed, adult relationship would involve sharing, on many levels."

"So you shared, with me," Beau remarked. He said he was both flattered and honored.

Valeria René nodded and averted her eyes. "You know Diddley...There isn't another man alive who knows as much about me as you do."

"That's because we're in a committed, adult relationship, for life."

"Albeit platonic..."

"Right. No sex, ever, baby girl."

Valeria René laughed, and it was a bell-like tinkling sound. "Isn't it great? It's the reason we're so free with each other. There's no pressure."

"No performance anxiety."

"Listen Diddley;" Valeria René twisted her hands, a sure sign that she was nervous, which made Beau feel cautious.

"Diddley, you and I want the same things out of life, but until today, I couldn't say it, not out loud."

Nearly sighing with relief because that hadn't been so bad, Beau also heard his roommate say she was sick of dating, with all its players and haters. "I just want security. You know?"

"Well I don't want anybody to take care of me," Beau put forth. "I'm a man. We handle our own business, so that's probably a woman thing."

Valeria René chuckled. "All women don't want sponsors, silly. I certainly don't, I just want to be secure in the knowledge that my man is there, that he's feeling me, and that he and I would back each other, even if it happened to be us against the world."

"Yeah, okay," Beau cogitated aloud. "I got you. And if *I* had a man, he'd be my steady somebody to go to the movies with."

"Yes, and *my* somebody and I would laugh, and mix drinks. Oh!" Excitedly Valeria René shook her hands. "I'd make my raspberry swirl cheesecake, and he'd help me eat it, and I'd lick his fingers. Then when we made love, I'd be comfortable."

"Yeeeah," Beau nodded. "There'd be no worrying or wondering where else, or with whom else, your partner's been."

"Trust would be key," the beautiful mocha brown woman added. Then she sighed, because too bad her roommate was gay, or *he* would have been perfect.

"You know Beau," Valeria René called as again she lay down and placed an arm over her eyes. "You and I want what most people want, to be loved and desired, *without drama*."

Seeing that his roommate was so wise, Beau just had to ask, "Val, tell me; how do I make the person I want, want me the same way?"

She dropped her arm to gaze at her friend. "Honestly honey, if I knew, do you think I'd be lying around here agonizing with you?"

Chapter 5

$\mathcal{R}$ONNI had haggled, and still wound up handing over the cash. Thinking about it, she knew she'd gotten gypped, because two days of borrowing Valeria René's car should not have cost so much, but oh well.

Pulling up onto the drive in front of the cabin, Ronni shut off the ignition. She hopped out of the sporty coupe, and leaned to snatch up her designer tote. Outside the car, she turned, to fetch her larger overnight bag from the trunk, and a male voice wafted to her on the mountain air.

"Yes I need help," she stated, because heck if she was going to carry both her bags while he walked alongside her empty-handed; even though he *was* tall and fine, she thought.

He appeared rugged, picture perfect, and didn't he mean business, Ronni mused. He had come out of the cabin in shorts, and nothing else.

"Be careful," she told her helper as he clicked Valeria René's trunk shut. "We can't have you hurting your back. Not when that's my job."

With a nod, the man fell into step and visually assessed Ronni. "You're kind of small aren't you, to take on such a large job?"

She became flippant. "No job's too large, but some are too small."

The man laughed and held wide the cabin door. He also confided that he had nearly believed she wouldn't show.

"And leave you stranded up here in lonesome country, with your cell phone or some other means of contacting a replacement?" Ronni humorlessly laughed, "No, big boy."

The man chuckled, and said he guessed he was in for a few surprises.

Ronni closed and latched the door, but before she could turn from it, her arms were pinioned above her head and she was kissed, roughly. She was also huskily informed that she was about to be done.

"Well quit talking," she saucily replied, "and let's get it started."

She was told to lose her clothing.

When every piece that she had been wearing fell to the floor, the mountain man's eyes wickedly gleamed. Quickly he pulled a hunting knife, and pressed the cold blade to Ronni's nude breast.

"If you're not planning on carving up dinner," she spat as painfully the reddening skin beneath the serrated edge began to tingle. "Then put that thing away, and pull out something else."

"Maybe," the mountaineer breathed and pressed the knife to Ronni's mouth, "we should have you put your *lips* on it." Without warning, he yanked her around so that her back was to him. Holding his weapon at her abdomen, he eased it downward. Scraping her skin with the blade he also said, "Why don't we see how your *other* lips like it? Open wide..."

"Look, we gonna do this, or what?" The butter-skinned woman fearlessly griped, "Because you said you had something; but all I've gotten so far is talk. Now either show me what'cha working wit' –or I walk."

"Show you? Shut up," the man growled and shoved Ronni forward. Yet gripping his knife, he pushed her head downward, toward the floor.

Bent over, Ronni still managed to produce a foil packet. Normally, she didn't like to deplete her stash. However, she figured this man might want to begin without preliminaries. So she sassily stated, "Put this condom on, or I'll do it for you."

Wryly her captor flung his gleaming plaything at a dartboard across the room.

"Bull's-eye," she unenthusiastically noted. She also asked if she should be impressed.

"Oh you will be," the man sneered and turned her so she could watch him wield what he thought of as his now-sheathed mighty proven sword.

"Look," Ronni spat, catlike and impatient, her feet planted firmly apart. "I could've stayed home if I'd wanted to chat, but I came up here, for sexation, and I don't need it in moderation. So get to work, and I want you to stroke this kitty like you mean business."

"Yo, you talk big for someone so small, but I'll oblige you," the mountain man said. "And since, as you put it, you want to be my nine to five, my work, you should know that around here little girl, overtime is mandatory."

Ronni sing-sang that he was *talking*, again.

Jerking his prey into position, he entered her from behind. Systematically he pumped her to delirium. With both hands about her neck, he near strangled her, as he barked out, "Yo, wuss my name? Call it out, like *you* mean business."

Absolution

When the mountaineer finally stood at his cabin window, a cigarette dangling between his teeth, Ronni gave him his props. Especially, she said, since she hadn't thought he had it in him.

The man smiled, because with all his happy campers it was the same. He was the mother-lovin' man.

"Yeah, I'm the man," he stated aloud, stroking his own ego while also thinking it was about time she sucked his dick.

"You could be the man," Ronni, the unrelenting taskmaster called out, unaware and lying spread-eagle, "if you'd get back to work...Vaughn."

Chapter 6

$\mathcal{I}$ still say this is a dumb idea," Ronni whined, from the front passenger seat in Kismet Staar's car. For crying out loud, it was a beautiful spring evening, a Saturday to be exact, and she should have been out, partying, *without* her family of friends.

"Yo, I'll say again: if you three were smart," butter-yellow Ronni moaned. "You'd have bought me gifts and let me be. Then none of us would be out here, trekking up to the Bronx, in the rain."

Curly-haired Valeria René narrowed her eyes as from the back seat she softly spoke, her slight lisp apparent. "Ronni, you are so ungrateful. Now I feel we *shouldn't* take you out, for your stinking birthday."

Kismet Staar agreed, because ever since the evening had been mentioned, a week ago, Ronni had given her Cohorts only grief.

"I said it was a nice *idea*," Ronni moaned. "But since *I* am the birthday girl, I should have the last say."

"Yeah, yeah," Beau interjected. "You say we should have given you our money and kept it moving."

"Right," Valeria René chuckled. "Like any of us would have done that."

"Yo, how come," Ronni whined, turning to look at her Cohorts, "none of you can see that I'm looking out for everybody? Your time could have been your own is all I'm saying."

Valeria René shook her riotous curls. "You know Ronni, with that attitude, if it weren't for Kiss, this year, you probably would've only gotten 'hello' and 'goodbye' from me."

Forgetting Ronni, the mocha-skinned woman looked over at Beau. "Diddley, you don't look too happy."

"I'm not," he snapped. He kept his eyes on the scenery passing outside the window at which he sat, behind Kismet Staar.

Feeling unfairly attacked Valeria René said, "Sorry I disturbed you."

"Oh come on Val," Beau mumbled. He knew she was working up a sulk. "I wasn't trying to hurt you." He faced the door and said he just wanted to be left alone. He groaned that it was bad enough that they were all out in the rain. "But y'all wanna pretend we're going to some glam-jam, and not one of us has coins to spare."

"I didn't deserve that," Valeria René softly retorted, still stuck on what she perceived as the wrong done her. "So Diddley, I will just leave you alone for the rest of this evening."

Beau kept his focus. "I said I wasn't being mean, Val. I just have stuff on my mind. Therefore," he called out, "I'd thank all three of you girls to be quiet—that is until we get to wherever we're going. Then maybe I'll *act* like I'm having fun." Heck, he really wanted to be out, or in, with Vaughn.

Through her rearview mirror, Kismet Staar eyed her cousin. "I told everybody where we're going. Oh, and I take offense at you saying we don't have coins to spare. *I* keeps cash, and I carry plastic. You would too, if you'd do one or two of them off-Broadway plays they keep calling you about. One of those would tide you over nicely, till you hit the big time."

"Look," Beau began, fully exasperated. "I didn't come out here with you three old hens to cluck over my personal life. What I do is my business." Heck, he could not take or cancel moneymaking ventures to hang out with Vaughn from now until...and it would be nobody's business but his. Even though doing so had been pointless and stupid, he recalled, fingering his dog tags.

In the rearview mirror his eyes met Kismet Staar's. "Would you turn up that blasted radio? Please."

Valeria René whined. "This song sucks, all these new kids sound alike."

Ronni jerked around. "Yo, you're on something, because lil' mama wore this song out."

"It sounds worn out," Valeria René quipped, "especially coming through Kismet's static-y radio."

"Yo you can walk," Kismet Staar quickly remarked, because never would she get used to her friends poking fun at her steel blue, late model sedan. It had been a gift from her grandmother. So what, it had rust stains, and a leaky windshield? Her Cohorts didn't have to guffaw themselves to tears when speaking of old Betsy, her four-wheeled baby. They didn't have to mention Betsy's snagged vinyl seats either, while admonishing the owner to get another ride. The truth was she wasn't ready, yet.

As she drove old Betsy, Kismet Staar felt just a little closer to Grandma Lacey who had only recently passed. Even though...ever since that fiasco last summer, Kismet Staar *had* been giving the new car-buying matter some real thought... Back then, Valeria René and Ronni stood beside the road,

beneath the brutal summer sun, as Kismet Staar attempted to change a tire. Well, if Kiss finished soon, butter-yellow Ronni thought, and if Kismet Staar floored it, they might make it to the Long Island wedding, only moments *after* the bride and groom said 'I do.'

Endlessly aggravated, the usually calm Valeria René eyed the expanse of Long Island Expressway that she and her Cohorts had yet to travel. Verbally she lashed out, albeit in a semi-soft voice. "Kismet Staar, what do you make? You have got to really be up there now, right? So there isn't a reason—"

"Penny-pinching Kiss," Ronni loudly cut in, to be heard over highway noises. "Makes big umpty-nine-n-change..." Ronni also announced that with Kismet Staar's up-coming promotion to Client Managing Director for Global Accounts at the I.T. Company where she worked, the curvy professional woman stood to make substantially more.

"She can afford another car, Val. Kiss is just cheap." Ronni kicked at the stilled heap, "And look at this wreck! The inside smells funny, and the tires are bald. No wonder this one just peeled apart."

"When I think about you driving, Kiss, I pray very hard for you," Valeria René sagely stated. She hoped not to offend as she also said, "Kiss, honey, you know this, but I'll say it again. Our possessions say things about us—"

"Yeah, and what has this wreck said to some of yo' clients?" Ronni jibed with folded arms.

Down on her haunches, Kismet Staar swiped at her forehead with the back of a bare arm. She also stated, sounding calmer than she felt, "Both'a you hush."

Ever itching for a brawl, Ronni became indignant. "Yo, who you telling to shut up?"

Since that was the way Ronni Brown wanted it, Kismet Staar retorted, "I'm telling you, Brownie! I'm also telling you I don't appreciate you blurting out my salary, or any of my business. And for both of your information, I don't *wanna* buy another car. End of discussion."

"You didn't *buy* this one!" Ronni screeched as several big rigs rumbled past. "Ya stole it, from your grandmother, 'fore she died!"

"She left it to me!" Kismet Staar hissed, as suddenly her eyes began to smart. "I just started driving it while she lived!" Insensitive Ronni knew it too, Kismet Staar angrily recalled, because Ronni Brown had known Grandma Lacey.

"Yeah, well, whatever Kiss. Walk into a dealership, or get on the Internet, lease something, for crying out loud."

"Why, Brownie?" Kismet Staar suddenly demanded, over the sound of speeding cars spraying pebbles. "So you can ride around in it, pretending like it's yours? Like you do with Val?"

"Kiss." Valeria René's was the voice of calm, as with a hand she shielded her eyes. "Do it for you." Then perhaps they could all be happy, since any time they went anywhere together, the ever-mothering Kismet Staar always opted to drive.

"Listen to her," Ronni continued. "Then you'll never have to crouch in the dirt again to change a tire, while wearing a beautiful, lime colored, silk halter-dress. Then *we* won't have to get in your no-air-buggy again, to sweat out the rest of the ride. That is, if you quit being lazy."

Kismet Staar's head shot up, because she just knew Ronni had not gone there. "*Lazy*? Lazy is standing idly by, while I break my back to change a tire. Lazier still was arguing about getting out in the first place—to make Betsy lighter, when you knew I had to jack her up to do all the work!"

Curly-locked Valeria René, who had initially offered to drive, attempted to diffuse the situation, but Kismet Staar pre-empted her, just as Ronni indignantly hollered.

"Kiss you're working needlessly because you won't let your money work for you!" Ronni pointed at her roommate. "Now Val? She doesn't have these problems; even though you, Big Mama, will never agree to let her drive."

Well, Val had no problems, Kismet Staar angrily mused, because Valeria René's black sports coupe was new, unlike Betsy. Val also kept the newbie serviced and squeaky-clean.

"Val's ride is a just get-in-n-go," Ronni taunted. "While yours Kiss, is a lessee-if-I-can-make-it-to-the-corner-'fore-my-shit-falls-apart, and you always gotz to drive."

Despite herself, Valeria René chuckled, and Ronni further sneered because now she had an audience, "Yeah Kiss, you drive—us mad!"

"Enough!" Kismet Staar yelled, shooting up to dust off her grimy hands. "Clamp it Brownie, because you don't even have a ride."

Valeria René laughed, "A point for Kiss."

"Yo you both clamp it," Ronni pouted. Wearing a coral cat suit, she eased around Kismet Staar's car, to carefully crawl onto the frayed front seat, the one she'd covered that morning with a blanket. She murmured to her self as the remains of the ruined tire thumped into Kismet Staar's trunk, "Dang snagged seats, even I can do better than this..."

Remembering that Saturday last July, Kismet Staar vowed to get ahead of the stinging comments before they started. Therefore on the current rainy evening she called out, "Val, say something thing about my car, or my radio, and all'a y'all will thumb your way back to Astoria."

Valeria René scoffed as Ronni, who only thought of herself, suddenly changed the subject. "So who's got my first gift?"

Valeria René chuckled. "Isn't it rude to ask for gifts?"

Beau broke his sulk to reply. "It would be courteous to wait."

"Yeah Brownie, demanding gifts is quite crass."

"Oh leave it to you Kiss," Ronni shot back in witty repartee, "to agree with your cuzin."

"Kiss!" Beau suddenly called. "Stop this thing! The light is red, and use your defogger."

"So you'll be able to see," Valeria René softly urged.

"Yeah," Ronni added, "through these steamed up windows."

"If everyone closed his or her mouth," Kismet Staar offered, "things would clear up nicely."

Despite not wanting to, Beau chuckled, because things would most likely never change. Perhaps he would always find himself in absurd situations with his Cohorts, who actually loved each other, although strange was their way of showing it.

Moments later, Kismet Staar brought old Betsy to a stop, and all became quiet.

Peering out of his foggy window, Beau contemplated aloud, "Where the devil?" because the building before them loomed massive and ugly.

"Maybe we can't really see," Valeria René whispered, her eyes darting everywhere. "You know, with the night being such a drip 'n all."

"I don't know Boo..." Beau shook his head because things appeared really bleak.

Valeria René discreetly pointed to the large, old-fashioned red and green Christmas bulbs. In the otherwise dark window of the structure she assumed they were to enter, the lights flashed.

Ronni eyed the sign furiously blowing in the wind. The writing on it was near invisible. Looking further, all she saw were more darkened buildings, and motor vehicles randomly parked. To her horror, there seemed to be no life in the surrounding area.

In the rear, Beau continued to stare, as did Valeria René, as slowly he stage-whispered. "Kismet Staar, I do *not* want to know how you know about this place."

"I don't wanna know how she knows a lot of things," Valeria René whispered back. Feeling suddenly chilled, she pulled her flyweight, tan, suede jacket close, over her sexy little leopard-print top. With an eye on her jeans and her tan suede boots, she also said, "I sure hope I don't step in, or on, something."

Wearing a black leather bike jacket, Beau laughed, and Valeria René joined him, because to them, suddenly their newfound predicament seemed pretty funny.

Unable to conceal her disappointment, Ronni girlishly whined. "This place, Kiss?" She sucked her teeth. "I thought we were going somewhere I'd be proud to say I went."

Peering out of her rain-spattered window Ronni further moaned. "Kiss, when you said we were going to the 'Boogie Down' I thought you meant someplace real, and not this Bronx back hole."

Seemingly unfazed by the reluctance of her Cohorts, Kismet Staar motioned for them to get out of old Betsy.

Ronni balked, and forlornly thought of her 'wasted' outfit. Now, there would be no man to appreciate her blue thong bodysuit, no one to notice the unobstructed view of her cleavage. Now no man would admire her from the back, as she stepped around in her stilettos and her shimmering, tight white jeans that displayed her bulbous booty.

"See? I knew I should have done my own thing." She moaned with escalating disappointment, "And on my birthday too, Kiss. You're cruel. You know I'd have *never* wanted to go here."

"How can you know anything when you haven't even set foot out yet?" Kismet Staar inquired.

"Tsss, any fool can see this looks bad," Beau quietly mocked, causing Valeria René stilted laughter. "Later for talking 'bout set foot out."

Kismet Staar turned to eye each of her Cohorts. Sincerely she asked "Don't we love down-home cooking?" Receiving only silent stares, she shrugged. "Well, this is the place."

Without another word, she got out, slammed her door, and disappeared.

Beau, Valeria René, and Ronni all sat in silence, until simultaneously Beau and Valeria René jerked on their door handles.

"I'm with Kiss," the curly-locked one announced as tall, buff, brown, beautiful Beau dashed alongside her in the rain.

"Me too," he stated. He also inquired, "But what about Ronni?"

"Oh she'll come along. You know how she hates to be alone."

"Hey, this is nice," Ronni piped, standing behind her Cohorts, who also found the inside a welcome surprise.

The neat Bronx Nook had an air of being exclusive, with two cozy dining rooms divided by a wrought-iron wall and privacy-affording greenery. There was also a snug inviting area on the lower level called the Blue Room where live jazz could be enjoyed. The upper level, above the dining area, housed The Showcase, an in-house nightclub and bar.

In each of the Bronx Nook's dining rooms there were fireplaces, and original artwork. The Cohorts noticed patrons too, who entered through the renowned eatery's front entrance. These people, some of whom were famous, were engaged in conversation and partook of sumptuous entrees.

The Cohorts noticed classic off-white dishes, as in the background, Blues diva Dinah Washington pronounced it *Time Out for Tears*.

Beau looked around, as he and the women were led to their crimson cloth-covered table. "Not bad Kiss."

Easily Valeria René agreed, but Ronni did not reply. Visually she honed in on each male that she and her party passed.

Seated, the Cohorts ordered drinks, and Valeria René remarked on the cozily lit mini chandeliers above each table.

Finished with her 'male survey' for the moment, Ronni announced her desire to open her presents before dinner.

"We didn't get you anything," Valeria René teased, accepting her Voodoo Doll, which included Vodka and Chambord.

"Yeah, bringing you here *is* our gift," Kismet Staar winked.

Not deterred Ronni sang and clapped. "Nope. Gifts, gifts, come on."

"Since you can't hear that we got you nothing, other than this, I'm thinking that maybe," Beau said with his eyes on his menu, "you really need an ear doctor certificate."

"I'm not going to stop." Ronni clapped, "Gifts, gifts, come on."

After a while, Beau raised his eyes, pretending to be fed up, "Somebody help."

"All right." Valeria René produced a beautifully wrapped box.

"Wow," Ronni gawked, snatching it from the woman who had intended to hand it over. Ronni fumbled with the wrapping, while Valeria René produced another box, and another.

Kismet Staar slapped at Ronni's hands, and Beau reached over. Ronni watched as the lid was gently lifted off the first giant parcel. The other box tops were removed as well.

"Voila!" Beau raised his cold gold.

"Oh!" Ronni's eyes were wide as she handled a designer purse. "This is to die for! But there's no card to say who it's from…"

Regardless, she was directed to look in another box containing assorted spirits, including gin, tequila and cognac. She was also told, "Don't stop there." In her final box, she found a basket, filled with bath salts and foams. There was a super-rich emollient, along with scented candles, a bath mitt, and a loofah.

The birthday girl looked around, bewildered. "This one doesn't have a card either. What gives?"

"Just say thank you, and enjoy," Valeria René advised, because why turn the fun of giving and getting into a price gauging competition? She also asked the busboy who was a man to send their server over.

When the wait staff appeared Valeria René requested a cup of hot water. "No teabag though, please." Settling comfortably, she folded her arms, self-satisfied.

Wearing a pearl choker, a starched white shirt with French cuffs, pearl cuff links, and sleek navy trousers, Kismet Staar drank whisky straight. She also asked why the water.

Valeria René shrugged, "To sterilize my silver."

"Bet you five dollars," Ronni predicted, her eyes darting to and from every man in the room, "our waiter brings a side of teabag."

"He won't."

"He will, Val," Kismet Staar nodded, "because you mentioned it."

Beau removed his leather jacket, to reveal toned abs in a crisp white tee over fashionably faded jeans. "Let's see…" he offered because again their server approached.

"Thank you," Valeria René said accepting the steaming water. She also attempted to hide the accompanying teabag. "Oh laugh already, you bubbleheads," she finally said while dunking her cutlery, "but *I* won't wind up diseased. So, she who laughs last will laugh last."

Ronni chortled. "The last laugher is supposed to laugh *best.*"

"And indeed she will," Valeria René innocently agreed, and caused more chuckles.

"Ooh, what have you got?" Ronni asked Kismet Staar who heartily dug into chicken and dumplings.

"I'll trade you a couple of forkfuls of this, for some of that." Beau held up his catfish and jumbo shrimp platter.

"Deal," Hurriedly Valeria René spooned up candied yams, macaroni 'n cheese, and fried okra.

"That for me," Ronni inquired, as she accepted seafood gumbo, black-eyed peas, and short ribs.

Later, she rested her fork on her plate. She was actually full, like Kismet Staar had promised when she'd suggested 'her little place' for delectably rich, down-home cooking.

"I'm going to check out the Blue Room," Beau announced, as with flourish he placed his napkin atop his plate.

"Wait, Diddley," Ronni called, wanting help taking her birthday parcels out to old Betsy. "Come with me. Then when we come back..." She was none too subtle, "You three can do your thing, while I check out The Showcase..." on the upper level.

Moments later, the Cohorts decided on a time to meet, just before Ronni sashayed off.

Beau, his cousin Kismet Staar, and Valeria René then descended the Bronx Nook's wide, polished wood staircase. They found The Blue Room filling for the second show.

In the darkly paneled, intimate, and smoky, smooth jazz lounge that boasted antique rugs, beaded lampshades, and comfy furniture, the Cohorts relaxed on an overstuffed sofa. Sipping coffee and *Eau de Vie* respectively, Valeria René and Kismet Staar could not believe Beau who had ordered dessert to go with his coffee.

As the headlining ingénue took the small stage, the chef's creation appeared. Beau's twice-baked sweet potato pudding was smothered in heavy cream, and enjoying it, he thought it as smooth as the voice of the reed-thin young woman seated on the stage.

"Ohhh, that's divine," Valeria René ecstatically moaned, following a whipped mouthful.

Kismet Staar licked a fingertip, "So light, with a hint of coconut."

On the upper level, in The Showcase, Ronni's birthday was now complete, and her outfit not wasted. With people gyrating to bass-thumping party jams, she sat at the bar nursing a cognac, while obvious male admirers approached and surrounded her.

Some time later, she surprised even her own self by leaving the assemblage. Descending two flights of stairs, she feverishly sought her friends. In the dimness, she worked her way through people enraptured by a girl and her band. Feeling welcomed, she found herself squeezed onto a plush sofa. With the hard-bodied Beau on one side, and the soft, ample-bosomed Kismet Staar, along with Valeria René on her other side, Ronni felt tears prick her eyes. Glad it was dark, so that no one would notice, she realized something. The Cohorts were more of a family to her than Cliff Jr., her own brother, whom she had not seen in years.

When the show ended, the foursome headed for home. Tipsy, Ronni rested her head on her girlfriend's shoulder. She breathed alcoholic fire into the curvier car owner's face as Kismet Staar drove. Ronni also slurred her thanks for a lovely evening. Then turning, she grinned goofily at the pair in the rear.

"Shush Diddley," Ronni sluggishly waved, and cleared her throat. "Just lemme say thisss." Her head dipped, but she jerked it back up, to continue speaking. "No matter what happens to me, I know one thing. I hev known it shince we became a family of friendsss. I kin count on you guys for the luuv I need."

Valeria René looked at Beau, and knew he thought the same thing that both she and Kismet Staar did. It was rare for Ronni to say what she really felt, and rarer still was it for her to say something touching.

Therefore, in the satisfied sweet silence, Ronni's Cohorts pondered her words. Each was also happy that their evening, spent mostly together, had turned out so well.

Chapter 7

ON a bright Sunday morning not long after her birthday outing, butter-yellow Ronni Brown sat at The Quarter's kitchen table. Leisurely, she thumbed through the weekend edition of the paper.

"Why can't I have the comics and the magazine?" Beau inquired.

"I'm not done with them," Ronni retorted.

"That's not fair," he pointed out because his roommate held all but one section of the paper on her lap. "Ron, you can only read one part at a time. So why not give me the circulars?"

She nearly sighed, because Beau was about to get on her last nerve, the way he did every Sunday morning. It was always the same thing. She got up early, showered and pulled on a snug jogging suit, while her roommates lay behind closed doors. Nosey Beau would hear her as she let herself out of the apartment. Then he would get up and follow suit.

Down at the corner bodega, she would chat up Carlos, the proprietor, who was a bit sweet on her. Then she would purchase a pack of gum, the Sunday paper, and accept a lidded, hot cup of coffee, compliments of her Latin admirer.

Then back in The Quarters, Ronni would pour herself a serving bowl full of cereal, and seated, she would attempt to enjoy her meal, and her paper. However, Beau, who by then had prepared himself a plate of waffles or pancakes, would not allow it. He'd break her concentration by begging for different sections of her paper, as he did now.

She huffed as slowly she shoved the comics across to the man who could have bought his own paper. "You are so cheap!"

"If you say so," he smiled, satisfied that yet another Sunday morning he had broken his roommate down.

Ronni dismissed Beau, as seated on one of his too high canvas director's chairs she hunched herself further over the table. Again, she became ardently engrossed in the Personals.

Glancing at furniture sales, Beau heard the slide of worn bunny slippers on hardwood. "Here comes Val."

Sleepy-faced, she entered the kitchen, dragging her feet. "Who made coffee?" she asked, just like she had every single Sunday morning for nearly three years.

Ronni fingered her place in the personals. "You don't smell any."

Valeria René waved and wondered why the seated pair could not allow her to enter the kitchen, just once, to be greeted by the scent of fresh coffee. Preparing to brew a pot, she asked why she always had to make it.

"Well, I get mine for free," Ronni announced and popped a toasted O into her mouth. She returned her attention to the paper.

Wearing an oversized sleep tee, Valeria René fingered the dials on the radio that was as old as she was. There. She'd found it, gospel singing. Settling with a hip against the counter's edge, she realized that she liked the sameness of Sundays in The Quarters.

Once or twice monthly, she and her roommates would go to church, but on the remaining Sundays, she would make coffee, and the others would partake. Beau and Ronni would bicker over Ronni's paper. Then when they were done, the three roommates would go fall across the furniture in the living room.

There, they would proceed to watch a movie, usually one like Lethal Weapon, that they'd seen a half dozen times. However, Ronni would have to be told to stifle, because lying on her ivory sofa she would make it hard to hear. Carrying on a conversation with her man—of the moment—she would get loud, and graphic.

Pouring the first cup of coffee, and adding cream, curly-locked Valeria René also cogitated on the fact that in The Quarters no one ever got fully dressed before two p.m., a fact that Kismet Staar found disgusting.

"So what, Kiss," Ronni had once said. "No one cares that you're up, over there in Elmont, running to 'n fro, probably driving your poor gardener crazy. We're not you. We like lying around."

Valeria René remembered Kismet Staar's retort. "Yeah, because you guys are lazy slugs." The curvier woman had also announced she did more by noon on a Sunday, than her Cohorts did all day.

Sipping coffee Valeria René smiled because no one was offended by the ever-mothering Kismet Staar. Looking over, Valeria René noticed Ronni's grin. She also noted that hungrily Ronni scanned the paper.

"Whatcha got?" Valeria René asked, peering over Ronni's shoulder.

Looking up, Ronni answered quickly like a guilty child might. "Oh, I—I I've got nothing." Then with feigned disinterest, Ronni attempted to turn the page; yet Valeria René knew she was onto something. She knew because Ronni only acted guilty when there was some type of sexual stimuli involved. Most likely, Valeria René thought, the behavior stemmed from Ronni's unnecessarily strict upbringing.

In Ronni's now deceased father Big Cliff's home, any thing that had to do with the sensual was considered a no-no, and it was ironic because the man had had more than his share of dirty little no-no's.

Valeria René forgot Ronni's father. Anxious to see what had piqued her butter-yellow roommate's interest, she set her cup down. She also tried to return Ronni to the prior page as she said, "Let's see, Ron."

"Stop, Val!" Ronni yelled. "Or you'll rip my paper. You know what?" Ronni suddenly huffed. "You and Beau both need to start purchasing papers of your own."

"Now why would we do that," Valeria René quipped, feeling like Ronni was unreasonably indignant; "when we have yours?"

The fight went out of Ronni, and abruptly she sat back. She allowed Valeria René to turn the newspaper page. No sense in further protesting she thought, because the nosy other woman would never let her be.

Valeria René sputtered with laughter, before she called out, "Diddley, listen to this ad," that Ronni circled.

"Attractive SM 6'1 looking for sexy SBF to enjoy erotic tryst. Also seeking SBM 6'1; must be Bi. Want to pursue innovative threesome activities."

Valeria René laughed again. "Now isn't that something? Some man who claims he's attractive and single is looking for a single black female, and a single black male."

"Does it give a number?" Beau asked; his grin spreading as he looked from one roommate to the other.

"There would have to be a number," Ronni sarcastically stated. "It is an ad."

With one jerky movement of her head, Valeria René tossed a curly lock from her face. "The things people do. If he's so attractive, why's he placing an ad?"

"Hey," Beau chimed, looking at Valeria René, and then at Ronni. "If that's what floats your boat, then why not?"

"Thank—you!" Ronni exhaled with the paper lying open before her. She was happy, because finally, someone was on her side. Yes, especially when she'd felt, for a moment there that she might wind up defending her self against two reprimanding roommates.

Ignoring her favorite gospel song as it played in the background Valeria René eyed Beau, and shook her head. She should have known he would join the multitude to do evil.

Rubbing her own hands together in contemplation, Ronni nodded at her new best friend. "Diddley, I'm thinking I could use a little newness in my life. Add a little spice, you know?

"There is that old adage," Beau pointed out. "It says variety is the spice of life."

"Stop it," Valeria René ordered pouring a second cup of coffee, "because there's nothing spicy about frolic hunting, which can wind up dangerous, Ronni."

"Oh please Val, if you look at it like that, anything, even leaving your home can become dangerous."

Listening, Beau stirred his own fresh hot coffee and shook himself. He then hollered without warning, like he was in church, and like he had just been caught hold of by the Holy Spirit. "Say amen somebody!"

"Not funny Diddley. This is serious." Perturbed, Valeria René turned to her female roommate who yet sat atop one of Beau's monstrous chair-stools. "Ronni you're not really going to call that number...are you?"

"Yes, I am." Ronni stared blank-faced at the woman who appeared mortified.

Turning, Beau eyed his feisty roommate. With his mouth agape he realized he had only said that other stuff to unnerve Valeria René who was ever more cautious than he or Ronni. He hadn't really agreed.

"Ron," he called, suddenly serious. "You don't know the placer of that ad, or others who'll answer. What if you wind up in a situation, where they change the rules, and gang up on you...or worse?"

Not him too, Ronni dismally thought. Her roommates were two little old ladies, and saddened by that fact, she shook her head. She also declared, "Well worrywarts, if 'ganging-up' is on the menu, I'll deal."

"But those big studs could do anything to you, Veronica." This Beau stated, knowing what some people were capable of. As a small child, hadn't he had to fight off most of the low-life sleazy men that his mother had brought home?

When Ophelia, Momma Dearest, had been trying to score drugs, she'd brought all sorts of vile creatures back to the dank hole she'd had her small son living in. When she had no money, she'd offered his little body—to get the drugs needed to keep her in oblivion.

In the kitchen, Beau tried to shake the creeping dread he used to feel as he said, "Say you won't do this, Ron." While awaiting her reply, for comfort he fingered his uncle's war tags, given him by his aunt upon the man's death.

"You want me to lie, so you and Ms. Holy over there can feel safe and good," Ronni scoffed and struggled to get out of Beau's canvas monstrosity. Clearing her breakfast paraphernalia, she gathered all of her newspaper. "I'm doing this," she announced while sashaying from the room. "If either of you has a problem," she called, "then too bad."

Remaining in the kitchen, Ronni's onetime Clark-Atlanta dorm mate Valeria René looked down and into the dregs of her coffee cup. "I don't like this Beau…"

"I don't either," he admitted, "but she's grown. We can only pray she knows what she's doing."

"Or better yet, I'll pray that she realizes what she's doing, before she actually goes through with it," Valeria René stated; "because what good can come of this?"

Beau forsook the coffee that he'd really wanted, because Valeria René wasn't usually the one asking questions. Normally she had all the answers.

Chapter 8

$\mathcal{L}$ADIES," Beau called as he entered The Cohort Quarters living room. "Can one or both of you help a brotha out?"

Valeria René raised an eyebrow, "Help?"

"Yeah, what does that mean?" Kismet Staar inquired, raggedly thrown over Valeria René's chaise longue. Eyeing her cousin's laden arms she also asked, "What *is* all that?"

Beau dumped the bungled mass on Ronni's sofa. "All that, as you called it, is my costume, for the contest." The annual Impersonator's Ball held yearly at Club La-*Laa*! "The only thing is…somehow its all wrong."

He stood staring downward as his heart gave a little leap because Phase I of his plan had worked, like a charm. His traipsing back and forth past the living room door had paid off in attracting the women's attention.

"You mean that's supposed to be a costume," Valeria René put in, "because at this point it only looks like leaves, and not like anything that you could win a contest wearing."

Time for the implementation of Phase II Beau thought and smashed a large fist into its opposite palm.

"Man! I really want to win that contest, this year." He looked beseechingly from one woman to the other. "It's why I need you girls to help me. Please…"

Kismet Staar raised herself on an elbow, "Oh no." She looked at her longtime sister friend. "Val, did you hear how he said that—like it's our duty to rescue him?"

"Yes, from his sinking ship of dilemma."

"I know Diddley and his 'help-outs,'" Kismet Staar curtly stated. "They always turn into all night sewing sessions." She shook her head. "I can't do it, bruh."

"Please, Kiss?" Beau begged, getting down on his knees. He wrapped his muscular arms about her legs. "Don't say no. I'll just die if I don't place this year. Help me, Kiss." On his knees, quickly he turned to the woman seated on the purple sofa. "Val?"

When she remained silent, Beau looked up. "Kismet Staar, you've had things that you've really needed help with—like putting together your bookshelves." This he quickly pulled from his mental hat, "And I was there for you. It took hours, but I helped."

"Saying I owe you won't spark much enthusiasm," Kismet Staar advised.

"I'd never do that," Beau replied, knowing he had his cousin, and Valeria René too...almost. "However, I have to ask you this." He appealed to Kismet Staar's competitive side. "Wouldn't you like me to beat the fancy pants off that dang Marçhand clown who won last year?"

His cousin's eyes narrowed, even as Valeria René softly stated, "Mar-SHOND won the year before that too..."

"I despise that arrogant little man," Kismet Staar announced, shooting up off the chaise.

Anger was good, Beau mused. It would work in his favor. "Well, ladies," he deliberately began, "I cannot possibly win, as Val pointed out—with that." He gestured to the faux leafy mess on Ronni's sofa. "So you'll help me, a little? Please? This is important to me."

"How important is it?" Valeria René asked, her eyes gleaming iniquitously. "Help us understand."

Beau dropped his boy-beggar routine. "Val," he called, towering over her, "if you're plotting, forget it."

Laughing, she raised an eyebrow. "You know me well, don't you?"

"I do," Beau nodded. "I also hear your brain clicking."

"No clicking, just yet," she sweetly sang, as warily her roommate watched her.

"Even if she *was* hatching a plan, Diddley," Kismet Staar put in; "who are you to get mannish," like her mother Nell would say. "You're the one who needs help."

In silence, Beau hung his head.

His first cousin laughed. "You are such an actor; cut it out." Folding her arms, she also asked, "Diddley, what do you really want from us?"

A smile brightened Beau's countenance, because he loved it when a plan came together. "You mean it Kiss?"

Without replying, she simply stared.

"Okay," Beau rummaged around on the sofa. "I'll need a few pointers, to start with." Then without warning, he grabbed his cousin's shoulders. Quickly he wrapped her in an elated embrace. "I love you girl! You know that?"

"Yeah, yeah, you too," Kismet Staar wryly remarked with her arms down by her sides, because if her cousin thought he was going to play her, by getting her to do a ton of sewing, he was mistaken. "Uh, Beau," she nearly gasped. "I need air."

Delighted, Valeria René clapped. "He forgets his strength."

"Look, both of you," Kismet Staar voiced, in her motherly no nonsense manner. "If this turns out to be a tedious task, I'm not doing it."

"There's nothing, really," Beau said feigning nonchalance, and praying that she'd think so too.

"Diddle-Diddle," his cousin called out. "Don't sit down. Hold that business there up, so we can assess it."

Quickly Beau picked up what appeared to be a leafy skirt attached to a long sleeved tee made of panty hose material. "I'd like to impersonate prima diva Josephine Baker, but this," Beau shook it, "is just not coming out right." Not yet anyway. He held the costume so that the women could better view it. "You think it can be fixed?"

"Think *you* can be fixed?" Valeria René teased as she went to sit across the living room before the large window. Pulling the curtain aside, she peered at people entering the building below. She also eyed the two brave souls in the park across the street. Amid a tennis match, they lunged and swung, in hellacious and stifling heat.

"Hey, when it cools off, this evening perhaps," she proposed, "Kiss, we should get out our rackets and swing them at Beau's balls."

Jerking to look at her, he fingered the dog tags at his neck.

"Your *tennis* balls!" Valeria René howled, laughing, because she well knew what her roommate had been thinking. "Gutter mind boo, racing heart."

"Quit playing," Beau squawked because he was on a mission. "I've only got a few more days, and I'd like to be done before then."

"Who're you rushing?" Valeria René cut her eyes. "Remember, it's not *our* fault that *you* wait till the last minute every year." Again she peered out of the window as she mumbled, minus malice, "You need to admit it, you don't have a clue, Sherlock."

"I do not wait until the last minute," Beau countered. "I've been working on this, but it just hasn't panned out."

A skilled seamstress, curvaceous Kismet Staar cut in, concerned, because she realized the contest and the costume meant a lot to her cousin. "What do you want to see Diddley?"

"Well..." he began, aware that he would actually have to open himself up. "You know the banana skirt Ms. Josephine wore?" He half expected to get laughed at, but he had to take a chance, to get what he really wanted. "That's what I was going for."

"You're speaking of the Josephine Baker movie, I suppose," Valeria René chimed.

"Correct." Beau became brisk, businesslike. "A replica of her skirt is what I'd like, and if you'll both notice, I've attached see-through fabric on top, to create an illusion, albeit sheer, to allow nipple peekage."

Valeria René chuckled, "Is that even a word?"

"Ahhh," Kismet Staar got the picture, "so you wanna shake yo' lil' fast tail." Fingering the portion of the costume that Beau held up, she acknowledged that her cousin hadn't done a bad job. Finally understanding what he aimed to recreate, she also turned to her friend. "You know Val, there's really not much left to do. Oh, there are a few places to whipstitch by hand but I'll do those, and reinforce others on my machine."

"Okay, but I have a question," the mocha-skinned woman called, yet seated before the window. "I'm not trying to be funny Diddley, but shouldn't you have put bananas on the skirt, instead of leaves? Since Ms. Baker's banana skirt is the basis for your design?"

Beau allowed the piece to fall. He searched his duffle bag. *"Voila!"* He produced a string of plastic bananas.

"Now you're cooking," Valeria René smiled, and stepped over. To Kismet Staar she remarked, "Don't those look like the fake ones that your Grandma had on her dining table when you were a kid?"

Valeria René also admitted that when she'd go to her Nenna's house, her dad's mother in South Carolina, she'd always creep around, to pinch and fondle Nenna's fruit; when her grandmother wasn't looking, of course.

Kismet Staar nodded. "For me it was the grapes. I finger them even now, when I go to my mama's house," in California. Turning to Beau,

Kismet Staar said without missing a beat, "Take off your clothes Diddley."

Seeing that his cousin gestured toward his work-in-progress costume, Beau quickly obliged. Stripping down to his zebra-striped briefs, he stood before the two women happy as a lark. "Okay, what now?"

Valeria René held up the little outfit. "Put it on, silly."

When Beau bent to do so, his roommate gave his backside a slap. "Oh I couldn't resist," she giggled. She did not divulge that what she had actually wanted to do was squeeze one of Beau's buns. Inconspicuously though, she looked him over, and could not refrain from declaring that he was just one luscious hunk of man, and he had a nice bulge too.

"Yeah and if my little Brownie were here," Ronni, whose libido was seemingly always in overdrive, Kismet Staar teased, "we'd also have to un-heat her."

Beau mocked a repulsed shiver for the women's amusement.

"Diddley," Valeria René called, looking up into her roommate's face. "You really are going to make somebody a fine life-partner one day."

"Val," Beau laughed, suddenly feeling self-conscious, "if I had a mother—that cared, you would sound just like her." Beau then eyed Kismet Staar from his peripheral as quickly he made amends. "I meant if I had a mother other than A'nt Nell, Kiss' mother who reared me, you'd sound just like her."

Beau dismissed the slightly uncomfortable feeling he'd momentarily experienced. "Look, you ladies have to forget my behind and fix me, because I just want to be the best darn Josephine Baker that club has ever seen."

Kismet Staar snapped her fingers. "Well, go 'head, wit'cha bad self."

"If Kiss will sew, Diddley," Valeria René proposed, "I'll do your makeup." She promised to beautifully transform Beau, but not before she advised, "Put your costume on, big man."

When Beau finally shrugged into the little outfit, both women gasped, and Valeria René ran her dark hand over the bodice of it. She studied Beau in the nylon top and attached frond skirt.

Kismet Staar grabbed the bananas and held them against him.

"Oh now it's coming to life," Valeria René gushed, the curly ringlets on her head falling into her face. Involuntarily she swiped them back. "Kiss look at Diddley's abs!"

"Six pack!" Kismet Staar sang out. Then with exaggerated effort, she inhaled, to flatten her own stomach. When she could no longer hold the big breath, she allowed air to whoosh through her lips before she sheepishly grinned.

Beau, who faithfully went to the gym and had boxed for years, shook his head. "Inhaling, alone, will never tone a body."

"I know that," Kismet Staar squawked as her friend continued to rave about Beau in his costume.

"Diddley," Valeria René breathed, running a finger over his nylon top. "You look so silky." Blowing out a series of short breaths, Valeria René hoped to un-titillate. Actually, she recalled, she didn't often think of her roommate in sexual terms, but a moment ago, again it had hit her. Beauregard DeVeaux really was appealing.

Watching Valeria René turn away for a few calming moments, Kismet Staar chuckled. Pinning bananas to Beau's leafy skirt she knew how her friend felt. As Beau's cousin, she had seen the very same chemical reaction to him many times. Most times she found it amusing because she couldn't really see her cousin in the regard that others did. She guessed that was because she often recalled him as the gangly, shy boy who'd begun living with her family when he was eight, after her mother hired a private detective to find her deceased brother's son.

Forgetting the way her mother Nell had nearly worried herself sick before finding small Beau, Kismet Staar announced, "You two wait until I sew these bananas on."

Suddenly she smiled and realized that Beau's excitement was contagious, because now in the eye of her own mind, she, like he, could nearly see the finished outcome. And it was fabulous.

Quickly forgetting her own and Valeria René's vastly differing perceptions of Beau, his cousin sang out, "Diddleee, those club patrons are going to *go* bananas when you step out in this get-up." Bent over the sofa, she rummaged. "Where's your head-dress?"

Beau joined the search while being truthful. "Actually, I didn't make it up, but see..." He pulled on something. "This is the fabric I'd like to use. It's iridescent."

"Metallic, yes, it'll catch light." Kismet Staar turned the fabric in her capable hands. "Lean over." Quickly she wrapped her cousin's head.

"Ahh Sukey," he grinned, having dashed to view himself in the hallway mirror. Back, and fishing again, he pulled other items from his duffel. "I bought this ceramic fruit. Here." he presented the multitude of berries to Kismet Staar. "Put 'em on me."

Acknowledging the genius of her longtime friend, Valeria René said, "Kiss, you have such talented hands. Hey—gimme a minute you two." She hurried off in the direction of The Quarter's bedrooms.

Upon returning, she held out a pair of earrings. "Diddley look," she eagerly coaxed. "You can wear these, if you promise not to lose them." Clipping both on his ears she pivoted. "They match, right Kiss?"

"Oh they do, and they're clips." Kismet Staar nodded, "Or you couldn't wear them, Diddley."

"These are extra," Beau stated, taking one down. Ever the lover of beautiful things, he gently handled an earring that was comprised of three faceted crystal balls. The first orb that sat just at the earlobe was the largest. From it dangled a mid-sized globe, and from that hung the smallest. Noticing the way the glittering pieces caught light, Beau thanked his roommate for the loan.

"They look like Austrian crystal," Kismet Staar remarked.

"They are," Valeria René nodded. She then stated that her life's love had given them to her, as a promise of marriage.

Though she had never gone fully into detail about the circumstances surrounding what had transpired all those years ago, Valeria René's friends had been able to gather a bits-and-pieces story about Marc McKennon, her boyfriend who'd passed.

Curious, Beau said, "He's the one you sometimes mention, right?"

"Yes..." Visibly deep in thought, Valeria René affirmed that Marc had perished in a car accident.

"He was crushed?" Beau further edged, before he realized he was prying. Quickly and sincerely he apologized, because he abhorred it when others did the same to him.

"No need to be sorry, Diddley." Valeria René shrugged. "Although it still hurts, many days, if I really think about it, it's something I experienced. The only thing is... there are times when any little thing can suddenly remind me of him."

"Oh baby I'm aware," Kismet Staar confirmed. She well knew, because at nineteen, she'd lost her beloved father. "Sometimes I'll smell a particular cologne on a man in passing, or hear a snippet of a song—"

"Or for me, it can be a particular flavor of ice cream, or a type of candy that I haven't had in years," Valeria René remarked; "even the color of the sky on a given day can prompt a long forgotten memory..." She acknowledged that the triggers were endless.

Then sounding so unlike the Valeria René that Beau and Kismet Staar had grown to know and love, the mocha-skinned one explained how Marc McKennon had passed...

Having attended a wedding where he had been the best man, he'd started out in the dark of the morning, early the following day to head for home. Shortly thereafter, a man drove toward Marc on a lonely two-lane stretch of road in Virginia. The man had fallen asleep behind the wheel of his vehicle. Waking up too late, the man watched and fought failingly with his wheel as his car careened, head-on, into Marc's compact car.

Moreover, as though she were yet entranced, Valeria René told her friends, quite possibly again, that Marc McKennon's severely mangled car had had to be cut from around him. "I believe they call the tool the rescuers used the 'jaws of life.'" Quietly she also stated that Marc had been pried, profusely bleeding and broken, from his destroyed vehicle.

"I was told he called for me, all up until I got right to the hospital."

Mentally she re-lived that horrific time as she mentioned running down the sterile hallway. "I was praying, and then, in an instant I just felt...I'd lost something."

Though she'd not known it at the time, indeed she had.

Breathing harder, and similar to the manner that she had when she'd actually been running, Valeria René's voice caught on a sob. "Marc just passed...away."

Sounding as though she still didn't believe, she also revealed that Marc had slipped into shock. "I was told that a couple of times medical workers lost him, but they managed to bring him back; however I wasn't fast enough. I didn't get to kiss my honey, or tell him I loved him, because the last time he slipped away, it was for good.

"I didn't want him to be gone," she softly moaned, a confused look in her eyes. "We hadn't had enough time."

Looking wistful and sad, Valeria René spoke in retrospect. "Maybe if I'd gotten there sooner so that Marc could have heard me say I loved him—because I really did—maybe he would have held on."

Attempting to release herself from the painful past, Valeria René took an enormous breath.

"Sometimes though, I think that if Marc had lived, he might have been miserable. You know? Or I'm thinking, right now: if he'd lived, I probably wouldn't have met either of you, because my life would have taken different turns."

Valeria René stared blankly at Beau. She remarked, as gingerly she took back her precious earrings, "Then *you* wouldn't have these for your glam-slam, now would you?"

"I guess not." Feeling melancholy, Beau watched his roommate turn the pieces in her hands. Perhaps in the crystal, she was viewing her life, as it would have been, had circumstances been different and fate not so cruel.

"Did you love him?" Beau couldn't keep from asking as he fingered his dog tags.

"I did." Valeria René nodded as sunlight caressed her sparkling tears. She even smiled with shimmering eyes as she said she'd loved Marc McKennon with her all. "I loved loving him, and I loved the way he loved me. Actually, I haven't loved another man the same since. Sometimes I even think that because I was young and idealistic, back then, perhaps Marc and I wouldn't have worked out, had he not wound up in that accident."

"You never know," Kismet Staar stated. "However, the one thing we do know is we can't lose ourselves in 'what if?' We can't keep looking back, not at things that cannot now be changed; or we'll miss the something sweet that could be just ahead of us."

"Enough!" Beau clapped his hands. He knew he had to break the dismal spell that now pervaded what had been an upbeat afternoon. Or he and the women would wind up at a pity party for three.

"Val, my Boo," he said, bowing to her. "I thank you for sharing. You didn't have to, but it was a gift." He looked at Kismet Staar, "And now, you girls have to fix me."

Coming back around, Valeria René smiled and told Beau that on contest night she would beat his face. "I'm gonna make you fierce. Then After I've done you boyfriend, you will give people *fever*!"

Beau's laughter exploded as he flipped a curly ringlet out of his roommate's face. "Well then, all I've got to say is: do – me – baby."

Beau began to sing and gyrate. *"Do me baby...* I wanna lick you up 'n down—"

"Till you say stop," Valeria René chimed, winding her hips because she remembered the song by the R&B group Silk.

Ever the mother, Kismet Staar advised, "Oh, cut it out you two."

"Hey, wait." Valeria René held up a hand. "You didn't mention our tickets."

"I've got them," Beau assured her, "and I need your money. Girls, on that night, I want y'all to cheer like never before."

"Oh, hard and long," Valeria René wickedly grinned.

"Yeah..." Kismet Staar licked her lips, appearing pensive. "I'll do *anything* for hard and long. I'll do a lot of things for big, too."

"Why Kiss," Valeria René laughingly scolded her sister friend, "you're a nasty girl!"

Kismet Staar winked. "I sure am. And with the right man, you would be too."

Flouncing away, Valeria René knowingly called out, "Oh, I *was* that girl; hoping to be her again, real soon."

Chapter 9

$\mathcal{S}$HE night of Beau's big bash, mocha brown Valeria René and her cohort, butter-yellow Ronni moved about, near frenzied.

At ground level, Kismet Staar buzzed up, and the roommates nearly stumbled over each other trying to let her in. Opening the apartment door, Ronni took a good look at Beau's curvaceous cousin and squealed. "Kiss you look ravishing!"

In her emerald green strapless dress, and bejeweled high-heeled sandals, this Kismet Staar looked so different from the other her. Having shed the savvy businessperson who wore tailored weekday pantsuits, tonight she was a vision. As always, her professionally cut hair was sleek and shiny.

"Going all out for boyfriend I see," Ronni remarked. "Got your nails done; ooh Kiss, you put a on a dress!" Ronni nodded, "And sparkly eye shadow, not bad Mama."

"You're not half-stepping your self," Kismet Staar commented, taking in the other woman's attire. Ronni had been poured into a tight, black, leather mini skirt. Like Beau would, later, she also displayed her ripe fruit, in a studded black bustier. She wore fishnet pantyhose and metal-toed, spike heels.

"I'm always sexy," Ronni immodestly offered, tossing her wavy-haired head. When she managed to perch herself atop one of Beau's canvas chair monstrosities, she pulled a cigarette from her small purse.

"You know, Miss Kiss," she began, her attitude big. "If we weren't going out tonight, I would still have to find a little something to get into."

Taking a seat as well, her friend inquired, "Why's that?"

"Just look at all this," Ronni gestured. "My hair is coiffed, and my shit is so snatched, until it would be a shame to waste it."

Kismet Staar roared with laughter because sometimes Ronni really was too funny; even to her own self. It was why she joined Kismet Staar and chuckled as well.

"Oh baby I know," Kismet Staar acknowledged, coming down off the moment's high. "Sometimes you just need somebody to see you, and though we've all thought that, only you have the *cojones* to say it." It was one of the many reasons Kismet Staar dearly loved her extroverted friend.

Ronni blew smoke rings, and looking around, she sang out, "It's time. We need to make this happen, y'all."

"Okay." Valeria René tripped into the kitchen. "Where's Boyfriend? All his stuff's still on the bed..."

"I passed him in the outer hallway," Kismet Staar revealed.

Squinting to keep smoke out of her eyes, Ronni deduced, "He must be at the Nunley's." The older couple lived across the hall, also in a three-bedroom apartment. Inhaling tar and nicotine Ronni addressed her roommate. "Val, you know how they are."

Valeria René nodded. "They believe in Diddley. So they show their love every time he performs."

"Oh they just think he's going to be a big star one day because they've seen him on a couple of TV shows. They don't fool me. They're just trying to get on the Beau bandwagon ahead of everybody else." Ronni crushed out her cigarette. "Tonight, they'll probably give him a bottle of champagne—to secure their place in his future."

"They might genuinely care for Beau," Kismet Staar advised and recalled something. "Don't they have a daughter?"

"They do," Valeria René nodded while adjusting items so they'd better fit in her makeup case.

However, it was mouthy Ronni who elaborated, informing Kismet Staar that the Nunleys, a sweet pair, had developed a special affinity for Beau.

"Yeah, even though as a tall African-American male, he scared the living daylights out of them that first time; they were on the stairs, and he was behind them, moving fast."

"As usual," Valeria René absently interjected.

Ronni further admitted that the Nunleys liked her and Valeria René well enough, but for some reason they desired Beauregard DeVeaux for the daughter they'd had late in life. "Lil girl recently got her Bachelors, and now her parents think she and Beau should marry." Ronni looked around. "All who know that'll never happen please nod."

"Mrs. Nunley has hope," Valeria René shrugged, before the butter yellow Ronni informed Kismet Staar that the older couple often eyed Beau with knowing little smirks.

"He told Mrs. N and her husband that his interest lies in men, but they feel he's just going through a phase, one that he'll soon tire of."

"The daughter knows better, right?" Kismet Staar inquired.

"She does, but still she flirts, and hopes, for the big black stud. You know how that goes."

"Well thank *you* very much, Ms. Information." Beau appeared, and spoke to Ronni whom he'd heard gabbing as he re-entered the apartment.

Valeria Rene looked up. "What'cha got there?"

Beau raised his latest gift, Australian Shiraz, and an equally as expensive bottle of *Roussanne*.

Ronni scoffed before she again indicated the time. "We should be leaving, now. It's full dark out."

Beau turned to Valeria René. "Val, please do not get so excited tonight that you forget to take pictures. Okay?"

"You guys will never let me live that down."

"How can we?" Kismet Staar laughed. She wagged a finger at the darker-skinned woman. "Bringing an empty camera home; not once, but twice."

"Hush Kiss," Valeria René waved. Unintentionally she changed the subject. "I heard Ronni making on over you, and I must agree. You do look like a goddess tonight."

"I told Ms. Couture," Ronni added, "that she should wear dresses more often."

"Kiss, tell Ronni," Valeria René called, zippering her makeup case, "Venus knows when to do it."

Ronni fingered a second cigarette. "Let me inform you two misguided souls, Venus was the Goddess of Love and Beauty. Therefore, Miss Kiss cannot possibly be her, because Love and Beauty are *my* department."

Mock indignant, Valeria René, whose hair was fashionably upswept, clamped a hand on her hip. "Ronni Brown, are you saying Kiss and I are the ugly twins 'n can't have love?"

"Forget Brownie," Kismet Staar waved. "I'm getting me some. It's why I'll now be known as Aphrodite."

"Nope," Ronni struggled down from Beau's monstrosity. "Venus and Aphrodite happen to be one and the same. Read up on Mythology. Venus is the Roman, Aphrodite is the Greek, from whence—I might add—we get the word aphrodisiac. So you see?" Ronni shrugged. "Both Venus and Aphrodite are the goddesses of Love, and Beauty, a.k.a. me."

Kismet Staar smoothed her emerald green suede strapless dress. "Enough Mythology 101, I'm leaving."

"Wait. Somebody zipper me." Valeria René bounced girlishly up and down in her red-hot number and strappy heels.

"Lemme look at the front of this dress," Kismet Staar, ever the mother, uttered walking around Valeria René. "Wow."

In front, the diamond cutout permitted one a generous view of Valeria René's glorious cleavage.

"The rear's the same, only larger," Kismet Staar announced, gently pushing the other woman because she was done with the zipper. "We can see your whole velvety, chocolate back." To the woman who also wore dangling, large rhinestone earrings, and a matching cuffed bracelet, Kismet Staar spoke. "Girl you look *fabulosa*—with your 'fire engine' red lipstick, and same-color finger 'n toe nails."

Breezing back into the kitchen in tennis shoes, a tee, and jeans, the buff, brown Beau carried a garment bag, and an army green duffle. "No time like the present," he stated.

"Oh please," Ronni scoffed, grabbing her keys from the kitchen countertop. "You should say there's nothing like *getting* the present, this year, even if you get second or third."

"Hey, where's your faith?" Kismet Staar stepped into the hallway. "Why not believe he'll win first prize?"

"I take what I can get." Ronni waved. "So should Diddley."

"That's a defeatist attitude," Valeria René proclaimed.

"For-give me!" Ronni yowled, "For wanting the man to place, once out of three years. Maybe you two aren't, but I'm tired of coming home from these things, disappointed."

"Tonight will be different," Valeria René knowingly stated. "I've seen it."

"Oh please, Val. You're no psychic. You saw Diddley's costume— you and Kiss, and I say no fair, because I didn't get to see it."

Valeria René calmly followed Ronni down the worn marble stairs. "I'm no psychic, but I know Diddley's good at what he does, *and* I prayed for him to have a little extra tonight."

Ronni dismissed what she often thought of as her roommate's religious mumbo-jumbo, "Whatever Val.

"Beau!" Ronni hollered, holding the rail and looking back upward. "Did you lock the door?"

"I did." He breezed past the women, in their slow-a-sista-down high heels. "Val, I've got your car keys. Ronni," he brightly called. "You get to ride with Kiss."

Instantly the mouthy spirited one whined. "Why? Why me?"

"Well," Beau appeared nonchalant, "Val and I have to pick people up."

Ronni spoke softly, as though to herself, "But her car smells like old gasoline, and her seat—that dang worn vinyl—it'll snag my fishnets..." She watched her male roommate exit the building. Standing on the marble landing she moaned, while gazing longingly at Valeria René's newbie through the staircase's large open window. Looking pretty, it sat in the glow of a street light. "Could things get any more unfair?"

"Yep," Kismet Staar nodded, as she reached the lowest landing. Stepping into the lobby, she called back upward. "You could have to walk."

Chapter 10

AT the overcrowded Club La-Laa! The women danced and mingled as though it was what they had been born to do.

Then the show began, with the announcer stepping into the spotlight, to crack jokes.

"Yo, get this party started!" someone in the audience bellowed. Others applauded, and someone else yelled, "Yeaaah!"

The Cohort trio chuckled. The women also noted the approach of a handsome dark-skinned man. Appearing five feet ten inches tall, he wore a well-tailored olive green, single-breasted jacket with a sleek jersey tee beneath that was a shade lighter. As a compliment, he wore quality black slacks and shoes.

Standing beside the table at which the Cohort women and a few friends sat, the well-dressed man questioningly searched each face. He also admitted he was looking for Val.

"Ooh, and *I'm* looking for *you*. Meet me in the ladies room," Ronni murmured, as her roommate, sipping gin on the rocks, wiggled her fingertips.

"I'm here." Valeria René daintily waved and smiled. "And it's Va-ler-REE-uh Ree-nay."

The man returned the smile and said, "Well, Ms. Valeria René, I'm Fabian. There is a Beau in the back who is calling for your expertise."

Fabian then held out a hand to assist the attractive woman.

"Where's my cosmetics case?" she asked, searching, near frantic, around and beneath her seat. She rolled her eyes. "Lord, please do not let that case be at home."

"You had it when we were on the steps, outside our apartment," Ronni reminded her.

Mireya, Beau's female friend since middle school, glanced over as Barry, a friend of all the Cohorts, raised something. "Is this what you're looking for?"

Valeria René breathed relieved. "Yes." She snatched the case from the man who had ridden with her and Beau. She turned then to follow her escort, but not before she purred, "Thank you Barrington."

Watching as she tucked the case protectively under an arm, Barry smiled and shrugged. "Val, sweetheart" he intimately called, "it was on my chair. Sorry for the scare." He gave her a sweeping once-over with his eyes. "Wit' yo' fine self," he added, for the benefit of that Fabian-fake-escort-character—the man he suddenly and viciously hated on.

Valeria René winked to show that no harm had been done, and was whisked away by Fabian who offered his last name, Sinclair. He also said he was a physical therapist.

"Nice to meet you," Valeria René nodded, and revealed that they both were in health and wellness, because she was an optometrist.

"Well how about that?" Fabian smiled.

Without flinching, Valeria René questioned Fabian Sinclair. "Are you gay?"

"You're pretty straightforward I see," the man remarked. "That I've always liked in a woman, and," he admitted, "I am not homosexual. Matter of fact, Ms. Valeria René, when I'm with that specific, special woman, I find myself insatiable..."

Fabian then chuckled before he said, "And Ms. V R, you're?"

"Straight." Producing another inquiry, she watched Fabian closely. "Why are you here then?" Persistent, she attempted to ascertain the man's angle, since he was quite attractive, and since he appeared to think the same about her. "Okay, you're bi, right?"

"Incorrect, again," Fabian grinned, sensing Valeria René's interest. "Like you, I came with somebody who's in the show; been coming for the past three years."

Fabian admitted he rather liked the crowd that the event drew. Most of the people were fun and easygoing, and a person didn't have to put on silly airs, like at other functions. Suddenly Fabian laughed aloud.

It was a rich *basso profundo*, the sound of which Valeria René immediately liked.

"My sister, the self-professed fag hag, and her 'girrrl friends' dragged my partner and I out here, the first time," Fabian revealed, "and the rest is history. Now, Brotha Man calls asking me when we'll attend again. He's into meeting all the brown sugars."

Fabian smiled down at the luscious lovely walking beside him. "I'll tell you. It was a surprise, our first time, to find that women like you attended."

In the dimly lit hallway, Valeria René raised an eyebrow. "I think that needs clarification."

"Women like you; professional, sexy, beautiful, together, cocoa-mocha women—who happen to be single." Fabian eyed her. "You do happen to be single, right?"

Valeria René nodded, and smiled. She stated that she too liked the sparkling, spontaneous crowd.

"Yes, and tonight," Fabian announced as they passed others. "I've even met a gorgeous lady. The very one with whom I'm speaking right now."

Beau came into view. Just ahead, he sat before a large lit mirror, wearing the costume—minus his headdress and shoes—that his cousin and roommate had helped him to perfect. In the room with him were scores of other people, each one readying their self for the night of the year, this week.

Eagerly Beau leaned forward. He beckoned Valeria René over.

"I saw you," Fabian disclosed, walking the lovely questioning female to within feet of the impatient man, "last year. I saw you the year before that too. I liked what I saw, then," Fabian told Valeria René as he licked his lips and tried not to stare at her inviting cleavage. "I like what I'm seeing now too."

"The only thing," Fabian divulged, "was that in the prior years, that Barrington-person seemed stuck to you, you know? It was a little too close for my comfort, so I didn't approach." Involuntarily, Fabian held his breath. "Was, or is he, your man?"

"No," Valeria René stated, her eyes on his, "but for a while he's wanted to be."

Fabian exhaled. "Well, I can't blame the brotha for trying, because you, lady, are *extra*."

Valeria René laughed. Then flirtatiously she allowed her eyelids and hands to flutter as she announced, "Fabian, flattery—against my better judgment—will get *you* everywhere."

The ever so attractive dark-skinned man tried hard then to keep the heat he felt from rising, and becoming apparent. Unable not to, he pulled his jacket, concealing what he called night stick. He implored Valeria René to let him buy her a drink, when they were out front. "And dance with me," more than once; "I promise, I'll make it worth your while..."

Eyeing Fabian from beneath her lush eyelash fringe, Valeria René confided that she knew he would, because he had promise written all over him.

Feeling like his evening had been made, regardless of anything that might later transpire; Fabian slid a hand down Valeria René's bare arm to lightly clasp her hand. With a wink, he reluctantly left her, so that she might attend to Beau, but walking backward, facing her, he mouthed that she should not forget. He would see her later.

"Oh, no doubt," she coyly whispered, before turning to Beau, and her task.

"How's the crowd out there?" buff and beautiful inquired of his makeup artist. Adjusting his banana skirt, Beau also semi-nervously fingered the dog tags that he ever wore, as his friend began to pull magic from her cosmetics case.

"Well," Valeria René sighed, "you know we picked up that cute girl—your friend Mireya, and your skinny friend Brett is here. I think I saw Jervais, your dancer friend too, and some others." She switched gears. "The crowd is pumped," she admitted, "and though they *think* they're ready for the show, ain't one of them ready for *you*, boyfriend!"

Running a dry cloth across the counter's edge to make sure it wasn't soiled; Valeria René wedged herself between it and Beau. "Hold still," she softly advised and hummed, while performing her little miracle.

Minutes later, satisfied that Beau-Josephine couldn't look any more glamorous, she helped him don his headdress and stockings. "Quit looking in the mirror, Diddley," she scolded. "I know you can't believe that's you, but it is. Now work with me, or I will have missed the whole first half. Use this, just before you come out. Oh, and," she pointed, leaving a few things for his use, "powder again before you come on stage."

The bald, attractive, ebony-skinned Fabian appeared, saying he would escort Valeria René back to her table; however, before leaving her to await Beau's coming with her friends, he whispered. With his warm breath feathering over her ear, he admitted that the hallway leading from the dressing room was long, and dimly lit. He reminded her that all sorts were in attendance. Therefore, he'd simply wanted to take care with the valuable—*her*.

Valeria René placed a hand at her breast, touched, because what a sweet and chivalrous thing for a man to say and do. Opening her arms, she hugged Fabian, and felt her body meld, oh so sensuously to his.

Reluctant to release her, he softly stated, "We fit."

Feeling slightly bereft when out of his arms, but nonetheless aroused, Valeria René agreed, before she watched Fabian walk away. While doing so, she felt her heart, like a door, creak open, just a bit. Then she became conscious of another feeling, anticipation. She could barely *wait* until intermission, because then she could again speak with the man, and smell his sinfully decadent cologne. Maybe they could even—

"So how's Diddley look?" Ronni asked, nudging her mocha-skinned roommate with an elbow.

"You'll tell me," Valeria René stated, allowing thoughts of Fabian to slip from mind. Proudly she tossed her head, "My advice, Ron? Sit up, because you don't wanna miss a thing."

Ronni spoke loudly, to be heard over the raucous crowd and the music. "I'm gonna stand." Climbing un-self consciously up and onto the table, she cupped her hands and called down to Valeria René. "Don't forget to snap-snap with that camera, or beat-down, tonight, for sure!"

"Don't you think for one minute," Valeria René saucily called up, "that I would forget to take photos of get my creation."

The crowd around the semi-bickering women began to cheer and roar. Many in the near vicinity stood, to get a better look at whatever currently took place on stage, and although they couldn't see, due to the mass of bodies wedged before them, the Cohorts and their guests could still hear the announcer.

He begged the capacity crowd to remain seated.

"Screwww you!" The audience loudmouth bellowed as finally, it seemed, the show would fully get underway.

The talent was staggering, the music loud, and the costumes were something to behold...

One contest participant in particular was quite memorable. He, or she, stepped robot-like onto the stage. Wearing a Darth Vader-esque spacesuit, the contestant proceeded to mid-stage where they stood, slowly turning the masked head, from side to side.

This elicited a few cheers. Then without warning, the accompanying music blared and stopped.

For a few seconds the house lights were lost, and in the dark, people began to murmur. "Hope there's a backup generator." "It would be a shame not to see the rest, after waiting all this time." "I want my money back." "Maybe its terrorists," someone else feared, until surprise!

The lights winked on and there was the contestant, again. The space gear however, seemed split down the middle, and the two equal parts fell clattering away. A nude man stepped from the discarded armor. However, only his right side was visible because he faced one of the stage walls.

To the astonishment of all gathered the nude man shook and wriggled.

"Oh shi-z-it!" Ronni yelled, joining the audience in going wild, "That's Marçhand, from last year!" With her phone she snapped photos.

Kismet Staar bolted upright and wrinkled her nose. Watching, Valeria René laughed, because that man was Beau's biggest competitor, his nemesis.

Marçhand, who'd been 'Vader' a moment ago, leaped around, for the further stupefaction of those congregated, and beholding his other side, the audience viewed a completely nude woman! Hers was a rounded naked breast, flowing hair, long fingernails, and bodacious booty. Cheering, and catcalling, the club patrons went wild.

Ending his stint, the unisex contestant turned. Cavalierly he left the stage, assured that the first place crown had again been secured.

The announcer stepped back onto the stage. Since he had no words, he threw back his head and screeched "Owww-ow!" and the audience responded in kind.

The show proceeded...with other impersonators and imposters alike, including: a Britney Spears, and a Milli minus Vanilli. After intermission, the list became endless.

Until...there came an original sounding score, from Josephine Baker's Parisian run.

"Oh Lord! Look!" The Cohort women and their guests began to clamor and babble. "This is Beau! Ooh oh, I'm so nervous—for him!"

The musical composition played on, unapologetic as it seized the audience. With its greatly enhanced bass and drum lines, the music magnanimously vibrated through all present, while a chorus of half-naked unbelievably fit male dancers wriggled. Wildly they gyrated to the beat of conga drums played by two topless, nearly flat-chested girls.

Positioned on the floor at the foot of the stage, the nearly naked female waifs wore leaf skirts. On their heads were woolen, lusterless black wigs, the hair of which was so long it partially covered their chests. In addition, the girls sat on great portions of the hair.

Given ample time to ogle those already present, the audience noticed eerie silence. Just before faintly, there came the sound of blowing wind.

During this seconds-long time-out, one audience member could not resist the temptation to yelp, which in turn caused others to join in. Yet the stillness continued, as the sound of the blowing wind steadily grew.

Intently the audience watched those onstage, as they stood stock-still in the dimness. Then audience members noticed the dancers, as one by one, they began to sway, at first imperceptibly. Then, like palm trees in a gathering storm, they picked up velocity.

By the time it was apparent that the storm had risen, with the 'wind' blowing loud and hard, the dancers swayed from side to side. Bending like limber palms, they nearly touched the 'ground,' beneath them. Behind them, though no one had seen it earlier in the evening, was a large screen. On this, a frothy ocean churned, under a vehement sky.

Then the wind died, the sea ceased to roil, and it seemed, as all in the audience waited with baited breath, that surely greater was to come...

Amid the impregnated silence, the two war paint-faced, savage looking conga-girls jumped up. With all eyes tracking them, the pair ran barefoot onto the stage. There, with their round bottoms jiggling, they rolled out a red runner as the dancers parted.

Creating two rows, the ripped and toned male dancers bowed as the percussionists passed. Quickly turning, the girls raced back to their instruments. There, the conga twins began a serious throw-down, their lusterless hair flying every which way. Their forceful blows on the percussion skins worked rhythm into every fiber of the audience's being, even as a light began to grow. From a pinpoint in the middle of the ocean, this light radiated outward, until it became nearly too bright for the natural eye to stand.

Then...there was *Josephine*.

Walking regal and proud onto the stage, seemingly stepping *through* the light, 'she' appeared; an object of desire and devotion.

'Her' skin was flawless, and true to their word, Kismet Staar and Valeria René had helped Beau majorly transform. He had become a creature so sensual, one he had previously only imagined in the recesses of his mind.

Noting this, Valeria René and Kismet Staar both appeared stunned, as on stage, 'Josephine' smiled tantalizingly and batted her super lengthy eyelashes, courtesy of Ronni Brown. Josephine moved too, enticingly, like a skilled houri, while the conga-girls' manes swirled and the dancers swarmed.

Around Josephine, each dancer revolved and whirled. Each was a dervish, never losing the beat, as singing, Ms. Josephine shook her bananas while the audience hooted and howled, going berserk for her club revue.

Then Josephine became super animated, and snatched off a banana, barely attached for just that purpose. She tossed it, out and into the midst of the cheering throng.

Up and on a chair, Valeria René snapped photo after pose-full photo. On one side she was supported by Barry, and to his annoyance, that fake-escort character—Fabio, or whoever—held Valeria René on the other side. Was his hand on her ass? Barry angrily wondered, peeking.

Up high also, Ronni stood on the table, yowling and screeching. Madly waving, she also stomped, with no fear or thought of falling.

At 'her' stint's end, Ms. Josephine bowed, as did her dancers. Naughty Josephine again shook her bananas, before she also lifted her skirt. In an ad-lib gesture, she scintillatingly mooned the audience.

Rooting and hollering, those congregated thundered, as quickly Beau left the stage. "Encore! Brava baby! More!" The audience chanted, "More, more, more!"

When the house would not be quieted, Beau and his troupe returned, to deliver a brief excerpt of the prior performance. Again, he and his cast left the stage with the audience caught in the throe of passion.

"*We love you Josephine!*" someone shouted, still clapping. "*We love you!*"

Chapter 11

AFTER Beau, there really was no need for the show to continue, but it did, a desperate struggle, which would inevitably lead to the showdown. In the audience, most people felt a bit anxious, and like the contestants, they too were eager to learn which participants had fared well, and which had not.

At long last, the announcer took the stage. Unnecessarily, he stated that all the contestants were worthy of honors. He also sighed, a preface to his 'arduous task' before he said, "We all know somebody's got to lose though, so somebody else can win, right?"

Receiving his fair share of boos and hisses hurriedly he raised both hands and yelled, "Qui-et!" He also said he would announce the third place runner up.

No one in the audience seemed to care much about the Little Richard impersonator. A few people clapped, almost unenthusiastically, as he received his due. Drinking and surmising, most people discussed who would take first prize.

"Second place goes to..." the announcer tried to strum up excitement. "Elllvisss!" One of the five present.

"But that one's got no rhythm!" the audience loudmouth bellowed, amidst laughter.

"Yeah," Kismet Staar whispered to her JaMerican friend Abigail, seated next to her, "but he sure is pretty, like The King, in his younger years."

"Now, for the moment of truth," the announcer contended as he was handed one envelope, and then another. He appeared baffled while ripping both open, and aimlessly he droned, about the hard time that the judges had had. "I mean just exactly how does one decide who will get the forte of distinction award?

"I don't know," he shrugged, "but when it all boils down; they've got to pick somebody, right?"

A few audience members hooted as the announcer continued. "Well, without further ado, I'm going to introduce this year's favorite, and get out of the way." Pretentiously, he coughed. "Oh, I'd just like to say—"

"Quit stalling and say the winner," the audience heckler bellowed, "bozo!

"Well!" the announcer huffed and smoothed his moussed hair. "I was *about* to say this envelope announces a tie—" "A tie?!" Hisses and boos abounded, as Ronni held her breath. Clutching her camera, Valeria René's lips moved as silently she prayed. Kismet Staar leaned toward her friends. Plaintive, she whispered, "Guess Diddley's going to be disappointed, "Guess Diddley's going to be disappointed…"

No one dared reply, while up on stage, finally managing to regain the audience's attention, the announcer hollered, "And the winner is…" Pleadingly he looked at the lifeless hair of one of the conga twins. "Think I can get a drum roll? Please?"

Sullen and catlike, the girl slunk over to her instrument. There, she obliged the announcer, who yelled over her cacophonous thumping.

"This year's winner…is none other than our own, our very spectac-u-laaar, our vivacious—"

The conga twin doled out thunderously loud blows.

"Jo-seph-feen—"

The crowd exploded with bluster and gale at having attained the winner that most of them desired. The Cohort women bounced and squealed too, along with their guests, as Beau walked regally onto the stage in his high-heeled size thirteen pumps.

Most of those present laughed as his entourage jumped wildly up and down. Visibly overtaken with glee, the dancers flailed their arms and madly hopped about. Hugging one another, toothily they grinned at the audience.

"Val!" Kismet Staar yelled, and pointed, nearly poking a screaming woman in the eye. "Photos! Get Diddley!"

Hurriedly Valeria René was again hoisted up and onto the table, with Barry on one side and Fabian on the other. Noticing though that she was shaky, Barry snatched the camera and began to click away. Standing up high, Valeria René liked that Fabian held protectively to her as she watched Beau's dancers clamor all over him. She laughed with the audience, as nearly losing his headdress he raised a large hand to secure it.

When his entourage and the crowd calmed down enough, he received his statue. He was also handed a jeweled plastic crown, and a humongous particleboard, five thousand-dollar check. Part of which would be donated to the club's two charities of choice, one of which was The Gay Men's Help Center of NYC. Beau liked that Gay Men's, as it was called, educated people on HIV/AIDS prevention, and provided resources and testing.

Broadly Beau smiled, and with his check, he posed for pictures. As he did, a diminutive blond woman was audaciously boosted onto the stage. There, she presented him with a bouquet of red roses interspersed with baby's breath. Handing them over, the small woman reached up.

Reaching down, Beau heartily hugged her, flowers and all, and the audience went wild.

As the woman's friends lifted her from the stage, jubilantly Beau smiled and took the microphone handed him by the announcer. When he spoke, a hush fell on the audience.

"Yo, everybody...I would like to give thanks, to God, for allowing me to be alive tonight. I would like to thank the judges who have bestowed this honor on me. I also want to thank all of *you!*" He pointed at the cheering mass. "You have made this one night I will never forget!"

Amid the rooting, hollering, and clapping, Beau continued. "Quickly, I would also like to thank three very dear friends of mine. These ladies," Beau sincerely stated, "are family, and I wouldn't trade them, for anything."

A member of Beau's dance troupe waved a tissue before him, and ever the actor, Beau dabbed his eyes. "I just want to say I have these divas in my corner when I'm doing well, and when I'm not. I want my *chicas* to stand up, so y'all can see how very ss-snatched they are."

When Beau's Cohorts obliged, there were tears in Kismet Staar and Valeria René's eyes. The crowd cheered as Beau and the women threw kisses back and forth.

Holding his statue high, Beau softly said into the microphone, "Val, this one's ours." To the audience he bowed, turning to go.

Practically out of sight, and nearly off the stage, he raced back. He grabbed the microphone. "Hey, I almost left without danking my thancers." Realizing his mistake, he made sputtering noises, and the audience laughed.

Again he attempted. "My bad," he chuckled. "I meant, I almost left without *thanking my dancers!*" Beau sincerely stated they were the greatest part of his act. He divulged that some in his troupe were professionals, dancers who'd studied theory and technique at the feet of the masters, Ailey, Dunham, Graham, and others. He said the list was longer than time permitted. However, he revealed, "Each person consented, simply because I asked, and for that I'm truly grateful!"

Beau bowed to his troupe, before he said, "And lastly I'd like to thank my friend, since we were little—Jervais." Beau bowed to the fragile-looking dark-skinned slender male. "I thank him for his wonderful choreography." Beau's true tenor then reverberated throughout the club as he called "Peeeace!" And with two fingers high, he left the stage.

His Cohorts clamored after him. Racing down the long hall, they converged on him in the over-filled dressing room.

"Beau!" Valeria René bounced up and down with elation. "You did it, boo!" Her joy spilled over to a man who stood aside, ravenously eyeing her cleavage.

"Yeah," Ronni pushed forward. "You're no weenie this year." Pulling Beau down, she noisily kissed him, leaving a fuchsia lip-print, which she attempted to wipe from his forehead.

Eyeing it in the mirror, Beau laughed. "Leave it," he waved, "it's our night, and who cares, right?" Cocking his head, he beckoned his cousin forward. When she stood next to him, softly he spoke while fingering his dog tags. "We've gotta call A'nt Nell."

"We do." Kismet Staar knew her mother would want to hear all.

Ronni then moved aside so that über-producer, Joseph Forrester, and his lady, Kismet Staar's friend Abigail, could congratulate Beau. Ronni watched as the famed pop music mogul pressed his card into Beau's hand. "Call me," the rugged faced man with the aura of power advised. "Let's see what we can make happen."

When the fabulous pair turned to go, Ronni pinched Beau. Quietly, but exuberantly she hissed, "Hohneee, you'd betta work!"

<h1 style="text-align:center">*Chapter 12*</h1>

$\mathcal{I}$T was nearly dawn. The women and Beau had just bid farewell to last of those who'd tagged back to The Cohort Quarters with them. The foursome had been followed from the club when people heard they were throwing an impromptu after-party...

In The Quarters' kitchen, Valeria René and Kismet Staar had made spinach dip, and warmed a large sphere of dark bread. They placed this, cheese wedges, fruit, nuts, vodka, cranberry, gin, juice, and beer on the dining room table.

Kismet Staar nodded as her longtime friend lit two tapers for the floral centerpiece. "Look at us, throwing a jam together in minutes."

Beau helped by opening additional bottles of expensive drink for those who nibbled, mingled, and danced.

Finally, the Cohorts closed the door on the last of the party people. Although exhausted, they couldn't imagine heading off to bed. Not cognizant of doing so, they had waited all evening, to be together, alone, to discuss the events.

And the time had come.

Wearing Valeria René's satin housecoat—that would not close over her ample chest, Kismet Staar lie on the purple sofa and spoke with a smile. "Beau, those people lost their minds when you appeared; oh Val, great job. Thanks to you, Diddley gave fabulous face." Again she spoke to Beau. "You worked it babe."

Across the room, sprawled on the man's flokati rug, Ronni agreed. "Didn't he though?"

Content, Valeria René lay on her chaise longue. Softly she stated that Beau had been too wonderful for words.

Ronni sat up. "Yo, I thought I couldn't hear when the space guy was there, but the noise level when you showed up, Beau! Stepping out of pure light..."Amazed, she shook her head, "And your face, boyfriend, it looked like Sam Fine or Kevin Aucoin gone-too-soon beat it."

Both Beau and Valeria René glowed with pride, because they too believed he looked like celebrity makeup artists had done him.

"Man, you looked prima!" Ronni added, "even though right now, you look sort of oily, and busted."

"Stop that." Valeria René laughed, a bell-like tinkle, before she offered, "Kiss nearly poked a woman in the eye, Diddley. The same woman who told me that *you* could teach a seduction class."

"Marçhand was pissed," Kismet Staar gleefully called out. "I don't know if any of you saw, but our space guy was in the back throwing stuff and cussing—about things having been 'fixed.' "

Ronni laughed, "Loser."

"Did you guys see his peops trying to calm him?" Valeria René inquired.

Kismet Staar nodded. "I loved every minute, because that pig won twice already."

Wearing drawstring lounging pants and a matching cropped top, Valeria René pushed a ringlet off her forehead. "I know, so why couldn't he lose gracefully? Why'd he have to be sore? Everybody knows—going into a contest that there's the chance that somebody else will win."

"Yep, and this time that somebody was Diddleee!"

"Can you believe it Kiss?" Ronni asked. "Oh, and did you two call your mother?"

"I did," Beau nodded. "While you three were dancing, and A'nt Nell said hey."

"Hey-aay," Valeria René chimed, before she changed the subject. "I cannot wait to print the photos, because I didn't look shabby! Forget Diddley. Give up some applause for *me*, people."

Kismet Staar chuckled, speaking to Ronni. "I guess even Val is entitled to an immodest moment."

Ronni changed the subject. Vociferously she called out, "Those were some men!"

"Them dancers?" Kismet Staar also became enthusiastic, "True dat!"

"Kiss danced with a couple of them," Valeria René informed no one in particular.

Kismet Staar nodded and deliciously shivered, "Danced with one, a couple of times." Lyle.

"The toned one from Belize, with the long locked hair," Valeria René acknowledged, "with the big pretty lips and biceps."

Again Kismet Staar shivered, "Big man felt good."

"It's a wonder *you* noticed anybody, Val," Ronni blurted, ignoring Beau's cousin. "The way you and 'the escort' were carrying on."

Valeria René waved. "So? We danced, and talked."

"Yep, bump 'n grind, slow 'n close," really close, "all night long."

Valeria René's eyes narrowed, because did Ronni sound jealous, or cynical, when she was always all over some man? The curly locked one shrugged, forgetting Ronni to remember the feel of Fabian's night stick pressed against her. "Our reaction was chemical. Now leave me alone Ron, because I gotta get back to Kiss, and her dancer. So...did you two exchange digits?"

"Puh-lease." Dismissively Ronni waved. "Kiss might have enjoyed that lil bit of attention, but she'll stick with her tired men who're less racy, and a lot less sexy."

Valeria René's eyes widened because ooh, that was raggedy! The sentiment, she thought, was quite mean, even for Ronni. Therefore, Valeria René didn't acknowledge it. Instead, she addressed Kismet Staar. "Did you get, or give, the digits?"

Without a word, the curvaceous woman pulled paper from her bosom and waved it. "I didn't just dance with the chiseled body, which was heaven; I spoke with him, half an hour ago. And get this—big *papi's* ready to see me again."

Talk about unfair! Speechless, Ronni could not disguise the fact that she was incensed.

At the club, she'd sidled up to that particular man, noting his chiseled physique and sculpted face. He'd been pleasant enough, but it had been clear, he'd not given Ronni a second thought. It had had indeed angered her because not many men brushed her off; the few times that one did, he was usually gay. Therefore, seated on the floor, in her home Ronni thought, who would have pegged Kismet Staar Moore for being able to pull *that* kind of man, Ronni's kind of man?

Shit, the mouthy one thought, Kiss probably couldn't *handle* that much combustion. Or could she? Ronni told herself she wondered because she was concerned, for Kiss. However, the truth was she was jealous. She was also unaware that her dark brows knit together, to reveal her true consternation.

Valeria René squealed, secretly happy that Kismet Staar had laid the smack down on Ronni. It had been needed, because Ronni thought she was the only woman that sexy men were interested in. Please. "Kiss, I'm happy for you."

"Hey—was that you Ron," Beau wondered aloud, unintentionally changing the subject, "standing on you guy's table?"

"It sure was," Valeria René nodded. She stated that Ronni had also kicked over his sexy friend-boy Kieran's drink.

"Kieran didn't want it," Ronni near-whined, referring to Beau's sometime lover. "He showed me. *Somebody's* curly Indian hair was in it."

"I am IndiAfricAmerican," Valeria René corrected, as she often did. "I'm a multiplicity of things and ethnicities, and I would thank you to remember that."

Facing Valeria René, Beau teasingly inquired if she would soon sport a baldhead like her new bean-grower escort.

"If you're talking about Fabian, then let me explain something," Valeria René huffed, feeling inexplicably protective of the man whom she really didn't know. "I think he's fine—black, bald, and sexy. And my hair suits me fine. See what you started Ron. But back to Diddley." She visually pinned him. "I'd thank you not to call Fabian out of his name."

"Or what? Don't get all huffy," Beau advised, amused. "I just stated what the man's name means."

Valeria René wrinkled her nose, "Bean-grower?"

Beau nodded. "Or nurturer, or farmer."

"Diddley, please, what are you droning about now?" Ronni asked while sleepily scratching an arm.

"I'm talking about reading," Beau articulated. He suggested that his cousin and his roommates purchase books of baby names. He advised them to study the meanings, because one or all of them could one day become mothers.

"Not me." Ronni leaned to scratch the itchy spot at her ankle.

"Diddley," Kismet Staar called. "I'm lost; what has becoming somebody's mama got to do with Fabian?"

Valeria René softly spoke. "Kiss, Diddley was explaining what Fabian's name means. Then he said you and I—since Ronni opted out—might one day become mothers, so he suggested we own books of baby names."

"Right," Beau nodded. He also said, "Don't get it twisted Val, because 'bean-grower' isn't a bad thing. You see, in order to grow something, a person must essentially start with what appears to be little or nothing. Then they cause it to become significantly something. So that means said person needs to be a nurturer, of sorts."

"Well," Valeria René thought aloud, "I *could* use nurturing..." I could use a 'beating' with that night stick of his too, she naughtily mused.

Beau chuckled before admitting he owned name books. "You girls can borrow them too," he said, "because it's insightful to know what a person's name means." It sometimes clarified why a person had certain personality traits or characteristics.

Beau also explained that names—contrary to popular belief—emitted power. He said the meanings often times even had profound effects on the wearer, whether or not the name bearer was aware of it. "In ancient cultures, and in many today," he continued, "it was, and is yet believed that one's name is linked with their destiny.

"Why do you think," he further proposed, "monarchs and royalty only bestow certain names on their offspring? They don't make up names, claiming they're from the motherland. Nor do they pick names just because they sound cute."

"If books of baby names are for mothers-to-be," Ronni sarcastically began. "Then what are you doing with them, Beau?"

"I might have a child, someday," the man smoothly acknowledged. "Anyway, Kismet Staar's mother was the first to teach me about names and their power. I came to Kiss and my A'nt Nell from a situation where I was greatly devalued," he divulged. "Therefore, my Aunt found value in me, by starting with my name, Beauregard. It means: to see, or behold, beauty."

Beau explained that after learning that, he began to feel marginally better about himself. He explained that his Aunt had also told him that at age twenty-six she had been expecting Kismet Staar. She had searched in Swahili name books, American name books; you name the book, for her soon-to-be-born baby's name.

"So what does Kiss' name mean?" Ronni inquired, yet sleepily scratching.

"Well," Beau explained, "Kismet is Islamic, for fate or destiny. For short, 'Kiss' means to touch, or press gently, most times in greeting or affection. A kiss can also be a sweet gesture, or a small candy."

"What about her middle name?" Ronni probed.

"Star means: any heavenly body, with the exception of the moon and the planets. It has also been documented that stars influence humankind and events. Kiss' last name, which she was fated to have," Beau nodded, "is Moore, it's Muslim. It means mixed, Berber and Arab. They were people who inhabited northwest Africa. To moor also means to fix firmly, or to anchor to a certain place. That's without the E at the end."

Valeria René nodded. "Well it seems like Kiss is what her name suggests. She can be sweet and she influences us. She has also been stable, our anchor, lots of times."

"What does my name mean?" Ronni asked, intrigued.

"I believe its strong counsel," Beau admitted of her nickname. He also stated that since 'Ronni' was a derivative of Veronica, he'd have to look up her given name.

Valeria René offered knowledge of her own. "I know that 'Beau' also means sweetheart, boyfriend, and beautiful—all of which you are, Diddley."

Ronni noted the wink that her male roommate gave Valeria René, and she rolled her eyes. Derisively she also said, "Leave it to you Val, to make anything romantic."

"Hush," Valeria René waved, and turned. "Beau, if this name business is so; I'll research it; then let me tell you, Fabian can nurture me any day." He can use that big stick of his on me too, she did not say.

Kismet Staar and her cousin laughed, while not particularly amused or sleepy any longer, Ronni spoke up. "Let's get back to Diddley having a baby. How you plan to do that, Mister? You're gonna make one, with a woman?"

"I might," Beau quipped, sounding perturbed. "How else would I have one, if I didn't foster or adopt."

Feeling upset, and not sure why, Beau did not mention that he'd extensively pondered the latter, after realizing that too many children languished, while desiring dedicated parents.

"But you'd have to have contact, I mean intercour—well, *you know*, with a woman," Ronni persisted.

Valeria René spoke on Beau's behalf. "Not necessarily."

The mouthy roommate cut her eyes at the unwanted interjection.

"Ron, you're thinking, but along the wrong lines. Like other people," Beau admitted, "if I too chose to have a child, I would use my God-given fluids. Just like you would use the mechanism you have. However, I wouldn't go about it like you think."

"Then why bother?" Ronni rolled her eyes. "You would probably have to carry 'your kind' of magazines, somewhere. You'd have to jerk off, then ejaculate, probably in a jar; then some poor woman would have to endure insertion. The woman would wind up an *incubator* for your sperm, and an egg."

Ronni shook her head. "It seems like one big hassle to me, when you could do it the old fashioned way. Not to mention the expense of it all." She thought for a moment, and verbally jumped back in. "Yo, what if after all of that, it doesn't work?"

"It's not *guaranteed* to work your way either, Ronni," Beau huffed. He said he couldn't believe it. He got the same narrow-minded thinking thing from other people, but he had honestly never dreamed he would receive it from a Cohort.

"I didn't mean any harm," Ronni near whined. She said she was just trying to understand. Sitting erect, she said she'd believed that all present could converse about anything, without offense, provided no one attempted to be facetious.

"We can." Valeria René spoke with her eyes on Beau. "Diddley, please don't clam up. I happen to be interested too."

Suddenly, feeling uncomfortable he asked, "Why y'all sweatin' me?"

Kismet Staar remembered the frightened pre-teen that her cousin had once been. She also remembered how he would lash out, anytime he felt he had been threatened. Therefore, ever-protective, she attempted to head off what could so quickly become a storm. She did so by gingerly calling, "Diddle-Diddle...baby... I don't think anybody's trying to gang up on you, about your life, or your beliefs." She spoke like she would have had she been counseling a troubled teen. "I think the ladies are sincerely trying to understand."

She shrugged, and gave her first cousin who was sometimes defensive, an out. "If this is uncomfortable though, we can forget it. I'll just go on home, okay?" Break up the party. "It's your call."

"I feel like a lab rat," Beau admitted, as his fingers inched up, to find his dog tags beneath his tee. He rocked, experiencing a multiplicity of unpleasant emotions.

"I don't believe that's anyone's intention," his cousin softly stated. "Remember, you know I wouldn't allow anyone to hurt you…"

Yet Beau rocked, and recalled aloud that while he and Kismet Staar had been growing up, she had beaten the crap out of many an adolescent, and a few teenagers. She had done so in the name of protecting him, although he too had done his share of fighting. He did not mention that his female friend Mireya had also been protective of him; *that* Ronni had found out some time back, having received a punch in the mouth.

"You know…" Beau said, fingering his dog tags. "I believe Kiss got her fighting spirit from her mother."

Knowing Kismet Staar's sweet round mother, Beau's aunt, Ronni and Valeria René exchanged surprised glances, before they gazed expectantly back at him.

"Bet you two didn't know that about A'nt Nell," he nodded, handling the silver dog tags that he always wore. "I'll tell you about one time in particular…"

He mentioned that his aunt had given him his beloved dog tags, on the day that she'd begun to call him Puppy. Around that time Nell also gave him a live dog that he'd named Pal.

Beau said he and his aunt, Nell, had gotten Pal from the pound, and Pal was skittish, because the pup had been abused, like Beau had. This his aunt pointed out; "but Puppy," she'd said, "neither you nor Pal ever have to worry about being beaten again."

Beau told his roommates that his Aunt also said that he, Kismet Staar, her half-sister Farai, and the little dog Pal were all her pups. Nell said having pups made her the mama dog—the bitch. She also said, "Puppy, if you want to see a real live bitch, a mean mama dog, then let your mother ever come nosing 'round here."

"My mother despised Diddley's mother," Kismet Staar interjected. Nell still did, "for the way Diddley's mother treated him."

"Yep," Beau nodded. Aloud, he recalled his aunt ferociously swearing she'd tear the skin from his mother's bones, should his mother ever darken their doorway.

"Why?" Valeria René wanted to know.

"I'll get to that," Beau stated, but first he showed his Cohorts how his aunt had puffed herself up, before she'd said, "Go'n back to sleep now sugar, because Mama Bitch is here."

"Beau," Ronni called, "I really want to get back to discussing you having a baby—and wait. Let me finish. I understand that discussing this might cause you to feel funny; but I feel funny too, sometimes. I do, because my life was a mess, and because I've been put on the spot, about...my beliefs and my behavior. So please know, I wouldn't do that to you."

Ronni placed a hand at her chest. "I just want to understand. How can yo' fine ass live here, with me and Val—two sexy sistas—and yet you're not attracted to either of us."

Seated on the floor, Ronni leaned forward. "Diddley, how do you resist, when we lean against you, or when I put my boobs in your face? I've sat on your lap too, wearing only a bra and panties, and you've refused—even when I've offered."

Beau sighed, and stroked his dog tags, as he pondered what to say.

When finally he spoke, he said it would be foolish if he did not at least try to help his friends to better understand him. "Not only as a homosexual male, but as a person..."

He admitted however, that he just did not know where to begin.

Chapter 13

BEAU momentarily excused himself and headed for the kitchen. He returned with a glass of water. He swallowed, and began to speak. "Okay. I'll admit I feel 'funny' like Ronni said. I feel that way because people react like I'm from Pluto or Mars when they realize I'm gay. It happens a lot. It seems, the moment a person finds out, they become negative or jaded."

Even Ronni had changed toward Beau the day he'd moved into the Cohort Quarters, the day she'd learned her new roommate was homosexual. This Beau did not say, but he did say he felt like opportunities that members of the heterosexual population received, he sometimes didn't. Therefore, he sometimes felt discriminated against.

"If you really think about it though," he said in his own defense, "I'm no different than anyone else. I want the same basic things that Val and I discussed a few weeks back. Like most people, I want to be loved, and respected. I also want a drama-free life; as a *person*, I just want the opportunity to live without being made to feel freakish or perverse."

Beau also admitted it angered him to hear people say things like those recently uttered by Ronni. It also hurt to hear that 'homosexuals had no business becoming parents.'

"What," he asked, "makes it ok for heterosexual's to parent—those who are abusive and mean?"

"But the bible says— " Ronni interjected, only to be cut off.

"Yeah, yeah, the bible," Beau shot back. "People use it to say that homosexuals are aberrations, but I've read the bible my damn self. I read that *all* have sinned and come short of the glory of God. I also read that God so loved *the world*, which means God loves even *me*. So I wish people would shut up, and leave people like me alone; I didn't choose to be this way."

"Beau," Ronni called with eyes wide. "You think you were born that way?"

"I don't know." He shook his head. "I only know that I was always different, from other boys. When I was younger, I thought it was because my home life was different—fucked up. I felt like I was the only different one. Now, I know there are countless other people like me. We're all human, and as such, we just want to be treated fairly."

Ronni leaned forward. "Were you ever...interested in women?"

"I've always thought them beautiful," Beau acknowledged. "I can see where they're sexy too; but I've always viewed women the way somebody would view lovely flowers."

Valeria René sadly smiled. "You don't want sex with flowers."

"Bingo." Beau said that didn't negate the fact that he had lots of love inside. "But I was unaware of how much until you three girls barged into my life—with all your shoes, cosmetics, chaos and confusion."

Smiling he said, "No, I'm kidding." Beau said he also wanted to make one thing clear. "Once, Val got bent because I called you three 'girls.' She said it was disrespectful, because you are all women. However, no one knows that better than I. So *I* call you 'girls' not to be demeaning, like some people, but because you're my *girlfriends*. I'm aware that you three are formidable women, and I address you as such when I speak of you to other people."

"Diddley you explained, when I mentioned it."

"I know Val," Beau nodded. "But I didn't say anything to Kiss or Ronni." Beau then reminded his family of friends that he could never forget that names mean a great deal. "It's why when I joke, or when I'm angry, I never call y'all bitches or ho's. That's disrespectful."

Ronni leaned forward, her eyes mirroring hardened pebbles. "Okay, so you don't call us those things—to our faces, but I *have* heard you refer to your real mother as a bitch."

"A spade is a spade," Beau retorted, feeling a spark of frisson. "And behind your backs, I don't say what I can't say to your faces. Look, I'm bigger than all of you, I box every day; I knock big-ass grown *men* down. So y'all can't beat me. Therefore, I have no need to be afraid of either of you, so understand, I say what I wanna say—to you, and to others."

Beau sighed. "As for that business about my so-called *mother*... maybe I need to start at the beginning, for you—Val and Ronni to understand.

"The woman who birthed me was named Ophelia, like the character in Shakespeare's Hamlet. I'm sure you know the literary Ophelia eventually went mad and drowned herself. I can only *hope* my mother has done the same," Beau bitterly divulged.

He said his father Emmett, Kismet Staar's uncle, her mother's brother, loved his wife Ophelia. However, Ophelia didn't love Emmett. "She didn't love anybody, not even me, her son, because she didn't love herself, to start with. It's why she was a whore."

Beau explained that his father, a tailor, went to work every day, and his stay-at-home wife Ophelia got into trouble. Often she claimed she was bored, so she tried to get Emmett to take her on lavish trips, like those she saw on television. "She wanted to go on 'The Love Boat' and 'Fantasy Island,' stuff like that, but my father just didn't have that kind of money. Hell, she'd have probably been glad to go to *'Gilligan's* Island' just to get with the professor, because that's how she was."

Forgetting venomous words, Beau said Ophelia began taking forays down into seedy areas, away from the nice home that Emmett strove to pay for. In the bottoms, Ophelia purchased drugs, so she could take mental trips. "Sometimes she even slept down there," Beau bitterly recalled. "I was three or four then, but I remember. That was when the fighting started, because my dad wanted her to straighten up.

"A round-ish woman came to get me," Beau said and smiled. The woman was his aunt, Nell. She had two girls with her. The girls who were a little older than Beau were his cousins, Kismet Staar and her sister Farai.

"Anyway, when A'nt Nell came for me, a big fight ensued." Beau continued, "My mother Ophelia was angry that my father had asked his sister to get me, his boy. Ophelia was angry that my father had also called his mother, my and Kismet Staar's Grandma Lacey—God rest her soul. My father called his mother and his sister many times, because he needed help. He had to work. I remember him telling my mother, as she sat looking dazed, that his son needed care, but my mother couldn't do it in her drugged-out state."

Beau's mother Ophelia pitched fits, one of which she threw when Nell arrived to get Beau. The women fought. "I remember being small, and up in my aunt's arms. That time my aunt shoved Ophelia into a wall.

A'nt Nell was trying to get me out to her car, but Ophelia was screaming, punching, pulling my aunt's hair and—just having a fit!

"Later she called my aunt, and vowed to get it together. She just wanted her child, she said. A'nt Nell was reluctant to return me," Beau revealed. "But she took me back, against her better judgment, and all hell broke loose. My mother became one of those abusive heterosexuals that I mentioned. She was so angry with my father, his sister, and their mother for interfering, that she began taking her frustrations out on me," her small son.

"Ophelia used to beat me, in places where it wouldn't show, and I had to keep it secret. Once she fractured my ribs, but I stayed quiet because I knew she would beat me more if I told. So with one secret under my belt, that bitch—yes Ronni, I called her that, she gave me another.

"I suspect she'd always let men frequent my father's home, but now, while he worked she did it more."

Beau stared at Ronni for a long time, because she had to know his point had been made. Remembering more, he told his roommates that his Grandma Lacey arrived after Emmett sensed evil-doing. Beau's grandmother sort of kept an eye on things.

"When she showed up, I loved it. She cleaned and cooked. She made me feel like I had a home, or like I did when I went to my A'nt Nell's house. Grandma Lacey bathed me, and she sang church songs while I splashed around in soapy water. She had the prettiest soprano voice. She would kiss me and say she was going to eat me all up." These things Beau said with an inner light in his eyes. "My grandma would hug me and wrap me in a towel. She would say I was her good boy. She always said 'Grandma loves you baybeh.' She was the person who started calling me Diddley, after the guitarist Bo Diddley."

As the ladies listened, Beau said his aunt came to get him a few more times, occasions where she literally had to fight Ophelia to get him out of the then-filthy house.

"The last time Ophelia got me back from A'nt Nell," drug-addicted "Ophelia ran away. She laughed and thought it would be fun to leave my father, who had just learned he had cancer. Then, for me," Beau softly stated, "life became *hell*…"

He gulped water, and forced himself to continue. "I've said my mother moved tons of times to keep my father from catching up with us.

I've even briefly mentioned how she abandoned me when I was eight... The truth is: she just left me in that last dinky apartment, by myself."

Beau voiced, minus emotion, that it had been days and days before it dawned on him that his mother was not coming back.

As an adult seated before those he loved, he had to summon all his acting skills to simply recite, like he felt nothing, that Ophelia had up and left, him, without a trace. He also shared with the seated women that old Mr. Fulton who'd lived in the apartment below, took care of him.

With widened eyes Valeria René asked, "Your *grandfather* lived downstairs?"

Beau raised a finger. "I'm getting to that. Now one day I was in the closet, where Ophelia left me. I was pissy and everything because I'd been in there so long, *and* I was hungry. So since I didn't hear anything, no fighting or sex noises...no drunken crying or laughing, I crawled out of the closet. I stepped over drug paraphernalia, beer cans, a pizza box and whatever else. I opened the apartment door. I peeked out into the hallway, and when I didn't see anybody, I ran to the steps. I ran down them. I was scared, but I remember hearing other tenants' televisions blasting game shows. A dog barked, off in the distance, and a baby whined while his mother hummed right along with him."

Beau revealed that he knocked on the downstairs door of his old neighbor. "I'd seen him many times before."

Mr. Fulton stood in his doorway, looking down; he asked, 'Where ya mama, boy?' The elderly man also asked why was Beau so dirty.

Making his voice gruff, Beau imitated Mr. Fulton. 'Weh, [well] don't just stand there, come on in, and close the door.' Beau said the older man fixed him soup, and spread newspaper on a chair so that he could be seated. Afterward, the old man sent Beau back upstairs, saying he didn't want trouble.

"When I kept showing up," Beau admitted, "Pa Fulton wanted to know why I wasn't in school. He asked where my no good mama was; so did the landlord."

Beau said he stayed with Pa Fulton for the remainder of that month. Then school let out, even though Beau had only been going sporadically, due to his mother's lifestyle, or lack thereof. Beau said, "Ophelia's apartment was cleaned and re-rented. Then, I sort of belonged to Pa..."

"Did he rape you Diddley?" Ronni blurted. She needed to know, because maybe that had been Beau's first experience with homosexuality. She was convinced that a person's first sexual experience determined their lifelong preference.

"No, Pa Fulton did not rape me!" Mentally Beau beat back anger as he spoke. "Unlike others, *that* man never touched me. He squeezed my shoulder occasionally, for encouragement, and he was gracious enough to let me sleep on his sofa. He even used his little money to buy me clothes, from thrift stores. Then he spent more money to launder them."

Beau told his roommates the older man was a churchgoer who also discreetly received other clothing for his small charge from a few church members.

"Pa taught me to shine my shoes—the ones he'd bought me." While speaking, Beau revisited all in his mind... "Pa told me that a man should always appear presentable. He gave me chores to do, like scrubbing the toilet, sweeping, and taking out the trash. He and I took turns. He said a man was supposed to work, make money, and pay his bills on time. He said a man was to save, and treat his woman nice; but Pa Fulton scared me too..."

Beau's fingers crept up to find his dog tags, and seeing it, the women became wary.

"Pa told me he was trying to locate my family," Beau said and alleviated fear. "I had a literal fit then. I cried and was so snot-nosed, until Pa had to explain."

The man said he wasn't seeking Beau's *mother*. He was simply searching for Beau's father, or anybody who could get him into school, come the fall. "You gotta get educated, boy. Or you'll wind up a plum bum, like your mama."

Unbeknownst to Beau or to Pa Fulton though, Beau's father Emmett had died. Emmett's sister Nell however, had begun a search. She'd hired a private investigator to locate her brother's child. Aware that it was what his relentless little wife had to do, Kismet Staar's father Brantley just shook his head.

"My aunt's search and Pa Fulton's collided. I was told I was going to live with my family. I remember being so scared," Beau stated. "I didn't know what to expect."

Beau said he'd grown to want the quiet of the days spent with Pa Fulton. The little boy grew to love shining his semi-new shoes too. Beau said since living with Pa Fulton, he hadn't even crawled into the closet as much when a big truck noise outside scared him. He didn't say that previously, he'd started crawling into the closet because it was where Ophelia threw him, for hours on end. He did admit though, that the closet was his 'punishment place.' "If I had a bowel movement or if I peed while I was in there," Beau divulged, "Ophelia would beat me, with a broom handle or a shoe, while she screamed that I was a nasty little animal. Now, I can't bear small spaces, or elevators."

Beau also seemingly digressed as he told of how one day while living with Pa Fulton, the older man had gone to get the mail. "I figured he must have got to talking with a neighbor, because he was gone a while." So, alone, and shining his shoes, Beau felt free to do what he had only done in the dark of the closet. He began to sing.

"I sang one of the hymns that Grandma Lacey sang when she visited and cooked at my father's house." Beau revealed that softly he'd also sung while in the dark closet. He did it to keep fear at bay, due to his mother's incessant shenanigans. "Stuffed in there, I'd sing and feel close to anybody who had ever loved me. Therefore, finding myself alone, in Pa Fulton's apartment, the song just bubbled up 'n out of me."

Beau said he hadn't known that the older man had brought his mail back into the clean, small, sunny apartment. Remaining silent the man had listened as small Beau, unaware of him, continued to sing. However, when Beau noticed, he fell silent.

"But I saw Pa Fulton's eyes," shimmering with tears they were, as wearily the old man sat. Softly he spoke. 'Boy, you got a mighty fine gift there. Got one of the purest voices I've heard in a long time.' Pa Fulton told Beau that his gift would take him far, and give others joy. "Yo' voice will let people forget they troubles, for a while—a good thang."

Beau admitted that soon afterward, he'd been coaxed to sing at Pa Fulton's church, for Men's Day. People cried and hugged the youngster. Beau revealed that living through what he had with his mother, he hadn't liked to be touched, but having people hug him, in sincerity, went a long way toward restoring his faith in people, adults especially.

Then Kismet Staar's mother Nell came. "I knew her on sight," Beau divulged. "I also remembered her fights with my mother. So as a child, I associated the two, thinking that my mother would be around if my A'nt Nell was around.

"I cried. Pa Fulton cried," Beau said, remembering. "A'nt Nell cried too, and she hugged Pa Fulton over and over. She kept thanking him. Then I looked over and saw my cousin, in the car, crying."

Kismet Staar's eyes filled as she admitted that back then she hadn't known exactly why she'd cried, "I just saw Mama, my lil' cousin, and an older man bawling, so I did too."

Reaching for Kismet Staar's hand Valeria René, gave it a squeeze. "Children can be so sensitive."

"They can," Beau acknowledged, before he again spoke of the older man who had been a savior for him. "I believe Pa Fulton kind of got used to having me for company. He liked having his little errands run. I would get him the paper, and gum, and a candy bar. He let me get candy too.

"Since I've been grown," Beau divulged, "Pa told me that he liked our long ago routine. It went like this, he would fix breakfast. Then after dishes, we'd walk to the park. He'd play chess. Then he'd meet me at the kid's park. We would walk home. He'd fix me spaghetti and Jell-O. I would do some homework that he had thought up so I wouldn't be behind when I finally got back in school. We'd watch 'The Brady Bunch' or play cards. Some days we'd go to the store, or to church, or to the post office and the pharmacy.

"That was our life, and since then, Pa has told me more. Back then, he wondered if he should contact my family because he really didn't want to wind up alone again, after I was gone. Thankfully though, that wasn't the case. A'nt Nell incorporated him into my life"

Beau looked at his cousin as he said, "She fused Pa into all our lives."

"So *that's* how he became your grandfather..." Valeria René whispered.

Kismet Staar nodded. "He's been 'Pa' ever since, and I can't imagine not having him, even though now he's getting up there. He's eighty-seven, right Diddley?"

Beau nodded. "But even when I transferred from Pa Fulton's home to my Aunt's, I was pent-up and frightened." Beau admitted that he suffered nightmares, and from the notion that one day his family would abandon him, as his mother had—and like he'd thought Pa Fulton had. Beau believed his aunt would one day call someone else to take him.

"Even though," Beau was quick to acknowledge, "I *now* know that raising a child—an emotionally distressed child like I was, might have shortened Pa's life."

Beau's eyes clouded, and he took a moment to regain his composure. "Pa was the proverbial little sweet granddad," he sighed, "and when he's gone to Heaven, I'll never forget him, or that it took so much love for him to rescue me. Then it took a greater depth of love for him to unselfishly give me back my father's family."

Beau went on to explain that he had never really known his father, Emmett DeVeaux, because he had been a young boy, and Emmett had worked hard, away from home. Beau also hadn't really known his father because Ophelia eluded Emmett and had started doing so when Beau was only months old. She claimed she'd done so because Emmett reprimanded her—for her cheating ways.

Knowing she wasn't maternal, Ophelia returned her small son to his father. Still, she fled many times over, taking Beau with her; each time to hurt Emmett.

"See?" Valeria René whined. "When parents do spiteful things, to hurt the other parent, it really hurts the child."

Beau agreed. He also revealed that being physically and emotionally battered, he'd begun to believe no one could love him. Things that had been said and done to him had only reiterated that he was unlovable.

"Did you girls know she'd ask me, *why are you here*?" Beau said he took that to mean why was he alive? "With me around, Ophelia couldn't really do her thing like she wanted to."

Beau also told his family, two of whom he'd met when all three had been college dorm mates, that his mother hadn't been very attractive. However, when she'd wanted to, Ophelia could clean up nicely. She got dressed, fixed her hair, gave good face, and fooled people.

"But was she the epitome of selfish and mean!" Beau huffed. "All she wanted was to get high, and chase men." When she couldn't do so she screamed that having him had been a mistake. "Do you know what words like those do to the worth of a child?"

Beau furiously fingered his dog tags. "Maybe now you can all understand why it seems like I sometimes crave love and attention; because there was a time when I couldn't bring myself to even reach for it," Beau divulged. "I didn't know how."

For a few moments he remained silent, wondering if he should tell the rest.

"I remember once," he said, having decided to tell. "I made Ophelia one of those corny little Mother's day cards."

He attempted to swallow bitterness. "You know; the ones we all made in public school, out of construction paper and glued-on paper lace. I was so happy about it, that I'd made it, until I rushed all the way home."

Again, Beau swallowed, as he re-lived the incident. At home, he the small boy pounded to get in, because he had no key. Ophelia opened the door... It all happened so fast that he couldn't remember every nuance. He only knew that one second he held his paper love-declaration out to Ophelia. The next instant, he was on the nasty floor, with a split lip.

The adult Beau moaned. "I felt like somebody had swung a bag of nickels into my face." He said that back then tears had flowed, stinging his eyes and the inner bridge of his nose.

"I just wanted her to *love* me," Beau choked out. Aloud, he also berated himself for being stupid enough to think that a little piece of pink paper could have fostered that.

Beau struggled and composed himself enough to say that Ophelia turned away. "She leaned to feel around on the couch—that was her bed, slash screwing spot when she was fired-up, to find her last broken cigarette. She lit it, while saying my 'dumb self' almost gave her a heart attack, bamming on the door like that. She asked if I was crazy.

"I was a kid!" Beau hollered and startled the women who felt so bad for him. "But I *must have* been straight cray," he acknowledged, "because I never ran away, and she caused me immeasurable pain."

The actor then bared his soul by admitting that all sorts of vile men trekked through Ophelia's apartment. They screwed her, beat her, and trashed the place; but not before some got at her son, sexually. They did things to him that no adult should even ponder doing to a child.

"She let them use things on me..." Beau remembered one scarred man in particular, one of the first. He pushed and held the small boy down, mashing his face into the sofa. Nearly unable to breathe, Beau felt the man fumble around behind him. Then he felt like he was being ripped open. He said the fire-hot pain spread from his buttocks to his spine and radiated outward, even to his fingertips and toes. "My whole body was trembling."

Recalling the man's grunts, Beau said he tried to get air while screaming and clawing, attempting to escape that awful pain.

In a somber voice, he mentioned Ophelia.

Nearby she sat, smoking a cigarette.

"I tell you Ronni," Beau ferociously whispered. "When I have the child that we spoke of, I will always provide a *safe* environment for him or her.

"I will never say things that might make my child feel guilty for being alive, and I'll never allow any of that hitting business! I was beat with a brush, and a broom, but heck; there are other methods of discipline.

"I promise this too. I will do what my A'nt Nell did for me, even over the phone tonight. I will tell my precious little one that he or she is loved."

Beau then closed his eyes, to block out remembered pain, and to keep from weeping.

Softly he said he would reveal all, because never again would he speak of such things.

"Ophelia and I didn't celebrate birthdays... To do so probably would have meant she was glad I was alive, when she wasn't. So I never even got a cupcake with a candle in it."

Beau leaned forward and looked each woman in the eye. "My mother could have beaten me to a pulp and I'd never have raised my arm in defense, if *just once* she'd said 'I love you.'"

Remembering and feeling old hurts, Beau then refrained from speaking, for fear of crying out, in the same manner that he had when he had been an abused boy.

Watching her roommate, so obviously in turmoil, Valeria René tried, unsuccessfully, not to absorb his pain. With tears blurring her vision, she tried covering her mouth, because never before had she truly understood Beau's heartache. She also wondered if his traumatic experiences with Ophelia—the first woman in his life—were why he was not at all attracted to women, perhaps he didn't trust them.

Across the room, the tall buff brown man released a ragged breath. "I always wanted to feel as though I belong. Sometimes I feel that, here."

He inhaled and was also able to mention the huge birthday bash that his female Cohorts had thrown for him the prior year. "None of you knows what that did for me... To have seen Grandma Lacey," who'd been alive then, "and A'nt Nell, and Pa Fulton... To have seen Jervais, Mircya, and all my friends, and you girls. When I disappeared, I was in the bathroom, shaking, and trying—I tried to stop crying."

Beau admitted, "I wanted to '*be a man*' like Ophelia had always told me. I wanted to be strong and not show emotion but I couldn't pull it off, because somebody was glad for *me*, at last. For the gay friggin' idiot boy, you know?"

Beau's throat hurt. His eyes shimmered with unshed tears as desperately he tried to compose himself. "I feel," he finally managed, "Like at last I'm finding my place, of belonging. I'm working on becoming a loving person too, so that I can not only give, but receive love."

Seeing Beau so torn up wasn't easy, so teasingly Ronni stated, "You could feel more loved, big man, if you'd go on in the back..."

Beau chuckled, aware of what Ronni was trying to do. It was why he said they needn't get physical. "We can keep our clothes on and love each other all our lives."

"Wait a minute," Ronni raised her hand. "Explain, and maybe I'll learn something tonight—no, this morning." She motioned to the window where dawn peered in.

"Yo, it's simple." Beau shrugged. "I love you. You love me; so we're lovers, people who love."

Ronni disagreed, but Beau continued, asking, "When one feels the passion that I feel for you girls, doesn't that feeling make me passionate?"

"It does," Kismet Staar agreed.

Beau spoke on. "I suppose my and Ronni's 'passion' is why we fight. Passion is a pendulum. It swings both ways, it can love or hate."

Yet Ronni frowned, and Beau attempted to further explain. "Ron, love isn't only physical. It's not only the 'act.' It encompasses us, inside. It's not our looks, or what we wear, or the jobs we have. Love is about us, as people. Love includes what we mean to each other. Expand your mind and grasp this."

"I'm there." Valeria René nodded. She articulated that love accepted others for whom and what they were. "Let me add this. Love also grants *absolution*. It pardons a person who has done wrong. Love forgives, and finds a way to remain, even when those who love can no longer be together."

Looking at each person present, Valeria René revealed that she and her boyfriend Marc had had that type of love. She reminded her family of friends that Marc had given her the earrings borrowed for Beau's contest. She said that all she and Marc McKennon had to do was be.

Fondly, Valeria René told her friends that with Marc, even the mundane had been special. When they sat beside each other, walked, or engaged in any activity, it had been so much more, perhaps because of something he had once told her. He'd said that anytime he and she were together, or anytime that he thought of her, he was making love to her. "And I've never had another man actually make love to me the way he did. He took time, he cared, about pleasing me, he satisfied me…"

Ronni Brown's breath caught in her throat, and she, the most cynical of the Cohorts, acknowledged that the sentiment was beautiful.

"Sometimes," she quietly uttered, reluctant to reveal her true feelings, "I wish somebody would love *me* like that; but you know what?" she asked, her voice hardening. "I can't imagine it. I can't even see myself really loving somebody back. Now, is that messed up or what?"

"It's not," Kismet Staar softly voiced. "It's just where you are right now, Brownie."

Ronni swore she would always feel the same way. She said she would never fully give her self, because she would never make herself vulnerable, to hurt.

Listening, Ronni's Cohorts realized what she failed to see that in being open, although there was the chance for hurt, she could also experience immense joy.

Beau, Valeria René, and Kismet Staar were also aware that Veronica Maria Brown's negative perceptions of love had been determined when she'd been a girl. Like Beau, Ronni had lived a loveless life, but unlike him, she had since, not altered her beliefs.

"I envy you Val," Ronni admitted. "Heck, I envy anybody courageous enough to love strong and long, because I can't. I can give the booty, but the inside me—" the real, softer Ronni, the person who longed for love? "That Ronni Marie Brown I keep for me."

Although Beau wanted to say it, he decided to keep to himself the fact that the very powerlessness experienced when in love was what made one powerful enough to love. Therefore, the Cohorts sat in silence, until finally Kismet Staar spoke.

"Val," she called. "I think you should love Marc until you die, because it's obvious, he left you lasting love."

Valeria René dropped her head and immediately began to cry, as though tears had just been waiting to claim her. Her little body shook, but somehow she managed to admit that sometimes she missed Marc terribly. She also said she felt like she was stuck.

"I feel like he never gave me reason to push him out of my heart. Now I'm scared he'll always be there and I'll have no room for anybody else; even though I want someone."

Kismet Staar understood. "Ohhh...You haven't received closure."

Valeria René nodded. Drooping in sorrow, with lowered lashes, she reminded Beau of a beautiful but wilted flower.

Leaning forward, Kismet Staar wanted to offer hope. "Val, baby," she softly spoke. "Sometimes our lives take unexpected turns; and even though Marc is in your heart, somebody else might slip in there too. Your new someone just might take up as much space, if you allow him to..."

Valeria René whispered that she sure hoped so, because there were times when she actually ached for love. "But lately, I keep meeting men who play games. I tell myself I don't care, but I do. I want somebody, but maybe I have all I'm going to have. Maybe I should just be grateful, because I have a lot. I've got a great family. I've got you guys; I make great money. I buy pretty things, and I go to glitzy parties...but somehow..."

Beau finished her thought, "None of that is enough."

Sniffling, Valeria René nodded, and admitted that what she really wanted was for someone to put his arms around her. "I want someone who doesn't want me for superficial reasons, somebody who will be willing to kiss my forehead and my temples as much as he'll be willing to sex me. I want him to be spiritual too, but not a fanatic. I want a man who is good, and honest, and unashamed of his beliefs—a man like my dad...a man like you, Diddley."

Dabbing her eyes with a crumpled tissue, Valeria René continued, saying she wanted her somebody to look at her with genuine tenderness. "I want to look in my man's eyes and *know* he cares for me. I'm tired of being dragged around, so some man's friends can see me. The suck-ey friends ooh 'n ah and ask bruh if I got my own loot. Then they inevitably ask did he tap that ass." She made her voice deep, "Yo bruh, you hit that?" Resuming normal timbre, she stated, "And they're stupid enough to think I don't know." Valeria René moaned that she wanted something ethereal. "I want the kind of love that's miles beyond all the lustful mess that people call love." Dropping her face into her hands then, she wept, again wishing that she hadn't lost Marc.

No stranger to heartache, Beau felt compelled to cross the room. Kneeling before his friend, he took her hands in his own as he murmured that he wished she wouldn't cry so. "I know you're hurt," he softly admitted, while pulling her from her chaise. Wrapping his muscular arms about her, gingerly he rocked.

After a few moments, in Beau's arms, Valeria René began to feel soothed, even as she wished her nose hadn't begun to drip.

Beau spoke, accepting the tissue that Kismet Staar handed him, "I'm going to tell you something Val." Wiping her nose he announced he was no longer looking for love.

Wrangling away the tissue, Valeria René proceeded to wipe her own nose as Beau spoke on. He announced that recently he'd realized that in her, Ronni, and Kismet Staar, he'd found the love he needed. "This that's between the four of us, lots of people long for."

Depositing the soiled tissue in her lounge pants pocket, Valeria René wistfully glanced up.

"Yo, we could all easily find somebody to sleep with," Beau mentioned, "but the love, the caring? That, we can't find just anywhere."

Valeria René managed a watery smile. "So you're saying that if we happen to add a sexual healer to our mix, we'd all be getting a bonus."

"Yup." Laughing, Beau nodded. "I don't know about you three, but I need a *big* 'bonus.'"

Kismet Staar approached the couple; while yet seated across the room, Ronni watched through narrowed eyes as Beau hugged Valeria René. Ronni watched him tickle Val's chin and a painful twinge slithered, snakelike, through her heart.

Quickly she turned, telling herself she felt no pangs, no anger, no jealousy. Ronni also stood. Attempting to sound nonchalant, she made herself call out, "Breakfast anyone?"

Chapter 14

$\mathcal{B}$EAU pulled on a denim jacket as hurriedly he walked.

"Hey." Valeria René stood in The Cohort Quarter's doorway, "Where you going?"

"To the gym," he called from the outer hallway. There he would box for a while. "But I gotta meet with my director first, so I'll be hungry when I get back." This Beau announced as he dashed into the stairwell. "So cook something okay—thanks!"

He actually thought she would do it. Valeria René chuckled as she closed the apartment door. "I'm going to cook alright Mr. Diddley, but only with my 'bean-grower.'"

Happily, Ms. Vee Reenay Thompson, as she sometimes referred to herself, headed for her bedroom. Recalling that she and Fabian Sinclair had become an item, she realized that she and he spoke often throughout the day. They managed to see each other a few times a week, and weekends were theirs alone.

On the night they'd met at *Club LaLaa!* they'd become fast friends. Now, that was developing into more, so naturally. Often Fabian told Valeria René she was exquisite, and she said he was charming and funny. The man was quite attractive too, sporting the clean-head look. Lord! She fanned herself. There was just something about all that visible skin on a man's cranium that turned her on as nothing else could.

In her candlelit, midnight velvet bedroom, a sensuous retreat in shades of navy and shimmering gray, she pulled lingerie from a drawer. Then, using her remote, she started her super-sexy Gerald Levert CD. Having forgotten Beau, she envisioned the dark-skinned sexy man that she would soon embrace.

In one of The Quarters' other rooms a phone rang.

Probably for Ronni, Valeria René mused as she also thought about the morning that 'the forum' had taken place. On that pre-dawn, in The Cohort Quarters' living room she and her friends had shared their inner most feelings. She believed the new knowledge was why things were now rolling along smoother than ever before.

There had not been one argument, scuffle, or near-fight between Beau and Ronni since, nor had she and Ronni had any tiffs. Valeria René believed these things were because now each person better understood the other.

It seemed that at last, everyone was respecting the space and property of his or her neighbor, and it was nice, Valeria René thought, as she shimmied into a long flowing skirt.

WHILE riding the train, Beau also pondered The Quarter's current peaceful period. It was cool because now when he looked at film or did research to give depth to the character that he would soon play, the apartment was quiet. Ronni was no longer disturbing him with the raw-n-ready, dirty south, big booty bama music that she loved. He didn't have to yell over 'Git it, Git it,' to tell her to be considerate.

At home, now, he could practice the enunciation and diction that he'd worked on with his vocal coach. He didn't have to holler that he couldn't even hear himself think. Now he could also hone things that his acting coach had mentioned. It was why later in the year, when he returned from acting abroad, he would take a few *big-screen* gigs! At last he felt ready, and his agent had been coming up with things, so he would start getting his feet wet...

Forty-five minutes later, Beau slung his backpack over a shoulder and headed toward the Pietro Brothers' gym. He'd been going there ever since he'd been fifteen. As he strode along, he cogitated on the fact that he didn't work out because he loved or wanted to. He did so because in his profession staying fit was necessary. People really did scrutinize celebrities and actors.

Entering the gym, he nodded at Andree, and others he always saw, but all he could think about was going home. Hopefully to quiet, and to the meal that Valeria René was most likely preparing right now; bless her Lord.

$\mathcal{N}$OT cognizant of what her roommates viewed as blissful serenity, Ronni was out. She perpetually was, seeking something she had not yet found.

Although she didn't rightly know what she sought, she felt she would know it when she found it.

$\mathcal{A}$LONE at her tidy ranch home in Elmont New York, Kismet Staar readied herself for the next day. She had worked late, as she often did, but she vowed to find time. Yes, very soon she would drop by The Quarters, just to keep abreast of things.

She would also inform Valeria René that she and that fine dancer from *Club LaLaa!* were still hanging tough...with his long locked hair and unbelievable 'licking skills.'

The dancer, whose name was Lyle, had even turned out to be a software engineer for a Fortune 500 company. He and a partner were about to open their own firm though.

Born in Belize, sexy Lyle the engineer said he'd worked his way through college dancing and waiting tables. He admitted that even though there had been no pay for joining Beau's entourage, he'd done it because a friend had asked. Lyle also said that dancing again, just for the heck of it, had been fun.

Kismet Staar had winked and said that *watching* him had been fun, for her.

Hopefully, Lyle said; not as much fun as when they danced together, between the sheets, and on the table, and in the car and— That reminded Kismet Staar. She had to connect with her cousin. He'd called, and during the conversation, he'd mentioned new career undertakings. He had also said he was yet seeking a steady.

Beau revealed he was hitting and missing with Vaughn Gruskin, the man who currently interested him. Kismet Staar didn't know how she felt about that. She wondered if she should rejoice, or feel bad, for Beau. He'd revealed that a couple of times he'd called, but Vaughn's service had answered. Beau also said that on the rare occasions that he spoke with the man, Vaughn had seemed rushed. Still, Beau was hopeful, because the other man claimed he was interested.

Although—Beau had admitted—he could barely hear Vaughn's words, because his contradictory actions were speaking a bit louder.

Kismet Staar prayed that her cousin would soon get his answer. Then if need be, he could move on. Then *she* would no longer have to hear about the man she didn't trust, for some unfathomable reason.

As he rode the train home from Sal 'n Luigi's, the Pietro brothers' gym where he boxed, Beau told himself he would indeed make his mark where Vaughn was concerned. He didn't care how lean things had been looking. Since Vaughn alleged interest, Beau would give things another go, because to do nothing would produce nothing.

Getting off the train, he climbed the concrete steps. Walking down his darkened street, he acknowledged the few neighbors yet out, as his mouth began to water. He could hardly wait to get at the meal he'd requested. He could almost taste the spicy Indian specialty that Val had whipped up.

Entering the building, he took the stairs—good exercise—two at a time. He also sniffed. Funny, he couldn't smell anything in the hallway as was usually the case. Inside the shared apartment, he smelled nothing either, and he found himself alone, with no home-cooked meal.

Plopping into one of his director's chair stools, Beau allowed disappointment to take hold. It had been such a long day, and he had honestly been looking forward to a satisfying feast. Had that been too much to ask? Now, he felt dejected, and like he would be reduced to poking around in the refrigerator.

"Like a raccoon in a trash bin," he grumbled.

Well, so much for good friends and good food, he wryly thought, as grudgingly he took Sunday's leftovers from the fridge.

When all was on the table, Beau saw that he had a container of cabbage, baked macaroni-n-cheese, and a few barbecued beef ribs smothered in homemade sauce.

Beau nuked his feast, such that it was, and he toasted a few slices of whole wheat. He hated the 'heels' of the loaf as his Aunt called them, but they were all he had, and dag-blame-it if the house phone wasn't ringing!

Ravenously hungry, Beau ignored it, even though the noise got on his nerves. Slamming the small breadbox shut, he told him self that voicemail would pick up.

When it did not, he snatched up the receiver. "Hello?!"

No one answered.

"Hello?" Beau nearly yelled. Frustrated, he realized he should have let the stupid thing ring, because it probably had not been for him anyway. He was about to hang up, when he heard a man call his name.

"Beau. Yo bro, what's going on?"

"Vaughn?"

"Yeah man, what's up?"

"It is what it is," Beau replied, not believing his luck. "What's happening with you?" Suddenly he felt more upbeat than he had all evening.

"I've got a few things in the works," Vaughn stated. "Consulting projects, you know; things I can tackle from home a few nights a week."

"Sounds good." For some reason Beau felt stupid as he said he had been meaning to catch up with Vaughn. Yet he asked why they didn't just kick it sometime. "We could hang out—do whatever."

Vaughn sounded interested. "Name the time and I'm there."

Beau modified his voice so that he wouldn't sound over earnest. "How about later this week, say Friday?"

"Ah, can't, bummer. S-sorry man," Vaughn stammered.

Beau tried not to push. "Well, you say when."

"Ah, I'll have to get back to you on that one. Good talking to you though."

"Yeah. You too. Peace." Beau slammed the phone down. He opened the microwave and got his hardened food. He really was interested in the tall blond, but for some reason—one he couldn't quite put his finger on, he was starting to think the feeling wasn't mutual.

Beau looked for a cold beverage to compliment his makeshift meal. But then again, why had the man called, if he wasn't interested?

Beau bit into a sparerib as his subconscious said *there was more going on*, something that he was unaware of. He licked sauce off his thumb as instinct said forget Vaughn; but how could he? He couldn't give up just yet. He had to give a hint of chase, at least. It was what some men liked.

Beau shrugged. If a little run-catch-n-kiss was what Vaughn wanted, then Beau could oblige the man, especially if it would lead to something.

Forget it, and him, Beau's conscience whispered.

Ignoring it, he sighed, and eyed the telephone. Maybe he should call Mireya. Or Brett. Putting his fork down, he picked up the receiver. But he replaced it. Biting into wheat toast heel, he wished he could call his longtime friend Jervais. But Jervais was out there...

Again he and picked up the receiver.

She picked up on the first ring.

"Can you swing by?"

The Quarters' buzzer sounded half an hour later, and Beau opened the door.

"Hey Diddle, Diddle." Kismet Staar shrugged her purse from a shoulder. "Talk to me." She headed toward the smell of food. "You need to. I heard it in your voice."

"Kiss, can the 'mother' stuff. You know I hate it." Beau took his seat, and his cousin struggled onto the opposite chair stool.

Eyeing her swanky camel-colored pantsuit, he began. "Look Kiss let's get one thing straight. I didn't ask you over for a lecture. I need you to listen. Only."

"Okay."

Beau sighed and wiped sweating palms on his jeans. "I spoke to him."

"Who? Oh..." She sounded disappointed, or disgusted, when she said the man's name. "Vaughn."

"Yeah."

Kismet Staar stared at Beau's plate. "And?"

"He did something puzzling."

"What?"

"He called, which was new, and since I was starved and nuking this, at first I wasn't gonna pick up, but I did and—"

"Him."

"Right." Beau sighed. "The thing is: he didn't respond, right away."

Kismet Staar looked perplexed.

"I almost had to *make* him speak. When I answered, he said nothing, like he was waiting."

Kismet Staar felt chilled as her eyes began to blur, a sure sign that a seconds-long visions would occur. Willing it away she asked, "Why would he wait, Diddley?"

"I'on't know." Beau fingered his dog tags, the ones that had once belonged to her dad. "But it was like when you've answered your phone, and the caller is somebody you know. Still, they weren't trying to reach *you*. They might have dialed your number by mistake, but they recognize your voice, and so they speak. This was like that."

Kismet Staar averted her eyes because she did not want Beau to see or sense that she'd had a vision. He knew about them, that they came true. Therefore, she feigned nonchalance, because she couldn't tell her cousin that in this latest sketchy revelation, she had seen *him*.

He'd appeared heartbroken, after peering through a half open door...

Attempting to act normal, Kismet Staar said, "Diddley this is bothering you," because it was surely bothering her.

"It's not."

"Diddley, please," she couldn't look at him so she took his fork and ate the last of his cabbage. Really, she didn't even want to discuss 'that man,' or her cousin's foolish and all-consuming infatuation with him. Shoot, it was preposterous, when all signs, for months now, had screamed *detour*; although hardheaded Beau wouldn't do so.

Without warning, he grabbed Kismet Staar's arm. "You know something," he charged. "Or you've had a vision. Maybe you've even seen Vaughn around your office building." He squeezed. "Tell me Kiss."

Silently she eyed Beau's hand, and he released her.

He had known she would say nothing, and it was all good, because if she did know anything, it wouldn't deter him. It would only make him more determined.

"I can't say anything that you'd heed."

Beau didn't deny it. Instead he said, "Well, wish me luck."

Kismet Staar looked away and mumbled, "I don't believe in luck." She reached for her cousin's glass. Drinking, she wondered why did she dislike Vaughn Gruskin, someone she didn't even know?

"Okay. I'll admit the call bothered me," Beau said as though she'd prodded him. "I'm blowing this out of proportion though; right?"

"Left. Oh no games Diddley." Kismet Staar waved. "You don't want my opinion."

"Give it anyway."

Beau could have kicked himself then because now he would have to hear Kismet Staar out. However long it took.

"Diddley, babe, if this is bothering you, leave it. Ask God for grace, and be out. Trust your inner self." Kismet Staar replaced her cousin's glass from which she'd drank. She admitted she didn't believe 'friend' was on the level. "I sense he's not truthful."

She looked away, not wanting to see the anger, or the hurt, quite possibly in her cousin's eyes.

"Yo, you've never liked him," Beau barked, "and you've got no concrete basis for your feelings."

Kismet Staar nodded, "Because they're just that, *my* feelings." She stood, announcing that she would go home. She also said she was finished, Beau was on his own.

"Just remember what our sage great poet Maya Angelou said," Kismet Staar called as she left the kitchen. "*When someone shows you who they are, believe them—the first time.*"

"Kiss, wait!" Beau shouted, because twistedly he wanted her blessing. "Vaughn hasn't given me reason not to trust him…"

Again, Beau could have kicked himself as he followed his cousin to the door, while fingering his dog tags. The truth was: he really didn't want to bounce and later find that he and Vaughn had missed out on the love of a lifetime. Therefore, he had to try.

"Kiss," he called. "Would you be surprised if he turned out to be on the level?"

She pulled her purse strap over an arm. "Yep, like you'd be surprised if *I* turned out to be Lola Falana."

Kismet Staar stood in the hallway. "Diddley, I'm not your mama, as you often tell me. So do what you wanna do."

"Yo, I hear what you're not saying, Kiss. I'll have to live with the consequences..." Irritated, Beau jiggled the doorknob. "If I make my bed hard I'll have to lie in it."

Kismet Staar shrugged. "Your words, not mine."

"You implied them. Ay!" Beau called. "Kiss! Turn around. Please. Thank you. I'll do one thing. I'll talk with him, and if he's in the stratosphere somewhere, I'll forget him. Okay?"

Kismet Staar did not appear troubled, although internally she had already begun to pray. Throwing up a hand, she turned into the stairwell, "*It's yo' thang.*"

"Then I'ma do what I wanna do."

"I can't tell you who to sock it to," the curvaceous cousin called, completing the popular song's refrain. Her voice floated back up to Beau, "Thanks Cuz, for them lil' forkfuls of cabbage."

As he stood in the open doorway, Beau hoped he wasn't about to make a mistake.

"Kiss!" He called, rushing forward into the outer hallway. "Tell me I'm not wrong!"

Beau realized she'd left the building when he received no response, other than the echo of his own voice. It reverberated in the stairwell.

Wrong...wrong...

Chapter 15

$\mathcal{T}$HE remainder of the week, Beau pondered the conversation with his cousin. Despite it, he felt there was something he needed to do. It was the reason that on the following Monday evening, after boxing, he made his way to Vaughn's neighborhood. Then he found himself on Vaughn's street, standing outside Vaughn's building.

He buzzed Vaughn's apartment. When he got no answer, Beau buzzed again.

Still no answer.

He was about to turn away when a woman exiting the building pushed the lobby door open. Smiling up at Beau she said, "Hey handsome." Dazzling her with his 'back at you babe' smile he was most grateful for the open door. Bypassing the elevator, he took the stairs, two at a time, all while his heart hammered with sheer excitement.

Beau stood outside Vaughn's apartment. Fingering his dog tags, he wondered if turning up, without having called, was a rank idea. Maybe he would be better off invited.

No, something inside him bulldozed. It told him to knock, because maybe Vaughn was in the shower, or maybe his buzzer simply didn't work.

Beau knocked, loud and hard, and got no response. He did so again. Nothing. Therefore, he turned away, and walked slowly toward the elevator, feeling let down.

Something creaked, and Beau spun on his heel. He also wondered if his mind played tricks, because had he really seen someone quickly push Vaughn's door to?

Instead of leaving, Beau went and pounded on the closed door. While he waited, a small inner voice advised him to cut his losses and go. Nevertheless, he chose to ignore it.

After a few moments, Vaughn's lock clicked.

So he was at home! Beau congratulated himself for waiting.

Vaughn opened his door, just a smidgen.

"Hey," Beau and attempted to peer into the apartment owner's face, through the crack between the door and its frame. "Hi'ya doing?"

"Hey." Nearly hidden, Vaughn inquired, "Uh what're you doing over this way?"

"Just passing through," Beau shrugged. He hoped he appeared nonchalant as he said, "I'ma bounce though. I just thought we could hang out." He lifted a hand and turned, because heck if he was going to stand carrying on a conversation with a barely visible eye. Shit, what did Vaughn think he wanted to do, rob or rape him? Please.

As Beau turned away, he thought, so much for giving chase. He guessed the party was over. Now he would move on, because he had already given this stupid situation too much time.

Unbeknownst, behind him, Vaughn had opened his apartment door. Slipping into the hallway, he called out. "Buddy, wait."

Knowing he should have kept walking, Beau turned, and blinked. The blond bad boy was nude, with a hand covering his genitals. His face and body glistened, most likely from physical exertion. Then when he approached, Beau felt heat radiating from Vaughn, and Beau also detected a near familiar smell.

"Yo, I'm not playing you close," Beau said, realizing the situation was preposterous. "Go on back inside, man. I'm out."

Vaughn caught Beau's arm, with the hand he'd used for concealment. He then positioned himself so that Beau would not miss his empurpled erection.

"Don't disappear buddy, stay a while," Vaughn suddenly coaxed. "Hey—come inside, because friends spend time. You know?"

Beau didn't entirely like the crooked, almost-smile or the new purring from the man who now considered them friends. Yeah, when seconds ago he'd been hiding out in his home like he was Goldilocks and Beau was one of The Three Bears. Therefore, Beau declined, feeling like the streets might prove safer than Vaughn's now rapidly unfolding, seemingly schizoid scheme.

However, the nude Vaughn blocked Beau's way, and the Cohort felt he would appear foolish if he ran. So feeling like a lamb led to the slaughter, he allowed himself to be steered back, into the darkened apartment.

In the living room Vaughn clicked on a lamp and gestured for Beau to be seated. "Give me a minute," the apartment owner suggested. Then flexing his buttocks muscles, he walked away.

Seated on the edge of a square sofa, Beau's fingertips again crept up to find his dog tags. He looked around. Decent place, he thought, in a functional way. The sofa wasn't comfortable though, and the place could have used his artistic touch.

Beau realized that never before had he been invited to Vaughn's home. Actually, he'd had the devil of a time prying the very address out of the man. So why, now... Beau's eyes narrowed. Why all of a sudden, did Vaughn want to be hospitable—although he had yet to offer a cold drink.

Beau shrugged away nagging questions, as his eyes fell on the end table to his right. In the lamp light, he noticed an ad, circled in red. Was Vaughn looking for more work? Beau wondered, beginning to reading, for lack of anything better to do.

The ad said to leave a message, at the number listed.

Beau closed his eyes and thought, hard. Something about the ad was familiar, even though he'd never perused the personals, or the classifieds. So where would he have seen something similar?

His eyes flew open! He looked at the number, recalling he had seen the ad at The Quarters, few Sunday's back. Ronni had been poring over it, and he and Val had told her to forget it.

Beau's heart began to pound when he also realized *he* had called the number listed, numerous times, because it was Vaughn's!

Beau frowned, because Vaughn Gruskin could not have placed that ad. He was attractive; and witty, dryly so—when he did carry on a conversation, and he was intelligent. So, why would he beg, in print—no less—for a single black female, and a black male? None of it added up.

Suddenly Beau needed to leave, but he also wanted clarity.

A small inner voice said he could *ask questions via telephone*. It told him, *vamoose, scram, now*.

Yet he remained, because he had to hear from Vaughn that Vaughn was bisexual.

Find out via phone, the inner voice prompted. *Now go!*

Feeling somewhat sick, Beau pulled himself up from the hard sofa. He guessed he would leave, because the apartment felt cloistered, and suffocating. Fingering his dog tags, he sprinted to the door; but he was not fast enough.

"I see you read my ad," Vaughn announced, re-appearing. The corners of his mouth turned up slightly in an acerbic smile. "So would you like to respond?"

Beau was dumbfounded because the man had asked like it was natural.

With his mouth dry, Beau realized he was not as aghast from Vaughn's inquiry as he was at the sight of the woman who'd followed Vaughn into the room.

"*Ronni...*" Beau gasped. Seeing her, with Vaughn, in his home, caused Beau to feel betrayed. "What are you—I mean how could...you?"

Crazily Beau's mind whirred, because Ronni, his roommate, the woman he'd thought of as a friend, had known all along that he was interested in Vaughn Gruskin. Should not that fact alone have made the man off limits, to her? And here she was, in Vaughn's home, sexually involved with him.

Beau scrubbed at his face, because oh Lord. The loud perfume that Ronni always wore, along with Vaughn's scent, and that of sexing...those, co-mingled, had been what he'd smelled in the hallway.

Beau's mind continued to dizzily whir, like a malfunctioning computer. Oh forget it, he told himself, not wanting to further grapple with the absurd situation.

Brazen and unapologetic, Ronni Marie Brown pulled at her cotton pajama top. With the act mocking modesty, she raised her head, to coldly stare into her roommate's eyes.

"You didn't finish your question Beau. You were about to ask how could I—what?" Ronni's bare feet were planted apart, confrontation-ready. "Did you mean to ask how could I—steal your man? Or how could I—sleep with 'your man?' Although we never *sleep...*"

Putting a hand to her face, she pretended to be shocked. "Or maybe your question is: how long has this been going on? Maybe you want to know how long I've been laying 'n playing with slim goody here..."

Dismissively, Ronni waved. "Just know this, roomie; I wasn't playing when I said I'd answer the ad that you and goody-two-shoes Val laughed about; now run tell that."

With iniquitously gleaming eyes, Vaughn watched Beau, as the mouthy butter-skinned Ronni chuckled, minus mirth.

"You...little witch..." Beau's voice was soft as he forgot Vaughn. "Ronni, you're a back-stabbing, double-dealer."

"Later for the name-calling Beau," Vaughn intervened because he needed to make a proposition. "Look buddy," he began, and took a condom from an end table drawer. "Why not have a glass of wine—or if you'd like, I've stocked up on malt liquor. Then when you've settled and digested all this, you can join us."

Beau blinked, because the man made it sound rational. He'd even offered malt liquor, like that was a treat for 'the black man.'

Beau frowned, insulted, because he had never touched the stuff, in his life. In addition, Vaughn's stupid statement showed he imbibed way too much stereotypical urban TV.

Beau turned. With steady hands, he unlocked Vaughn's door.

"You'd be perfect," Vaughn called, his greedy blue eyes roaming Beau. "Since we all know each other..." he continued, "no one would be uncomfortable. Buddy, haven't you ever wanted to do your roommate? She's hot man and here's your chance, you can get all up in it. What happens here, stays here."

Loudly Vaughn laughed, and to Beau it sounded sinister. "Diddley—"

Beau faced away, his hand raised. "Only friends call me that."

Vaughn shrugged. "Okay buddy. Well then listen. I now see that when I placed that ad, I had *you* in mind."

Beau the pugilist's eyes narrowed as he refrained from punching Vaughn in his lying mouth because heck, if Vaughn had ever thought about *him*, his ass would have called, once in a while. And he definitely would *not* have hooked up with skanky Ronni, a woman.

"You are perfectly it," Vaughn gushed, licking his lips as hurriedly he fit the condom onto his erection. "Beau, you're maybe a few inches taller, or longer—however you'd say it—but man, you're my specification, exactly."

"Yo *y'all*," Vaughn called, sounding silly, as he looked from the scowling Ronni, to the sickened Beau. "My dawgs, this is perfect!"

"It's not," Beau croaked, and wondered if the other man snorted glue. "Insanity is flawed."

Vaughn shrugged because he didn't want to argue. He only wanted to stick somebody, to make his fantasy reality. Therefore he stated, breathing heavily, "People say taste is acquired... So what do you say?" He took a step toward Beau, while handling his 'jewels.'

"Screw. You." Beau jerked the door open.

"Beau. Buddy!" Vaughn called, "Stay and watch, then..."

Quickly the tanned man grabbed Ronni. He bent her backward on his dining table. Dipping his head, hurriedly he stepped between her legs and snatched open the nightshirt of his that she wore. Grabbing her breast, he squeezed and bit. Then he thought better and flipped her over, as though she was nothing more than a rag doll. Grabbing her butt cheeks, with both hands, he pulled her apart and mightily thrust.

Seeing Vaughn enter Ronni like that, Beau thought he would throw up.

Relishing the idea of an audience, both Vaughn and Ronni instantly became all grasping hands, seeking lips, locking legs and gyrating hips, in a tangled heap.

The whole scene reminded Beau of a snake pit he'd seen in some movie. Disgusted, he stalked away thinking; like he would touch a woman, and his roommate at that! Grossed out, he shuddered, because *he* didn't do 'cat fish.' He never had. Never would.

Realizing he'd left Vaughn's door ajar, Beau shrugged as he flew down the stairs. He knew that depraved pair he'd just left wouldn't care. They *wanted* somebody to view their antics. It just would not be him.

Chapter 16

VALERIA RENÉ laid on her favorite piece of furniture. Feeling warm and sexy she reminisced on her evening spent miniature golfing with Fabian. Oh-oh; she heard something.

Sitting up, she listened. When she heard only the steady hum of the refrigerator, she leaned back resuming her trend of thought. How the man had kissed her. How he'd stood behind her, surrounding her.

There, again! That was the noise that had initially startled her. Praying silently, she got up, and tiptoed to peek into the front hallway. Perhaps, she thought, she should have first gone to get her Ginsu knife.

Someone moaned, and nearly scared her witless, but she had to see. So she craned her neck and peeked into the front hallway.

Moments later, she relaxed because it was just Beau.

Leaning against the wall beside the front door, his head was back and his eyes were closed. He appeared about to slide right down to the floor.

She crept forward. "Diddley... Honey, what's the matter?" She peered into his face, and wrinkled her nose. Ooh! He *reeked*, of liquor. "Oh Diddley," she moaned. "You're plastered."

"Ain't life grand?" he asked, and waved, like he smelled his own fetid breath.

Attempting to aid him to stand, Valeria René quickly found that without his help, she could not. So she huffed, "Look, you have got to help me."

Slowly Beau stood, and tottered, and Valeria René placed her arms around his waist. Huffing beneath his weight, she also attempted to propel him forward. In the living room she pitched him onto her purple velvet sofa, and prayed he would not throw up.

"Whew!" He blew, sounding winded. "That was rough."

Valeria René smirked as she bent to pull Beau's boots off, with no help from him. Tossing them, she said she would make coffee. Headed for the kitchen, she guessed doing so had become her second job. She also called out that Beau shouldn't move. "If you do," she stated, using the voice she reserved for young patrons. "You'll wind up on the floor—where you'll stay, because you're too heavy for me."

As the scent of java rose, Valeria René placed her palms on the kitchen countertop. Something was unfurling. This she knew because she could feel it. Therefore, since her paternal grandmother, sweet Nenna in South Carolina had often told her to handle fragile issues with prayer, she did so, now.

Afterward she re-entered the living room, carrying a tray, and noticed Beau who held his head. She wondered if it hurt.

"Good ole Val," he drawled. "You ain't the devil. You's a good, *clean* woman. N-no sss-skanky shit for yooo."

"Here, drink this," she coaxed, carefully holding a cup, minus its saucer, out to Beau.

He placed a heavy hand on hers.

"Don't," she commanded. "You'll make me tip it." With her free hand, she slapped at both his clutching clumsy hands. "Stop, I said. Just drink. It's hot though."

When he'd had enough, Beau closed his mouth, and turned his head like her sister Sonji's chubby baby did, to indicate he wanted no more.

Setting the cup aside, Valeria René sat, and heard Beau hum. She wondered what had sent him, this time. She knew he rarely drank; however, he *would* drink himself into an irresponsible stupor at the end of, or at an impasse, in a relationship. So which had happened?

Mentally Valeria René ratcheted around. She attempted to recall things that had recently transpired. Had her roommate mentioned being involved with someone? She wondered, wanting to figure out what currently ailed the man whose eyes were closed.

Since she could recall no mention of a lover, lately, maybe, she concluded, this was just the lonely acting up, again.

Lying on her chaise, occasionally she glanced at the tall brown man who began to appear fatigued. Well, she thought, she'd get no information out of him tonight, so she got up. Noticing he was about to keel over, she forced him back into the cushions, despite his protests.

When he seemed good and asleep, she clicked off the living room lamp. Headed to her bedroom she figured if he wanted to share, he could always do so tomorrow.

Absolution

@T nearly three a.m., Valeria René was deep in a dream; but she also heard walking.

Slowly she ascended, waking, due to the awful back and forth.

Realizing someone wore boots, she nearly screamed, because she had been amid a deliciously real-seeming, erotic scene with a ravenous Fabian Sinclair!

As she stared into the darkness, the clomping continued, along with an added racket, and why?

Turning over, she prayed to get back to 'Fabian' in the recesses of slumber. There she could lie back down for him; while hovering over her, he would resume doing deliciously enticing things to her. Therefore, toward that end she pulled a pillow over her head.

But sleep eluded her, and she felt frustrated. Heck, she wanted 'Fabian' back, with his muscular dark chest visible. She wanted his hunger. She wanted his night stick that had been pressed against her belly, then her thigh, then right at her—

No. She couldn't feel him any longer. She couldn't 'see' him either, as her dream man began to disintegrate. No!

Now she felt anger. Heck, her roommates knew she abhorred losing z's, yet one of them did this—this stupid, incessant, noisy, clomping back 'n forth!

Well, she would say something! Valeria René sat up. With her toes, she felt around for her bunny slippers. Pulling her oversized tee down, she flung open her door and with her lips angrily knotted, she marched toward the other two bedrooms.

"Okay, I am stinking mad now," she articulated, pushing at the door with the light pooled beneath. "What is so important," she demanded, shielding her eyes from the invasive brightness. "...That it can't wait until daylight?"

When the burn lessened, she removed her hand, and stood with her mouth agape.

There was Beau, fully clothed, at the foot of his bed, and he wore the boots she had removed earlier! So it had been him; noisy sod.

She watched as haphazardly he threw belongings into two large open suitcases, and into assorted liquor store boxes.

What shocked her more than his doing that was all the shredded material strewn about the room. With rounded eyes she realized...those 'shreds' were the remains of Ronni's sexy lingerie collection, some of which she'd had since college.

It was apparent Beau's anger was directed at the mouthy spirited one, and Valeria René just had to wonder if Ronni was home. She also wondered if something had transpired between the roommates while she had been asleep.

She blinked, unable to recall if she'd heard scuffling or quarreling. Nope, she'd been so deep in with 'Fabian' until The Quarters could have been on fire and she'd not have heard. Forgetting that, and surveying the mess, she was sure something had happened. But what?

Not now, Valeria René told herself because sleep called. Hanging out with Fabian was making her tired for work. Verbally she'd acknowledged that earlier, when he and she had been out, and now this. Well, tomorrow evening, she promised herself, she would listen as the details were laid out.

She turned to go, and heard Beau jeer, with his back to her. "Ronni Brown, she's a clown. The biggest 'ho in the whole damn town."

Watching him fold a pair of jeans, Valeria René remembered that earlier she'd felt something brewing. In the kitchen she'd prayed about it. Now she knew it was big. Placing a hand on the doorknob, she heard Beau derisively laugh.

"Wonder what our roommate will think," he gleefully proposed, "when she finds out her 'Hollywood' collection is no more."

Had she slept through the fray this one time? Valeria René really wondered. She also realized something, and softly she said it. "Diddley, despite whatever happened; you yet had *no* right to destroy Ronni's property."

When Beau retorted, Valeria René raised a hand. "I don't want to hear it. I'm not listening, or lecturing. If you want, we can take this up after work, when I get home."

She turned to go. Again, she noted that this thing between her roommates had taken on a life all its own. She could only hope that when she returned from work, the two of them would have the mess worked out.

Although, Valeria René thought as she headed to her room, she just could not see how, not after so much destruction.

In the darkened hallway, she bumped into something.

Absolution

"Ouch!" It wailed.

Chapter 17

$\mathcal{R}$ONNI stood in the doorway of Beau's room, aghast.

He liked that she couldn't speak. Guess she was surprised, huh? About as surprised as *he* had been, at Vaughn's place. Well, *winning*! What was good for the goose was good for the gander.

Beau nodded, satisfied. He also said everything now made sense. "You and your low 'ho profile." He acknowledged that although Ronni had kept quiet, yet he'd learned that *she* was the one Vaughn had been trying to reach the night he'd called. "The night I ate them hard ribs and the bread heels." Beau admitted he hadn't known it then. "...But that's why he couldn't say anything when *I* answered the phone."

Beau said he was aware that he'd been a mere distraction, a side piece for Vaughn, while stunt girl Ronni had been the main attraction.

"Knowing you," he accusatorily stated, "if the man suggested it, you'd let him shoot you out of a cannon."

"Shut up," Ronni snarled, unable to take in what she saw.

"Yo, you and King Dong figured I'd never find out," Beau surmised aloud, "but how long did you clowns think you could keep me in the dark?"

Not awaiting an answer, Beau also accused Ronni of knowing about Vaughn's ad all along. Beau mentioned 'that Sunday morning' and the paper. "Hey, the two of you could have composed that ad together. Ya probably did."

He tossed a few magazines into a box. He said he should have left Vaughn alone. For crying out loud, the two depraved varmints worked at the same place! And Kiss had kind of warned him from the get-go.

Beau walked toward the closet and his few remaining clothes. He kicked aside a portion of one of Ronni's teddies.

Seeing him do so, she bent to retrieve what appeared vaguely familiar. Then she trembled, with rage.

"Why, you little pussy!" She howled. She also growled that she could kick Beau in the privates, because "I've told you not to touch my stuff! Now look!" Ronni shook the lace rag. "Look what you've done."

Beau smiled. "Oh that? I saw it already. You can take it away now."

Incensed, Ronni screamed that Beau had to go. He was an animal, and could not possibly stay a moment longer in her apartment!

Mentally tallying up the damage, she also yelled, "You know you're going to pay me, right? You need to write me a check, now!"

"Take it out of the rent," Beau suggested and sidestepped the enraged woman. He almost laughed, because he'd just thought of something. Ronni was going to feel it, when she wound up having to pay his portion of the rent, from now on. That would serve her right.

Experiencing more fury than she knew what to do with, Ronni flicked her purse aside, because she intended to help Beau out. Hell, the sooner he was packed, she ruminated, wrangling a painting of his from the wall, the sooner she would never have to see his crummy face again.

Beau was speaking with his friend from childhood, Mireya. With the phone at his ear, he told her to hang on. He dashed over to Ronni. "Gimme that! Don't touch anything of mine," he ordered, as gingerly he handled the framed piece.

"Who the bloody hell are you to tell *me* not to touch *your* stuff?!" Angrily Ronni told Beau he needed to reverse the principle, for himself. "If you'd done so, earlier, maybe you wouldn't have destroyed my shit!"

Feeling tremendously angered, Ronni also rushed Beau, screeching that she had a good mind to disfigure his face.

He held her off, no problem. Sounding calmer than he felt, he also explained he would hurt her, if she put her hands on him. Lord knew he wouldn't hesitate to strangle her because on this wee morning, he really didn't know if he could manage the self-control that he'd exercised with her in the past; so not to be provoked, he turned, and clomped across the room.

Picking up his phone, again he spoke to his friend from middle school, the cinnamon-skinned, female, Mireya. "Sorry about that Reya." He listened; then said, "No, I'm not coming there. Quit worrying about me." He paused. "I know. It *is* late—or early—whatever, but I got this…"

"I hate you," Ronni spat, her eyes filling with tears. "I probably always have, because you're no man—with your pristine little ways—you're a zero!"

"Takes one to know one," Beau quipped, placing folded tees in a suitcase. With the phone wedged between his ear and shoulder again he told his friend not to worry. Disconnecting, he didn't glance at Ronni whom he passed. He simply wished she would leave, so he could leave, when he was done.

Ronni's eyes widened because Beau was too calm! She wanted him to feel like *she* felt, distraught, and hurt. As she watched him she became angrier by the moment because hell if he was going to clomp back 'n forth in her place, while calmly chatting on the phone, *after* he'd destroyed her belongings. And double hell if he would ignore her—the stiff-backed faggot!

Unaware that she would, Ronni screeched, like a banshee, "You cock-loving woman hater!" Livid, she also attempted to claw Beau's eyes.

"Yeah, yeah, suck my dick to you too," he dryly offered, avoiding the fake talons slashing the air around him. Belying his own churning wrath, he maintained his calm façade to begin taping a box.

Incensed, Ronni realized that she had not been the only one with a secret. Beau had also had a hidden agenda. He had not recently decided to move! From the looks of things, he had been planning—for a while—because who kept umpteen boxes and tape in a room so small? He had even found sturdy old suitcases in which to carry his clothes. She guessed he'd gotten them into the apartment on a day when she'd been working, and he, off.

The little cunt! He probably never would have mentioned leaving, until the last minute, *if* he had said it then. He might simply have snuck away in the night.

Ronni's eyes widened, because she realized. Beau thought his leaving would hurt her! She knew it, and wasn't that just like a man? To think some woman needed him 'n his lil bit of cash.

Without thinking, she hissed. "Yeah, dickhead, you were just gonna up and go. You were gonna slink outta here...like your *mama* slinked outta your life all them years ago."

His mother?! Beau had been carrying boxes, but he stopped. Having forgotten his phone, he stood riveted, because why had Ronni dragged

Ophelia into this? Why use something he'd told her—in confidence—to try to hurt him? Why not simply fight about their current situation, instead of flinging up the past—*his* past?

With fury buzzing chaotically in his ears, Beau dropped his filled boxes to grab Ronni's neck. Maliciously he squeezed, as wildly she flailed.

"Get off! Get offa me!" She screamed and hunched her shoulders, "Oh God! Get off!"

Sounding eerily calm, Beau sing-sang. "Who's gonna make me?"

Ronni's eyes narrowed in scrutiny of the man she had not known she could only push so far. "I will call the police," she spat, as pain radiated outward and pulsed even in the fingertips that she inched closer to her purse.

Aware that she tried to reach her cell phone, Beau released Ronni. Purposefully, he kept his face expressionless. He knew it was probably some of the best acting he had ever done in his life.

"Go on, call them," he coaxed. He spoke like Ronni was a witless child. "The only thing is: you'll have to do it outside of this room. In here, I've got work to do. So go someplace else, okay? Go call from Vaughn's maybe."

With her thumb hovering over the keypad of her phone, confused, Ronni warned Beau not to play with her.

"Yo, *you* play games, I don't," Beau reminded her. He bent to retrieve his boxes. He also picked up his cell phone and sounded exasperated

"Look, I really have things to do. So just, get out, will you? This room will revert to being all yours the moment I'm gone."

Ronni's eyes narrowed, because the big switchie had nerve! Talking to her like *she* was the one wrong. "You know what?" she asked, dialing 911. "I'm calling the cops, because you're into mind games. You think you can destroy shit and then hang around like—"

Suddenly seeing hazy red, Beau lunged at Ronni because there were only so many times that a person could threaten an African-American male with the police.

Knowing she was in for it, Ronni tried to lurch away, and her cell phone went flying. When it hit the hardwood, like she did, her phone cracked open, spewing out her battery.

Down on the floor, amid the shreds of what had once belonged to her, Ronni's eyes filled, while her knee throbbed. Tearfully she massaged it, while she moaned that Beau was a misogynistic bastard.

"Am I now?" he asked, placing a booted foot on her outstretched hand that had again neared her phone.

"Beau!" Someone called from behind.

With his foot yet on Ronni, he turned, just slightly. "Hey cuz," he said and told whomever he had been calmly speaking with on his own cell phone that he had to go.

Frightened and eyeing him, Ronni really believed he was straight crazy, as she too saw Kismet Staar.

Wearing a nightgown, Beau's cousin stood in the doorway. Her sleepwear hung from beneath her hastily pulled on paper-thin jacket. She also wore tennis shoes, and her shapely legs were bare. Her stylish hair was hidden beneath the colorful jumble of a silk scarf, and she appeared to have fallen straight out of bed.

Beau nodded. "Come to join the party?"

"Doesn't appear to be much fun," Curvaceous softly stated, stepping into the small room. She noted her cousin's bloodshot eyes, having already seen the fear in Ronni's. Therefore Kismet Staar said, "Diddley, remove your foot, okay?"

"This…" Beau cautioned, "does not involve you, Kiss." Turning back to the woman whose wrist he kept beneath his boot, Beau nudged her. "This is between game girl here—whorelina—and my self." He nudged harder, "How you like me now, heifer?"

Kismet Staar firmly stated, "Diddley I was roused from sleep, because it involved you, so now I too am involved."

"I'd have left you alone, because this," again he put pressure on Ronni's wrist, "is nothing to lose sleep over."

Kismet Staar could not possibly say what she thought: that it was most likely something utterly stupid that her cousin and Ronni were distraught over. Now was not the time. Now, she had to make Beau understand that the neighbors had surely heard the commotion, and who knew? One of them had probably already alerted the authorities. Lord only knew what would happen if the wrong pair of blue uniforms pounded on the front door.

These things Kismet Staar pontificated for Beau, and for Ronni whom she was sure had done something. The butter yellow mouthy woman had definitely provoked her cousin, of that Kismet Staar was sure. "Look Diddley," she stated, "you'll hurt Mama; if you get thrown in jail, over this piddling shit. She'll feel she went wrong, somewhere."

With a sigh, the cousin tried another tactic. "Diddle-Diddle, you and Ronni need time apart." Kismet Staar held out a manicured hand. "So come with me. Okay?"

Beau pondered his cousin's words; but realizing they didn't have moments to lose, again Kismet Staar spoke. Her voice was no longer soft or cajoling. "Do what I said, Beauregard DeVeaux," she commanded, her voice hard; "or three people will wind up hurt in here. You and Ronni are already hurt, and I'll get hurt, trying to drag you out of here." She spoke slowly, emphasizing every word, *"But – I –will.* If I have to..."

Seated awkwardly on the hard floor, with her knee aching, Ronni realized she knew that tone of voice. She'd heard it a few times, and each time the subsequent situation had not been pretty.

Actually, Ronni recalled, Kismet Staar had used that tone just a few weeks ago...

A man, quite possibly angry about his life, had walked up to Ronni and Kismet Staar as they'd pumped gas into Val's newbie. With Valeria René inside, the man had become a nuisance, handling his privates and saying vulgar things that he had no right to say to any woman, decent or otherwise.

Seemingly calm, Kismet Staar had advised him to go on; yet the man had become belligerent. He'd called Kismet Staar names.

Without warning, she had gone upside the man's head.

Recalling it, Ronni knew Kiss hadn't meant to, but she'd laid her big fists on that man, like Sophia had done Harpo in *The Color Purple*. It had taken a gas station attendant, a police officer, and a stocky bystander to pull the then-vicious woman off of her offender. Even so, she'd managed to forcefully kick the man in the chest, one last time, knocking him backward, along with those who had attempted to rescue him.

Seated in Valeria René's car afterward, Kismet Staar had blubbered that she'd believed she was past whupping up on folk. With tears streaming, she'd blathered that after much meditation, and prayer, she'd finally felt relieved of the fighting demon. Now, she'd moaned, her face in her hands, 'that man' had stirred it up again.

Seated on Valeria Rene's little back seat, Ronni had been amazed that Kiss had only seemed sorry that she was once again in fight mode. Did she not comprehend, Ronni wondered, that she had surely sent someone to the E.R.?

Valeria René had cried too, when moments later, angry, Kismet Staar smashed her hand so hard onto the dashboard that no one dared look.

Recalling that incident, Ronni chanced a glance at Beau. He must have recalled his own incident, because slowly he removed his foot.

Forgetting butter-yellow whom he believed had provoked him, Beau sweetly said, "Kiss, you and I never have to fight—over *outside* stuff."

Knowing her cousin sounded cray-cray, Kismet Staar still suggested, "Then let's go home."

As Beau rode shotgun in old Betsy, he pondered the word 'home.' Was that not a place of solace and peace?

If it was, Beau surmised, then The Cohort Quarters had never truly been his home. Therefore, he guessed, he would have to keep searching, until he found one all his own.

$Back$ at The Quarters, it was quiet. Valeria René had again gone to bed.

However, Ronni remained on the floor, in Beau's room. Amid her ruined possessions, occasionally she shivered. She was not cold though, because it was nearly summertime.

She also found she couldn't move, although her limbs worked just fine. She'd checked. Her knee ached a bit, but she knew it would be fine, in a day or two.

Still, she felt...like...she had lost something, vital. So, she'd decided, she would sit, until she figured out *what*?

Chapter 18

𝒲HY did Kismet Staar persist with the same question, over and again? This Beau wondered as he said, for the zillionth time, he did not want to talk about it.

Tearing her eyes from the Manhattan Street before them, Kismet Staar again griped that she wanted to know what happened. It was big she said, because Val had called her.

The curvaceous cousin remembered it so well. When her phone rang, nude, in bed she'd turned over in 'the dancer,' the software engineer's arms, to see the time. Four a.m. With Lyle sleepily, seductively running a hand over her, she'd experienced trepidation while peeking at her caller I.D., because the truth was: wee morning phone calls usually meant trouble.

She remembered picking up the phone and hearing Val say in a barely audible voice, 'Kiss, you're needed here, *now*. We've got trouble, involving Beau, and that's an understatement.'

Kismet Staar recalled scrambling up, telling Lyle to do so too. She'd pulled on a nightgown, a jacket, and footgear. Telling him he couldn't accompany her, she'd gently pushed the dancer from her home. Kissing him, she'd left him to start his car, as in the dark, she'd hurriedly made for Astoria.

Wearing a long sleep tee, and those hideously old bunny slippers—that needed to be trashed —Valeria René opened the apartment door. Then together the women rushed to Beau's room, where all had been chaos...

Seated on the steps of the New York Public Library on bustling, beautiful Fifth Avenue, Kismet Staar reminded her cousin that she'd told him her part of the story. Now she wanted his. She wanted to understand what had transpired, prior to her arrival.

Beau got up from the concrete steps. He'd met his cousin after work to sit and people-watch. The last half hour had been glorious, with a picturesque sky and fluffy white clouds. With low humidity, the seventy-eight degrees had been most comfortable, but now, the sky threatened rain. Warm winds were picking up, and most smart New Yorkers were heading off to remain dry. So towering over his cousin, he spoke. "Kiss, let's go. Or soon your beautiful turquoise pants and top will be all wet."

When she didn't budge, Beau finally huffed that The Quarters' mess was really none of her business.

Kismet Staar squawked. "I know you're not telling *me* that. Not when *I* was called over, to the rescue."

"Yo hol' up," Beau advised; "you ain't had to rescue *me*. Get that straight." He said *he* hadn't been the one on the floor fearing for his life. Disgusted, he also blew cigarette smoke.

"Stop it," Kismet Staar waved. She admitted perhaps it hadn't been him she'd been called to rescue. "But I was called, so tell me why, and that's a nasty habit." She eyed the smoke streaming from Beau's nostrils. "Why're you fooling with them cancer sticks again anyway? You'd quit, for two years."

"Why, why," Beau mocked. "Is that all you can say? Just face that I'm trying to spare you." He put a foot on the step below him.

His cousin did not budge. "I'm not leaving without answers."

He looked back at her, having stepped down yet again. "Why's it so important?"

"Because whatever happened," Kismet Staar began, "made enemies of two people who are very important to me."

Distracted by a fabulous pair of sandals, Kismet Staar, a shoe fanatic, swiveled to watch the wearer strut.

Beau called her. "Kiss. You know what happened." He said that although he hated to admit it, he had been on the verge of beating Ronni down, like Ophelia had done him, many a time, years ago.

Kismet Staar appeared stunned, because never before had Beau seemed even remotely like Ophelia. "Oh Diddley, you're not unkind, and she was."

"Kiss you don't understand," Beau said as he tapped out another smoke. "That little light-skinned former college dorm mate of yours brought up something in me that even *I* didn't know was there. And this wasn't the first time."

Kismet Staar said she understood, because occasionally Ronni pushed her buttons too.

"Don't try to justify what I did," Beau remarked. "It simply wasn't acceptable." He went on to explain that since manhandling Ronni, he had ruefully gone over and over it, and had seen the similarity. His actions mirrored Ophelia's, when he'd been a child.

"Please explain."

"I pushed Ronni around; even though she could provoke a saint. Still, she's still smaller than I am." Beau said he outweighed Ronni by at least fifty or sixty pounds. "It was like that with Ophelia and me; it's why I can't forget, or forgive myself."

Beau said he no longer pondered Ronni's actions, but he re-lived his own. "Kiss, if A'nt Nell knew about this, she'd be ashamed of me." Feeling quite culpable, Beau admitted that now he could see how ugly actions could rob a person of dignity.

Kismet Staar beseeched her cousin not to berate himself. She said she'd been there, many times. "Lots of people have," she assured. "Why do you think meditation exists? Higher self-reaching teaches us to guard against ugliness. Not that it helped me…"

She mentioned beating that man down, at the gas station. "I see, now, that I could have handled it differently. I could have gotten in Val's car, or reported the man. I could also have kept my hands to myself."

"I keep thinking those things too, about my situation." Wearily Beau scrubbed a hand over his face. "I just pray I'm not like Ophelia."

Kismet Staar stood, as rain appeared imminent, "Me too."

"We've got a few minutes, I think, so sit." Beau patted the step beside him. "I'll tell you, briefly, what happened."

Kismet Staar waved. "It's no longer important. Actually, I spoke with Ronni, and she remained closed-mouthed. So we'll let it rest."

Beau sounded belligerent while eying a dapper man and his dumpy companion as they exited a dark sedan. "Maybe I feel like telling you."

Forgetting the impending rain, Kismet Staar sat back down, and sighted more shoes, these worn by a savvy female exec who hailed a taxi.

Beau said he didn't want to speak ill of his cousin's friend. He claimed he hadn't said anything before now because it could have appeared he was attempting to ruin the women's relationship. Therefore, he said, now, he would make the telling short and simple.

The actor succinctly said his ex roommate was many things, young, hip, smart, and assertive. She was also trifling.

Kismet Staar chuckled. "You know that word only applies to men."

Beau shook his head. "Nope, it applies to dawgs, a.k.a. your friend."

Beau didn't tell Kismet Staar all the particulars, but he did say that the eruption had been building, for a while. He said it was because Ronni had no respect, for him. "She feels I can't take a joke, but I don't feel like someone's joking when they constantly verbally attack me."

Beau said Ronni had often claimed he should leave 'those men alone.' "But 'those men' my men, are the very ones she's always trying to get with, behind my back."

He explained that it had been hard, feeling like he was always being judged. "Your girl even scrutinized my relationship with Val. She hated that we cliqued, from day one."

Beau divulged that on move-in day, he knew the arrangement would end as it had.

"What was the indication?"

"There were lots of things," Beau shrugged. "One was the way my 'new roomie' tossed herself at me and Tony." Beau had barely known Ronni, he'd briefly spoken with her only twice before. He'd visited Kismet Staar at college. That was when he'd been introduced to Ronni. Then on another day he and she had discussed becoming roommates.

"She tried to holler, while you and blue eyes were moving in?"

Beau nodded and said Ronni had worn tight, cut-off jeans shorts, and a halter-top. "But Kiss, that outfit wasn't eye-catching enough, so she changed into a teddy."

Semi-shocked, Kismet Staar pushed Beau, "Underwear? Lingerie? Stop it!"

He appeared amused. "Yes, and it was midday too."

"Brownie knew you didn't have time for games."

Beau eyed ominous clouds, and told his cousin they might have to dash to the train. He also said time-schime, Ronni had gotten underfoot like a frisky puppy.

Engrossed, Kismet Staar attempted to ignore the wind.

Noting a trio of wide-eyed tourists hailing a taxi, Beau suggested that he and his cousin leave.

"No," Kismet Staar waved. "What happened after Brownie got all gussied up?"

"She put a leg up on one of my boxes. She complained about a Charlie horse, and she rubbed her calf, up 'n down, slowly."

Kismet Staar guffawed.

"She asked if I'd 'stretch it out' for her."

"What did you do?"

"What could I do?" Beau inquired. "I know I should've told her to move her leg." Perhaps then, he mused, Ronni would have been deterred from the full-blown circus acts that had become her modus operandi. He chuckled. "I have to admit, ol' girl has the balls that Nero and Napoleon could only have prayed for."

Kismet Staar well knew. It was why she'd often teased Ronni about her *cojones*. The butter-yellow woman's indomitability was part of why Kismet Staar loved her.

Beau continued. "Even with her coochie peeking out, I wasn't amused, or aroused." He mocked a shiver. "Heck, I don't want nobody's—*cat*—and that's not to say;" he clarified, "that she doesn't have body, because a blind man couldn't miss those curves; but her practices are unsafe."

For all Ronni knew, Beau said, he and blue-eyed Tony could have been serial killers in training. "Even now, for all she knows," Beau continued, "any of the men she drags back to The Quarters could pose a threat to either her or my little Val."

Beau became silent, and Kismet Staar knew what she had not before. For Beau, living with Ronni had been akin to living with Ophelia. It was a wonder he had stuck it out for so long.

Beau said on move-in day, the soft-spoken, southern Tony had said, "Miz Ronni, you're pretty 'n all, but *we* actually prefer *men*."

The cousins howled with mirth, before Kismet Staar inquired. "Why did you never tell me this before?"

"There wasn't any need to." Beau shrugged as his cousin dabbed her eyes. He said after Tony's revelation, Ronni's smile faded. With her eyes flickering disdainfully over Beau, she spoke. "I just hope your—uh– *situation* won't keep you from having your rent on time."

Kismet Staar's eyes widened and Beau nodded. "That was the beginning."

"Diddley," Kismet Staar called over the wind. "You think Ronni's *wanted you* all this time? Could that be the reason for you guy's crazy back-n-forth?"

Beau said he'd pondered it. "But I really hope not, for her sake," because he knew what it was to want someone who didn't want back. "Even she doesn't deserve that."

Kismet Staar agreed, as the first few fat raindrops fell. "Diddley you still haven't mentioned DaVon–or whatever his name is, Mr. Gala Attendee. He figures into this, somehow. I know it."

"His name is Vaughn, and you're right." Beau and his cousin hurried down the library steps. "He was with Ronni."

"Huh? With her, how?"

"All tangled up. I saw them."

As she trod down the train station steps, Kismet Staar wanted clarity, but her eyes began to blur. She prayed it was due to the rain, and not because of an oncoming vision.

Earlier, she had been thinking about her visions. The day that she and Ronni had gone to lunch, she'd seen Ronni in something steamy, with gala man. Then when she'd eaten Beau's cabbage, she'd seen her cousin heartbroken, after peering through a door.

Now, on this rainy evening, while hoping she didn't fall on the concrete train station stairs, she saw...Ronni and Beau. She saw herself and Val too. All four of them were...*crying*, of all things.

Chapter 19

ꝞALERIA RENÉ invited Fabian the physical therapist out to dinner.

When asked if he should drive, she replied, "Fabe, with all you do for others, I think you've earned a ride."

"That being the case," he stated, "then I want more than a *car* ride."

Laughing Valeria René said that was all she was offering, right then.

ꝊN Friday evening, Valeria René arrived in her newbie. Then at their destination, she parked and said, "This is the Bronx Nook."

As she and Fabian neared, she admitted, "Kiss turned us on to this spot." Briefly Valeria René explained celebrating Ronni's birthday, not long ago, there. "We had consternation, because we entered through the rear, a no good scene."

Inside, Valeria René and Fabian were led to a small table in a cozy corner of one dining room.

Laughing and talking, they shared succulent shrimp and lobster.

Afterward, Fabian took Valeria René's hand. Gazing into her eyes, he admitted that he had almost given up the hope of ever finding a woman like her. He also said he had not known her long; "But I'm not worried, because at my age, the criteria for the person I want is etched on my heart."

Kissing her fingertips, he whispered, "And you, baby-girl, are everything, and then some."

Valeria René smiled, thinking, ditto for you too, sexy.

Holding her hand, Fabian's eyes held hers, even when to their inquiring server he replied that all was fine.

Gently Valeria René extricated her hand. Pushing her chair back, she motioned for Fabian to do the same. She said, "I want to show you something."

Together the couple ascended the stairs, to The Showcase, The Bronx Nook's in house nightclub.

Fabian noticed the gleaming bar, and the dance floor filled with people. He was aware of the pumping bass coming through the sound system that caused the room to vibrate. Gently, he prodded Valeria René to turn so that they might leave. But, he confessed he never would have guessed the nightclub was on the premises, due to its mostly soundproof outer walls. He said he was impressed.

"Not enough to stay though," Valeria René chuckled as they descended the stairs; "no worries, because there's more." They came upon the Blue Room on the lower level, beneath the eatery's two dining rooms. They stood, along with another man, outside frosted glass and stained wood doors, reading the marquee. "Fabe, maybe we can go in here a while. It's comfy, and you can order a drink, or dessert."

Fabian was again impressed. He also noted that in moments the venue would host a soulful balladeer, one of his favorites actually. This he mentioned. When Valeria René winked, he knew she'd planned for him to see the artist.

Inside the Blue Room Fabian and Valeria René chose a bistro table. Pulling the wrought iron chairs together, they sat side by side. She ordered espresso, and he a beer.

The crowd cheered when the love song singer was introduced. The house lights dimmed, and on the brightly lit stage, the drummer tapped his sticks one against the other. The band burst into the intro of the artist's current single, and the audience clapped and whistled their approval.

When the band segued into the third number, Valeria René excused herself. Not long after, she returned. Using the light from the stage, she found her seat. Settled, she became enthralled by the magic of the artist and his band. She blinked and felt confused, because why did it seem like the soulful balladeer's eyes held hers? Why did he croon of being her moon, because she was his sun, shining bright?

Valeria René knew it was ridiculous to believe the singer pointed at *her* when he melodiously sang he knew their love was real, by the way she made him feel.

She was aware that the song was ending. Yet for some reason she felt like she and the singer both were spotlighted.

April Alisa Marquette
133

When he said her name, she gasped. Holding his cordless microphone, the crooner told Valeria René, before the audience—some of whom were seated, while others stood—that he knew someone who had something to ask her.

In the darkened room, the spotlight expanded to include Fabian, who held out a ring. Stunned, Valeria René's eyes darted between Fabian and the stage, as the singer asked, for Fabian, in song, "Will you marry me?"

Valeria René looked from the stage, back to Fabian, while her heart beat frenetically. Then seeming to move in slow motion, she clasped his hand as holding out the sparkling ring, he asked, "Meet me at the altar?"

"Yes." She nodded. Yes! She shouted inside, she would. She would marry him!

It was not something she'd mentioned, to anyone, but indeed she had dreamed of it, of this, she recalled. She vaguely heard the singer tell the audience, "Yep, that's it people, you can applaud for love."

With clapping all around, Valeria René felt cocooned in Fabian's embrace.

Lord, did he smell wonderful, she thought as she held tightly to him. And if this was a dream, she prayed, she never wanted to wake up.

ALL of those things Valeria René mentally replayed as she rode, while Fabian drove. She recalled disagreeing with him about paying The Bronx Nook bill; she said she'd asked him out, therefore she would pay.

After doing so, she'd stood outside, while chivalrously he retrieved her car from the valet. Several people who had also been in the Blue Room earlier, congratulated her before disappearing into the night.

Riding along, she remembered something else. Fabian told her, before she could ask, that he'd set up things when she'd gone to the ladies room. "I spoke to the stage manager."

Fabian also admitted that he had been carrying the newly bought ring around for nearly a week. "I just couldn't figure out when to give it to you."

He had then asked Valeria René to spend the remainder of the evening with him.

She must have agreed, she mused, again eyeing her sparkling ring, because they were headed to his home.

Although she had been to Fabian's place, never had she stayed the night. In some respects she was old-fashioned, therefore in the beginning she and he had promised to become friends, before allowing sex to enter the picture. Thus when she had to mention that she had no change of clothing, she became nervous.

"No problem," Fabian shrugged. Shortly afterward, he pulled into the parking lot of a brightly lit all-hours sundry store. "Come," he said and reached for her hand.

Inside, he led her to the bath and shower aisle. "Pick things you'd ordinarily use," he instructed, "or something similar."

Valeria René did, before she and Fabian found the toothpaste aisle. After hitting a few others, they headed for checkout. At the register, she pulled her card, but Fabian was quicker.

"Use this," he told the older woman. He whispered, "Since I sprung this on you Ms. Vee Ree-nay, I might as well pay."

Wasn't he special? This she thought and laughed; Fabian grinned, because he was growing to love that sound.

At Fabian's home, that was by no means the typical, unkempt, mostly bare, bachelor pad, Valeria René realized something. She and he would have more privacy than at The Quarters.

Sure, only she and Ronni lived in the big apartment in Astoria, now that Beau had moved into his own digs, but being at Fabian's just felt better. He lived alone, so they needn't worry about anyone else coming and going, or paying attention, a nicety.

Again, Valeria René noted Fabian's impeccable taste. In his living room, the pearl gray, modern leather sofa and love seat sat atop a geometric design rug. A darker shade of gray, the rug boasted squares of burgundy, and a sphere of black. Mod lamps highlighted abstract and African works of art, while sconces highlighted pale gray walls.

In Fabian's cozy bedroom, the somewhat nervous Valeria René was told to get comfortable. Therefore, in a niche she sat, in one of two wine-colored plush chairs, before a small table.

Looking about, again she noticed the mahogany poster bed and matching dresser. She forgot that in a few moments she might *be* in that bed, with Fabian, doing Lord only knew what.

Suddenly she almost could not wait, to feel the weight of him, his hands, on her; her own and her lips on him, everywhere…

Pushing exciting thoughts from mind, she noted Fabian's nightstands, on one stood a lamp, on the other, a stone vase.

She turned. Wearing lounge pants and no shirt Fabian re-entered his bedroom asking if she wanted a drink. "You get nothing to eat though," he teased, "because *I* had to finish your dessert."

Barefoot, he turned from his mahogany armoire to hand his non-thirsty guest the remote. "For the TV, DVD, and MP3 player..." Aware that she was nervous, he gently squeezed her shoulder. Since this was the first full night they would spend together, he coaxed her to simply, "Relax...babe. I ain't gon jump you." He kissed the crown of her curly head. "Just lean back, put your feet up, and pick your pleasure."

$\mathcal{L}$ATER, as she lay snug beneath Fabian's duvet, Valeria René could not believe the man who slept beside her.

Earlier, while songstress Jill Scott had softly played, he'd gotten on his knees before the mocha-skinned one, wrapping his arms around her. As she toyed with his chest hairs, quietly he'd revealed something.

"I've been thinking about it, and I want to be your man Ms. Vee Reenay, for as long as life lasts." Fabian also said he was done. He promised there would be no more running around, not for him, "Because now that I have you, what would I be out looking for, other than trouble?"

In addition, he divulged that sure, he wanted to make love to her, tonight, but that type of ride she hadn't offered, this evening.

"That's cool though," Fabian stated, "because I really just wanted you here, with me, doing nothing. You know," he shrugged. "It's what couples do, or not, sometimes."

With that, Fabian got up off his knees. Bending over, he took Valeria René's face in his hands. Sensuously he kissed her, causing every nerve in her body to respond, before noiselessly he walked away.

Lord, if she'd doubted it before, she well knew now. She was in love, with Fabian Adare Sinclair. Unbeknownst to him, he had cemented her growing feelings when he'd said they could do nothing. Valeria René knew this was so was because her deceased love Marc—God rest his soul. He'd taught her that love wasn't always a flurry of activity. It was sometimes quiet, and like the calm after a thunderous rain. Or it could be...like it was turning out, with Fabian.

Carrying a clean set of towels, the nurturing dark-skinned man returned. On a hanger, he also carried a striped shirt. "For sleeping," he said, and exited, to take a shower.

When Valeria René stood beneath the warm spray, she was grateful that her host wasn't like others she'd encountered. Fabian hadn't tried to push up on her, and turn her shower into a prelude to a wild and raunchy screw session. He respected what she and he had discussed in the beginning: that they would get to know each other, minus the complications of sex. They'd laughingly admitted there'd be plenty of that, if life lasted.

Lying on Fabian's bed, Valeria René also recalled that he'd not crowded her. He didn't talk, touch, or attempt to kiss too much. He simply allowed her to find her stride, which was good.

She smiled, because after brushing her teeth, she'd entered his shades of mahogany bedroom. Despite feeling self-conscious, she had forced herself to climb onto the big poster bed where he lay wearing lounge pants, and listening to a jazz CD she'd previously selected.

As she and he stared at the ceiling while talking, he took her hand, placing her smaller fingers atop his. "You're mocha, and I'm ebony."

"Well you know what they say," she offered. "The darker the berry..."

"—The sweeter the juice." Fabian turned, and with bed covers rustling, he pulled the lady close. Under his striped shirt, the one that she wore, he caressed her soft nude back and derriere. He also smirked when he announced, "I do have 'juice' you know."

Valeria René laughed, and wrapped a leg around him. "Then I guess we'll make beautiful, midnight-dark babies."

Rising on an elbow, Fabian peered into the face that he grew to love more each day. "Oh, so you've decided to give me some?"

"Maybe..."

"Now?" he asked, and pressed his flagrant erection to her.

"Maybe...not, yet."

"You want babies?" Fabian asked, suddenly serious. He smoothed a curly lock from his wife-to-be's forehead. "Tell me how many, and when we can start making and having them."

"I do want, and I'll say how many more after the first one. Oh, and maybe that one should come after one married year."

"Yeeeah," Fabian nodded and rubbed Valeria René's hip. "That'll give me time, to learn every inch of this beautiful body."

Unbuttoning her shirt, he dipped his head, to lave the firm full breasts of which he had incessantly dreamed. Holding them in his hands, he reverently suckled and weighed them as though they were crafted of spun gold.

Kissing and caressing, pushing and prodding, glistening and stroking, the couple sporadically spoke, until finally they slept.

Awakened by the rays of sunlight that peered through the slatted wooden blinds, Valeria René opened her eyes. She wondered. Where was she?

Oh, Fabian's, in his room, at his home. She glanced over, at her friend, her protector, her companion, her sexy husband-to-be, and she smiled. She gazed too at her cushion cut diamond, before she slipped from bed, needing to relieve herself. She also had to make two quick calls.

Moments before she ended the second, quietly she said into her cellular phone, "Kiss, I've got to get back to Fabe, but yes, this is it. I just told MaMa the same thing— "

Valeria René glanced toward the bedroom. "Girl, lemme go; maybe get me some."

Yes, she wanted to get all up on and underneath the man who'd had her bent over the prior night. Behind her, with palms and fingers, he'd polished and squeezed her lush little derriere. He'd also thrust, and wound up inside her, and content, she'd sighed, and felt as though he'd touched the very heart of her.

Recalling she was yet on the phone, she told her longtime sister friend, "Quit laughing. I'll call you later—we've got a wedding to plan!"

Feeling tingly and ready, she returned, to the man who had proved to be more than willing...to sensuously kiss, caress, and oh yes, ride her.

$\mathcal{I}$T was hot and sunny when Kismet Staar ran up and grabbed the other woman's arm.

"Get off me!" Ronni screamed, drawing the attention of passersby.

Standing before the Cohorts' building, Kismet Staar dropped her hand, as she softly spoke. "Don't play me Brownie. Don't try to make people think I'm accosting you."

"Hey," Ronni shrugged. "It ain't like I know what you're up to. Your cousin could have sent you over, to beat me down."

Kismet Staar bit her lip, to avoid spewing the mean words that suddenly welled within her. She forced herself to calmly speak, to the woman with whom she had been friends since college. "I came over here on my own Brownie, because I wanted to see you. I had to, because all of a sudden, you don't return calls; oh, *and* you ran down the train station steps the other day when you saw me. Why?"

"Yo, you always did think you had to be in everybody's business," Ronni snidely remarked. Turning away, she knew she had been rude. Yet she quipped, "I don't get it Kiss. You're asking what's up wit' me, when I should ask you that, because who jumps out of a car, and rushes up on a person like the got-durn Gestapo?"

"Save the drama," Kismet Staar advised, feeling nearly as nasty as the diminutive woman whom she had previously been worried about.

Taking a deep breath, Kismet Staar began afresh. "Look, I was driving by, and I saw you leaving the building." She did not say that she hadn't known whom she was seeing, initially. With a satin headscarf tied beneath her chin, Jackie O style, Ronni's face was nearly hidden, and her eyes weren't visible behind her huge tortoise shell shades.

Kismet wondered. Was her friend *trying* to appear incognito?

"Look Brownie." Kismet Staar returned to the matter at hand, "You've been avoiding me. Why, I don't know. So I didn't want this opportunity to slip away." She breathed deeply, so she could ignore Ronni's look of boredom. "So Brownie, how you been?"

"Yo, you need to move your car." Ronni gestured at the vehicle awkwardly stationed at the park's entrance, across the street. "One of these loud-music-playing kids will swerve around that corner, and ol' Betsy will be history."

"She's fine." Kismet Staar felt her friend was more important. Sure, Ronni had erected a wall of toughness, but Kismet Staar saw past it. She knew Ronni feigned nonchalance, and hardness, whenever she felt hurt, deserted, or even simply sad.

"Look Brownie," Kismet Staar began. "I know stuff happened, between you and Beau, but that shouldn't have anything to do with you and me."

Kismet Staar didn't know what else to say, or do. Neither could she just blurt that she'd had several visions of Ronni being in a hospital. She couldn't truthfully say she knew something was amiss. Pleadingly she did say, because she felt like she was purposely being shut out, "Veronica, talk to me. Or tell me when to call you."

Ronni frowned, because why couldn't Kiss just let shit go? Why did she have to care? Why couldn't she forget being friends? She could so easily go on with her life. She could continue to hang out with her cousin, at his new place, like she had already. Ronni had heard that Kiss had been to Beau's the same day that Val had.

Both women had gone over to help Beau choose window coverings. Ronni heard too that Beau's friend, the cinnamon-skinned Mireya, whom Ronni did not like, had been there too, along with his slender friend Brett, whom Ronni wondered about. Ronni had heard that Beau was making real money now, and that his new co-op had parquet floors, high ceilings, closets forever, and large windows. She'd heard his place was perfect.

She didn't know if her sister friends, or that other chick that Beau had known since middle school, or the skinny one had actually gotten around to Beau's window stuff, but Ronni did know that she wanted Val and Kiss to *do them*—tend to their own business, so they could leave her the devil alone.

Couldn't their stupid selves see it would be better, for all involved, if they did?

"Babe, don't leave..." Kismet Staar reached for Ronni's arm. "Hey." She had a thought. "Maybe I can drop you off someplace." That would give them a few moments together.

"Yeah, like where I'm going is any of your business." Ronni pulled away. Taking backward steps, she called "Quit sweating me, Kiss." Then before hurrying away, Ronni became snide. "Oh, and don't call either. I'll call you."

Tears stung Kismet Staar's eyes. With her throat aching—due to unshed tears—she wondered why Ronni was so mean, lately.

Why also, did it look like she'd had a *black* eye? Kismet Staar threw up her hands. "You know where I am Brownie, every day," she called. "Nothing with me has changed. I'm always around."

I love you; Kismet Staar also thought but did not say.

"Yeah, yeah." Ronni scurried toward the train station up the street.

"I'm not like other people, Brownie..." Kismet Staar called. "I won't give up!"

𝒩EARING the train station steps, Ronni's eyes filled, and placing a hand on the rail, she quickly descended. She also mumbled as if to Kismet Staar. "Yeah, you not giving up is exactly what I'm afraid of."

Ronni did not want her secret to get out, because God only knew what would happen then...

At the bottom of the concrete stairs, thinking about her friend, Ronni collided with a young man on his way up. Her partially open birthday satchel flew from her arm. Quickly however, she attempted to retrieve the scattered contents.

Dang sixteen year olds, she thought, rushing around; probably just itching to get into devilment.

Ronni shook her head, because *when* had she started thinking like 'old lady' Kismet Staar?

Down on his haunches also, the young offender aided Ronni, as profusely he apologized. "Miss if I had seen you..." he looked into her face.

Ronni watched as the young man's eyes clouded, and speedily she dropped her lipstick and her keys back into her purse. Then she realized, too late, that her sunglasses had slipped down her nose. Hastily she attempted to push them up, but the young man gingerly caught her wrist.

"Miss, you're too pretty…too precious, to let some knucklehead mess you up, like *this*…" With a gentle hand, he turned Ronni's head; stunned, she actually let him.

"Come on, I'll help you," the young man said, and temperately pulled her to her feet.

Her train was approaching, so she turned to go, acutely aware that the youngster watched her. Why'd he have to be so nosey? As she went through the turnstile, she heard him call out.

"Miss, I'm young, but I have a mother and a sister." He ran alongside the turnstile. "I got a father too," he yelled. "My dad says real men don't lay hands on women! Miss, that's not right! It—ain't—*right*!"

$\mathcal{B}$ACK at The Cohort Quarter's, after correctly parking her car, Kismet Staar buzzed upstairs. Valeria René let her in, and Kismet Staar admitted she would have called, "But I didn't know I'd be stopping over."

Valeria René nodded. "Then you must have been on one of your maybe-I'll-spot-Brownie drive-by's."

"Val, I hate that you know me so well," Kismet Staar said and sat. "I hate that Brownie's got a black eye, I think. Who did that to her—and why?"

Valeria René shook her head. "I honestly don't know."

"Jesus," Kismet Staar winced and scrubbed a manicured hand over her face. She felt so frustrated she could cry. "That little yellow woman keeps me praying! I saw her downstairs, and I tried to converse with her—"

"I'm sure she was rank," Valeria René calmly surmised, headed toward the kitchen.

Kismet Staar followed. "What's going on Val? What am I missing?"

Handing Kismet Staar a glass of ice and a canned natural beverage, the mocha-skinned one hoisted herself up. Since Beau had taken his canvas chair-stools, the countertop sufficed for seating.

Valeria René sighed before confessing she did not know who had punched her roommate. "But I do know she mentioned, before this, that she'd been horsing around, and got her collarbone hurt, when things got rough."

"Horsing around, with whom?" Kismet Staar asked, leaning against the sink's edge.

"Vaughn, and others," Valeria René calmly stated.

"Not more scum from that ad."

"Maybe, maybe not," Valeria René shrugged. "I only know Ronni said she and—*whoever* were playing. Still, I've other assumptions, because of things that have lately transpired around here."

Kismet Staar pulled at her long black slip dress. She also attempted to change the subject. "Val how's Fabian?"

"He's good; but I see through you Kiss. That's not what's on your mind."

"You're right, but downstairs I was nearly informed that I'm nosey. So I'm attempting to mind my own business."

$\bigcirc$N the train, that would take her to her appointment at the clinic, Ronni tried to forget how rude she had been to Kismet Staar. Ronni didn't want to think about the hurt she'd seen in Kiss' eyes or the way Kiss had said she would not give up. Ronni adjusted her sunglasses. With the motion of the train lulling her, she inadvertently thought of times gone by...

There had been the day she'd found the Cohort Quarters. After seeing it advertised in the paper, she'd gone over. She fell in love with the wood floors, the layout, and the location. However, she'd had only had one paycheck to her name. That she'd had, only because she had gotten paid that morning. On the phone, she mentioned the place to Kismet Staar, gushing that she could see herself living there.

Riding the train, Ronni recalled Kismet Staar graciously lending her the requisite app fee, rent, and the security, so that Ronni could get her dream apartment. Motherly, Kismet Staar had also advised Ronni to hold onto her own ducats for other sure to crop up expenses.

Ronni shook her head, because she did not want to think about Kismet Staar, or other things the woman had done for her...even though Kiss really was a good friend, the best a girl could have.

Forgetting all of that, Ronni watched passengers exit and enter the train, and still she remembered things...

Back, while in college, Ronni's mother Minerva had taken ill. Although Ronni had not seen her mother in years, yet she'd felt the need to visit. Contacting her brother Cliff, Jr. together they'd ridden to see Minerva.

Soon after, Ronni's mother died. Her ailments had been minor, but her life had been lonely. Mostly deserted by her children, she had also quit hoping for anything from her cheating husband.

Oh God. Ronni remembered. She would *not* have been at her mother's bedside were it not for Kismet Staar. Once again, curvaceous had shelled out money, this time so that Ronni could visit Minerva.

A few years before that however, Kismet Staar had also entreated Ronni to get a life insurance plan, one for herself, and one for Minerva. Kiss revealed that she had done so for herself as well as own mother, because a girl never knew. And Kismet Staar had been right. Ronni had been able to pay for Minerva's funeral, no struggle, and pay off Minerva's medical bills, with cash to spare…all due to her pesky sister-friend's wise counsel.

Ronni rolled her eyes because really, she didn't want to think any more. She wanted to forget all the times that Kiss had gone the extra mile, for her. Desperately she also wanted to forget feeling like she'd betrayed and hurt Kismet Staar, the mothering woman who would give a person the shirt off her back if they needed it.

The truth was, Ronni told herself, she was actually doing what was necessary, to spare Kiss and even Val. She, Veronica Marie Brown, was keeping her friends from pain. The kind they would surely experience, if ever the truth got out…

$\mathcal{B}$ACK at The Cohort Quarters, Valeria René let Kismet Staar in on a little secret. She and Fabian had been house hunting.

"Actually, Fabe had been looking before he met me, so I joined, and we've all but settled on a place."

Kismet Staar was happy for her friend. "So you'll move in when you guys make it official?"

Valeria René shook her head. "Nope, I'd move in *tomorrow*, if I could."

Kismet Staar appeared puzzled.

Valeria René explained that she and Fabian had already planned for her to live in their new home, before they were married. She would live there alone, but Fabian would be back and forth because they didn't want to break his apartment lease. Their new home would be their love nest. She could see it now; sexy days and sweltering nights... She could hardly wait!

"Oh I get it." Kismet Staar nodded. "That way you guy's won't have to spend extra money."

"Right."

"Then, why not stay *here* until the wedding?" Kismet Staar inquired.

"I can't." Valeria René revealed that Ronni had opened The Quarters to 'such garbage' since Beau had been gone. "I come home now, and never know what to expect. There could be a communal orgy going on," Valeria Rene stated, "or just some guy lying around, on *my* furniture! You see it's covered," with sheets, "because I'm trying to dissuade infection, and germs."

Count on Val to worry about catching something, Kismet Staar smirked. With saucer-wide eyes, she also admitted she'd had no idea things were that bad.

Valeria René shrugged. "Now you do." She also requested that Kismet Staar join her in prayer for Ronni, because roomie was very different now. "She even keeps to herself, when she's not entertaining."

Valeria René said she almost didn't want to move out, and leave Ronni. "I guess because I've been taking care of her for so many years— since Clark-Atlanta, but I do have to think about me. It's no longer safe here, not for me, anyway."

Valeria René said that when Beau had been present she'd had a big strong pal. As a bona fide boxer, he worked out and sparred most days, so most people who might have gotten stupid thought twice about it, especially after getting a good look at his buff body.

"When Diddley was here, I felt protected, because like you, he won't hesitate to knock the fool out of somebody. He and I had fun. We cooked, took trips, and did stuff. When he was here, I also had help keeping the place clean. Now, I'm just an unpaid maid. So...since this is Ronni's place, and since she won't let anybody forget it, I'm looking to bounce; hopefully soon."

Absolution

$\mathcal{A}$S she pulled on the door, Ronni felt a blast of icy air. Cool, it felt so good against her skin, after the heat of the sun. She hated that antiseptic smell though...

As she walked down the sterile hallway, she desperately hoped she wouldn't receive bad news. Not today.

She watched as a nurse got on an elevator. When the doors closed, Ronni returned to her own thoughts. Bad news. That's what she'd been pondering. Quite frankly, she didn't know if she could take any more, and especially not on today.

Chapter 21

ℑN September, a month before Valeria René's wedding, she and Kismet Staar met at a trattoria. While planning the outing, they had agreed not to mention Ronni, or the fact that she insisted on not being included in upcoming festivities. The other two women had simply established that they would share an Italian meal, good wine, and upbeat conversation.

At the eatery, while awaiting their table, both longtime friends indulged in a cocktail at the bar.

When finally seated, Kismet Staar started with the tomato and mozzarella platter. Crunching on a toasty polenta crouton, she asked a question.

Replying Valeria René gestured. "I told you before, Kiss. You're my maid of honor because I want you, and because I couldn't choose one of my sisters." The curly-locked one again stated that she and her four siblings were close. Therefore, to choose one would cause the others to feel slighted. "This way, there's no seeming display of favoritism. This way, everybody's happy."

Kismet Staar nodded, and popped a tangy Kalamata olive into her mouth, "Gotcha." Leaning forward, she mentioned wanting to ask something.

Looking sexy in a dress, Valeria René also leaned forward. "Ask away."

Feeling silly, Kismet Staar sighed.

"Oh come on, Kiss." Forking into their shared appetizer, Valeria René placed slices of creamy fresh mozzarella, basil, and garden tomatoes on her plate. "Talk," she coaxed, drizzling all with vinaigrette.

"Okay. Here goes." The rounder woman leaned closer. "Val, how do I get a certain man to be as committed to me, as Fabian is to you?"

Supremely happy, Valeria René laughed. "Kiss, honey, I don't have a magic potion, and I already told you what Fabe and I did."

"You said y'all vowed not to have sex, not until you were sure you really liked each other." Kismet Staar sniffed her bubbling hot sausage rigatoni covered in melted Asiago cheese. "However, I need another answer because Lyle and I are too far along now for that 'no-sex' stuff—which by the way—would run any man off."

Valeria René sampled chilled tortellini. "It didn't deter Fabian." She also whispered, "But Kiss, we fell off the wagon..."

Curvaceous frowned. Wrinkling her nose, she appeared puzzled. Then it dawned on her. "No!" She chuckled. "Not your 'no-sex' wagon."

Valeria René nodded. "Yes, and girlfriend, 'falling' was like drowning—in chocolate. You *know* how I luuv chocolate."

Playfully Kismet Staar covered her ears, "T. M. I. mama; too much information. You're giving me too much!"

"Kiss, that's *just* what I told Fabian." Valeria René made her voice breathy and sensual. "Yep, right before I said oh yeah daddy, that's it. That's my spot; do dat. Do it again."

Kismet Staar waved while laughing. "Stop—it—right now!"

Spooning up another bite of her lemon-chicken tortellini with its jewels of fresh fruit, Valeria René spoke. "Kiss, I love that man." She softly admitted that she still loved her dear departed Marc, "But Fabian understands. He said I'm supposed to cherish my memories." With a sigh, Valeria René dreamily said her fiancé was so sweet, until she could eat him all up.

"Sounds like you tried," Kismet Staar remarked, spearing a chunk of hot smoked sausage.

"You know I did, girl." Valeria René then revealed that Kismet Staar had helped to cement her decision to marry Fabian.

"Me? How?"

"Remember the morning I called you from his apartment? I told you we were discussing spending our lives together. You said something that stuck with me. You told me not to ask myself if I could live *with* Fabian. You told me to ponder whether I wanted to live *without* him. I realized I don't."

"Girl, put like that, I get goose bumps."

"He and his family met mine," Valeria René gushed.

Kismet Staar knew it had been memorable. Valeria René's family, who'd once lived in St. Albans, just streets away from where she too had grown up, were close-knit, and Val's mother was one great cook.

"Did your Mr. Sexy get to eat?" Kismet Staar inquired. "And did you make your icy, orange-pineapple cocktails?"

"Yes, and yes."

"Did Ms. Chitra make tandoori chicken?" Kismet Staar asked, her eyes bright. "Did y'all have lassi too?"

"She did, and we did," Valeria René nodded, "and Fabe got to eat your favorite, MaMa's pakora," spicy batter-fried vegetables.

Valeria René gave details, and Kismet Staar envisioned the piquant IndiAfricAmerican feast which had also included homemade fruit ice cream, and naan, flat bread made from the dough of super fine flour.

Valeria René laughed aloud as she mentioned how Fabian's eyes had watered upon his first mouthful of her mother's fiery shrimp masala. Quickly however, he acquired the taste.

"Were y'all inside or out?" Kismet Staar queried.

"Out," in her parents' back yard. Overhead, there had been the usual draped canopy of royal blue, purple, and emerald green. Beneath the chiffon that swayed in the breeze, the two large families had been on the patio. Before them, in jeweled holders on the long low glass table, votive candles flickered while everyone sat amid overstuffed pillows, Valeria René's mother's handiwork.

The curly-locked one also said that following the meal everyone lounged, while her mother told of growing up in India. Then her father regaled all with tales of his boyhood in South Carolina. In the twilight, a breeze gently spread the fragrance of night-blooming jasmine; and Kismet Staar was also informed that Fabian had said that he had never felt so comfortable with any family outside of his own.

"That was when MaMa reminded him that our family is now his."

Valeria René mentioned that after most of the guests were gone, she'd walked Fabian through her parents' lovely home. Seeing it, he'd suggested that he and she similarly decorate their own.

Massive and wide, her parents' living space had low, comfortable, earth-toned custom-made furniture. There was a large cocktail table, glass-topped, and from the ceiling, sheer fabric hung in billowy drapes. Topping the windows, the fabric fell to the floor on each side of the room's arched entrance.

Her parent's treasures had also intrigued Fabian. The masks and solid brass candleholders caught his eye, as did a clay sculpture of two nude toddlers. Leaning on each other, with closed eyes, the rounded babes appeared sweetly fatigued.

Passing through the room, Valeria René's father noticed his daughter's fiancé. The younger man seemed as taken with the piece as he had once been. Therefore, the tall, chestnut-dark, imposing-looking Horace Thompson opened the glass casement. He then handed the piece to his son-in-law-to-be.

Surprised, Valeria René glanced at her father, because never did he allow anyone to touch his treasures.

Smoking a cheroot, Horace told Fabian about the master artisan who lived in a Central African village. The old sculptor said he'd had the children's likeness in his mind long before he'd carved them. Then closing his hooded eyes, Horace told Fabian that the piece reminded him of Valeria René's sisters, Sonji and Magi, pronounced MAJ-eye.

Horace revealed, "Magi, whose name nearly sounds like magic, was named for the Zoroastrian Mystics."

"The Magi, also known as the Bible's Three Wise Men," Fabian interjected, nodding.

"Yes." Then Horace divulged that so badly had he wanted the sculpture, because it reminded him of his two middle daughters. Chuckling, he also admitted that he'd ceaselessly cajoled, but to no avail. So he returned, to begin again the next day. "I finally paid, dearly," he divulged, "for that little piece."

Looking at the work, Fabian thought it magnificent. The babes were so lifelike, and detailed, down to the eyelash fringe; thus he disclosed, "I'd have paid too."

"I'll tell you something," Valeria René's father said. "Some time back, when I was a younger, more naïve man," he winked, "I had that same type of go 'round with an artist. Well, that man *said* he was the artist of another piece I'd wanted. I was in India with my wife at the time and she couldn't see paying such a ridiculous price for 'some clay.' As her man, I ignored her." Horace gave a little chuckle because he was being funny. "I forked over my hard-won money to that artist. Then when we got out of that little village and into the seaport city of Paradip, what did I see?"

Fabian grinned, aware of what was coming.

"I saw *hundreds* of those little statues, just like the one I'd fought to pay so dearly for. As you can imagine, my wife laughed, and laughed."

Fabian did too, and Horace appeared sheepish. "Heck, man, if I'd just turned that thing over, I'd have seen that mine, like all the others, had been made in China."

"Ah," Fabian raised a finger, "but your seller *was* an artist—of sorts. A *scam* artist."

Valeria René's fiancé and her father guffawed, and upon replacing his treasured baby sculpture, the older man disappeared, leaving only fragrant smoke in his wake.

Though she did not mention it to Kismet Staar, Valeria René also remembered standing alone with Fabian on her parent's lanai. Turning, he had taken her face in his hands. With a lasting kiss for the woman he had looked for his life long to love, Fabian pulled Valeria René close, allowing her to feel his rampant arousal. He then traipsed warm hands over her until finally they were beneath her flowing skirt. There, he slid them up her slender thighs.

Ohhh... While seated in the restaurant, she re-lived the way he'd touched her, there. With Fabian opening her, and caressing her, back and forth; his fingers inciting and igniting, she'd ridden a wave of ecstasy.

Just recalling it, she nearly did so again, as with desire, her nipples began to pearl. Seated across from Kismet Staar who continued to eat, Valeria René mused. Just *maybe*...she could see Fabian later, the man that she had so quickly and irrevocably become addicted to.

Pulling herself together, Valeria René sipped her pomegranate martini. She also told Kismet Staar that in a year, she and Fabian would try for a little brown baby. "Now *that's* going to be fun!"

Kismet Staar looked up. "Val, you're turning into a nympho." Beau's cousin then announced that not only would she be maid of honor, but she would even become an auntie; she raised her glass, "Because of continued sexual activity on your part." She grinned. "Lucky me."

Less exuberant, Valeria René sincerely stated, "I'm just glad *you're* sharing this with me."

"I am too." Kismet Staar knew though, that without Ronni, the celebration was incomplete. Also aware that neither of them would mention it, curvaceous again lifted her sparkling Italian wine. "Val we'll keep praying. Not for Brownie to do what we want, but for her to receive peace."

Absolution

Valeria René nodded as again Kismet Staar sipped *Prosseco*. "You know Val, this could just be a case of when someone's not doing well; they feel bad if you are..."

Valeria René said that Kiss was probably right. Then in a voice more conducive to conducting business, she mentioned her upcoming nuptials. She divulged that she had a charming simple ceremony, with dinner and dancing planned. "I'm hoping for smooth, even though we do have to meld the faiths of two different families."

Valeria René explained that her mother and sisters were followers of Islam. "Not of radical ideals," but her family adhered to the Hadīth, the rules of right behavior. They submitted to Allah, praying and giving alms as directed in the Qur'ān.

"The rest of the wedding attendees are Christian. Oh," Valeria René remembered. "Fabian's best man Eli; and others are Jewish."

Revealing concerns, she mentioned the September 11th destruction of the World Trade Center. Since that appalling and heart-wrenching devastation, she and other born Americans who looked like her, now experienced a type of hatred they had never known.

"I had a man say to me, in passing, 'Shouldn't you be somewhere with your crock pot...making bombs?' I know he was ignorant Kiss, but that really stung. Similar incidents also cause me to wonder if carry-over hatred will ruin my wedding..."

Sympathetic, Kismet Staar acknowledged that racism and ignorance knew no bounds. However, she advised, "Just must make it known that only mutual respect and tolerance will be permitted. Then if somebody gets stupid, you and Fabian can have that somebody thrown out."

Valeria René smiled, yet Kismet Staar noticed the sadness, and she reached for the mocha-hued hand. "Val, you've got a lot going on...and I know you're worried about Ronni—"

"How can I *not* be?" Valeria René cried. Lowering her voice, she said, "I know we said we wouldn't get into it, but she's *supposed* to be *with* us, walking down the aisle too!

"Kiss, there's a reason she's doing this. And I know that reason has more to do with other things, things she's not saying, and those things are probably way beyond that stupidity that took place between her and Beau." Valeria René shook her head. "Whatever it is though, I just can't figure it out."

Kismet Staar glanced around. Although she agreed, she dared not say so, not this close to Valeria René's wedding. She also couldn't mention her visions. She'd had so many in the past few months, and she hated that they were always the same.

Either Ronni was in a hospital, or all four Cohorts were crying.

Go figure.

Attempting to forget what she'd seen, Kismet Staar offered, "Since we can't fix any of this, not tonight anyway Val, we'll keep praying. Right now," she squeezed her friend's hand. "Why don't we order a sinfully rich, gooey, dessert? Something bad, a real sugar and butter bomb."

"Something chocolate?" Light seeped back into Valeria René's eyes. "It'll mean more time on the treadmill," she said more to herself, "but what the heck."

Hadn't she read somewhere, she suddenly cogitated, that *sex* burned calories? Believing she had, Valeria René piped up, "Hey Kiss, let's try the cake you mentioned when we were at the bar."

"The chocolate buttercream one with cocoa shavings on top?"

"That's the one." And since she fully intended to get Fabian to help her 'work it off,' Valeria René voiced her decision. "I don't want to share, either."

"Val," Kismet Staar blinked. "You do realize how big those pieces of cake are, right?"

"Yep." She sure did, but since she and Fabian would work it off, Valeria René happily mused, why not?

Chapter 22

$\mathcal{I}$T was late October—Indian summer.

Valeria René could not believe it was Friday already, the evening on which her wedding rehearsal was being held.

Standing outside her parent's home, she felt like summer had sped by. Then fall had come, and Diwali the Indian Festival of Lights. Now, on tomorrow she would marry her lover, her friend.

The ceremony would be held on the grounds of a Westbury Long Island estate. Friends of her parents owned the vast and meticulously cared for acreage called Canterbury Walk. The friends had insisted that Horace and Chitra's daughter have her ceremony at their house, a three-story brick mansion, gratis, their gift to the bride.

Standing beside her parents' home, Valeria René watched as her friends and family members rehearsed for her nuptials. She smiled at the great-aunt who stood in for her, because superstition dictated that a bride should only walk down the aisle once, at the actual ceremony.

Visually Valeria René hunted for her sisters, Kira, Sonji, Magi, and the youngest, LorRen. Her eyes sought them in the crowd. She found the older three, but it took her a moment to locate LorRen. What beautiful bridesmaids they would make.

Watching the vivacious nineteen-year old, Valeria René wondered if her baby sister LorRen, also called Lovey, actually flirted with Fabian's two brothers. It appeared that both the eldest, Richard, a dentist, and Drew, the youngest, a physical therapist, like Fabian, enjoyed Lovey's animated conversation, and ever protective, Valeria René sighed.

She noticed Fabian's sister Michelle, who would not be in the wedding, unlike her brothers who were groomsmen. Seated uncomfortably on a lawn chair, Michelle too watched all. She longed to be a participant, but she hadn't the fortitude. Fanning herself, Michelle conserved her waning stamina. Constant fatigue was her companion, a result of eight hard months of pregnancy. Still, she had to keep up with her busy three-year old, Chondra, the flower girl.

As she stood beside her parents' professionally landscaped Lindenhurst township home, Valeria René's eyes drifted from Michelle, to the woman's beautiful small daughter, Fabian's niece. Reminded of her sister Lovey at that age, Valeria René suddenly remembered her first day in the split-level ranch.

It had been beautifully breezy back then too, the day her parents moved the family here. They'd wanted a new start, after the death of Horace Jr. Valeria René's beloved brother.

Placing a hand at her throat, as she stood in the shade, Valeria René envisioned getting a second start from Lindenhurst, on tomorrow.

Come Saturday, she would rise early, do a few things; then she would don her wedding gown and ride to meet her groom.

Wow, she breathed. This was really happening! She was actually going to marry Fabian A. Sinclair, and to think, she had all but given up the hope of ever finding him.

Chitra saw her eldest standing alone in the shade of the house. Walking over, she took Valeria René's hand. "Isn't this exciting?"

The daughter agreed, even as her eyes clouded.

Noticing the joy, and the sadness, Chitra looked wistfully over her lush lawn. She noted the wedding party, her husband, her in-laws, and her four other offspring. She saw the surrounding foliage, now autumn gold and red, and in the drawing dusk Chitra turned. "I know," she softly admitted. "I know."

The daughter squeezed the mother's hands and with tears in her chameleon eyes, she spoke. "Then you know I *wish* MaMa...for Junie to be here, to enjoy this...with us."

Chitra spoke into the hair at Valeria René's ear. "We all wish my darling, but," Chitra said, her voice brightening. "You'll soon have two new brothers, and a new sister, Fabian's siblings."

"They're nice, right? Almost as nice as we are," Valeria René teased, just as someone nearby spoke.

Mother and daughter welcomed Valeria René's baby sister who dramatically began.

"Val I am so glad 'your friend' Ronni's not here; because if she was, she'd try to make this her own little circus."

Chitra's point of view differed from that of her outspoken last child. "Perhaps Ronni's going through something, Lovey. We don't know."

The mother faced Valeria René. "I still think her absence is a shame, especially when you, she, and Kismet Staar have been through so much together." Chitra sighed. "Perhaps if we pray, Ronni will change her mind."

"Don't do that. Leave her alone," LorRen sassily advised. "Things will go smoother, and Val needs smooth. She's supposed to be happy. She doesn't need anybody around to mess shi—*stuff* up."

"Watch it young lady," Chitra scolded, eyeing those who adjusted foldaway tables on her lawn. The activity and the twinkling lights reminded her of the soon to be served meal. "Listen Lovey, if Ronni shows up, you are to behave. She deserves decency, just like we do."

"I didn't say she didn't," LorRen flippantly whined. With folded arms, she bumped shoulders with Valeria René. "I'm just glad she's not here, and I'm entitled to my opinion. MaMa, you 'n dad taught me that. And my opinion is: I don't like Ronni."

"Just behave, Lovey," Chitra commanded, "or I'll box your ears." Then magisterially the mother announced that the nineteen year old's feelings about a person should not dictate the way she treated that person. "You act decent Lovey, because you are decent, and remember. Ronni's mother isn't present—like our Junie. Those things hurt. So perhaps when you dislike Ronni the most, maybe then, she's hurting the most."

"MaMa's saying," Valeria René diplomatically chimed, "just be respectful, Lovey."

"Yeah," LorRen muttered, "whatever Ma." Sick of the singsong, she flounced away, to seek someone to flirt with.

Chitra slightly raised her sari. With wispy tendrils of hair floating wind-borne, she started toward the main serving table, but turning, she offered advice.

"Valeria René, you pray for Veronica. I know she's going through something, because in here," Chitra pressed her fingers to her torso. "I feel anguish for her." With a hand yet at her solar plexus, the concerned mother spoke on. "I have the same feeling I had just before we found out your aunt Malka had cancer...so earnestly pray."

Those words the bride-to-be pondered, even as she began to aid her mother and others to bring serving dishes out of doors.

"Don't shoo me," she told her father's sisters, her two favorite aunts. "I may be the bride, but I'm not incapacitated."

As she set a steaming bowl on the tablecloth that threatened to float away on the breeze, Valeria René forgot taunting her father's sisters. Her mind drifted back to her most recent conversation with Ronni. Again the woman had refused to participate in the festivities.

She claimed she had no friends, and much less to celebrate.

Yet, Valeria René found herself daring to hope...even at this late date.

Chapter 23

THAT Friday night, following the rehearsal dinner, Valeria René prepared to sleep at her parents' home, in their bed.

Carrying his pillow, her father Horace walked toward the guest bedroom, muttering. "Kicked me out of my bed; worked all these years, for them, and this is what I get."

Watching him go, Valeria René smiled, knowing her father didn't really mind, because it was a tradition *he* had started two years prior.

On the eve of another daughter's nuptials, Horace told his wife to call 'the girl' into their room, "After I leave." He'd also said, "Then Chee, you can tell Sonji what to expect."

Chitra had heartily laughed because their daughter and her then-fiancé were already the parents of a nine-month old.

"Horace," Chitra chided, "if Sonji doesn't know what to expect, now, Allah help her."

"I love you Dad..." Valeria René called watching her father enter the guestroom.

Not facing her, he threw up a hand, "Yeah, yeah."

Chitra chuckled. "Your father doesn't fool me."

LorRen who lay on her mother's bed, watching music videos, piped up. "He doesn't fool me either. He's gonna smoke, in that room. He'll think we can't smell it because he'll open the window and use that fake 'smokeless' ashtray of his."

"He'll drink too, and watch his DVD of naked women wrestlers," Valeria René offered. She joined her sister in a robust laugh at the antics of the man they adored.

Suddenly she remembered that the young woman with the heavy fall of curly hair had once been the chubby baby ever on her hip. Feeling suddenly wistful, Valeria René wondered if her family would also hold dear the memories of this special time spent together.

ON the morning of her wedding, Valeria René woke before sunrise. She blinked, and wondered why she felt nothing, no excitement, no nervousness…not a blessed thing.

Oh well. Mentally, she forged on to list things that she, her mother, and her sisters had to do, one of which was go to the salon. At ten, they would get their hair, nails, and toenails done. They would take Fabian's small niece too, since she was the flower girl.

The child's mother wanted the hairdresser to wash and curl the toddler's long kinky hair.

Afterward, Valeria René mused, they could all again relax, at her parents' spacious abode, until Ms. Makeup arrived. Then it would be time to get dressed.

Just beyond the bedroom window, morning birds began their vivacious chatter, and Valeria René's mother rolled onto her back with a groan. Her daughter laughed. "You will never be a morning person, MaMa."

"Shhh," Chitra only wanted to sleep.

"Neither will I," Valeria René announced noting the lightening sky, "not on any day outside of this one."

"Thaaat's right," Chitra said, as remembrance crept into her voice. With a thumb, she eased long dark hair away from her face. "Today my baby marries the man she loves."

"That's later," LorRen moaned reluctant to wake. She turned over on her pallet, down on the floor. "Now, we need quiet."

"Yes, quiet," Chitra agreed.

"Did I wake you two?" Valeria René covered her mouth. "I thought I'd been quiet."

"With all that sighing?" Chitra inquired with closed eyes.

LorRen added, "And with them clanging bangles that my new brother-in-law bought? Please."

Valeria René apologized. Then without thinking, she sat bolt upright in her mother's bed and pulled back the curtain. Peering out, she had a thought. "We should all go to breakfast! Wouldn't that be nice?"

"Nice?" LorRen groaned. Most weekends, she and her mother never got up before nine, although today they would do so. "Yo, you should go *somewhere*, with your talking self." She also said she hoped Fabian knew that with his new wife he would never sleep again.

"But not because I'll be *talking*," Valeria René retorted as she got out of bed, wrapping herself in a silk robe, a shower gift. She turned. "You guys really don't want breakfast? Or coffee?"

"Your father will prepare it! Even though I'm sure he's not up yet," Chitra snapped. "Now please...remain silent."

Wearing her raggedy bunny slippers, Valeria René sounded hurt. "I feel like you two are trying to get rid of me."

"We are—since you won't clam up!" LorRen pulled the sheet over her head. "Too bad we have to wait till this evening to do it."

*A*T five fifty-seven, on the pristine grounds of Canterbury Walk, Kismet Staar, the maid of honor appeared. In a champagne-hued, sleeveless dress, she walked down an aisle created by rows of alabaster chairs. Feeling disconcerted, because all eyes were on her, she lost her footing.

Wearing his Yarmulke, Elimelech Hertzberg, Fabian's best man jumped to her aid. As he helped to right her, Kismet Staar became cognizant of some fool who snapped her picture. Forgetting Mr. Photo though, she kindly thanked Eli.

Safely ensconced with the bridesmaids, she turned. She watched for the flower girl, whom she believed would deflect attention from her.

And that she did! The toddler ran down the papered aisle, her basket of floral petals in hand. Midway, she stopped. Then solemnly she marched back the way she'd come. Smiling, small Chondra also reveled in the fact that she held captive an audience.

As the wedding coordinator and others tried to coax her back down the aisle up which she'd come, the imp bent her wreathed head. Putting a hand in her basket, she turned in a circle, to slowly distribute flower petals to the floor around her. Then without warning, she darted behind the last row of chairs, and raced to the obscure aisle at the opposite end. With long curly ringlets flying, she proceeded, at breakneck speed, toward the altar—where her uncle Fabian, the groom caught her.

Handsome smiled, as the audience laughed, and embarrassed, his sister, the child's mother, lowered her eyes.

Then...*she* stepped out of an allée of decades-old oaks. A vision in white, Valeria René emerged, passing trees, the trunks of which were tied with festive bows.

Her father met her, and on his arm she serenely floated, down the papered aisle. She also softly spoke. "Dad, you do know...you'll always be my first love, right?"

Nearly choking up, Horace could only nod, grateful for his tinted glasses.

At the altar, the bald and glowing groom wore a white tuxedo boasting tails. With baited breath, he watched as his betrothed, carrying orchids and oriental lilies, approached. Standing beneath a garland of the same flowers, Fabian realized that not even in his dreams had his bride appeared so exquisite.

Wearing a fitted a halter gown, her mother's creation, Valeria René stepped to face her groom. As she looked up and into his eyes, she did not hear the murmurs of those that marveled at her white silk garment. Sand-washed and beaded, its mother of pearl clusters mirrored her earrings. Her mules, white silk heels, were the envy of her bridesmaids.

As his heart beat double time, Fabian noticed Valeria René's bare arms. On one, she wore a four-strand pearl cuff, a gift from her four sisters. On the other, she wore his gift, a tennis bracelet.

As the wedding Officiate announced they would pray the Fattiha, 'The Lord's Prayer' of Islam, Fabian reached to touch Valeria René's hair. Piled beautifully atop her head in a frenzy of large bouncing curls, a few locks spilled over into her expertly made-up face, and the groom whispered. "You're beautiful."

Before beginning, The Officiate explained that the Fattiha was recited for all new beginnings.

"In the name of God, the Merciful," he intoned, "the Compassionate..."

At the prayer's end, Fabian touched Valeria René's smooth-skinned back. Unable to pay attention to anyone but his bride, he also took her in his arms. Very nearly, he crushed the flowers she held between them as facing her he whispered into the ear that their guests could not see.

Radiant with joy, the bride held to the groom with her free hand, smiling as he promised to love and cherish her.

He also reported that he'd pondered it, and he *guessed* he could live with her ugly bunny slippers.

Valeria René laughed. Gazing up into Fabian's eyes, she informed him that she would, from that day forward, bequeath him, her soul mate, her most precious gifts and virtues to last always.

Noticing the exchange between the bride and groom, the Officiate ceased to speak. He realized, as did others, that nothing that had taken place so far, had been as planned.

Remembering him, Fabian spoke to the copper-skinned man that he and his bride stood before. "Sir, I need you to anoint us. Or whatever comes now, because I have *got* to kiss this woman."

Horace laughed, and some of the groomsmen cheered.

Quickly obliging with a toothy grin, the Officiate stepped aside as Mr. Sinclair picked up the new Mrs. Sinclair. He kissed her, lasting and sweet.

When the newlyweds released each other, the wedding party converged on them.

Finding himself surrounded by well-wishers, Fabian raised his diamond-banded hand. Holding his wife at her small waist, he laughed as all were directed to the reception tents, where on each table a bevy of lilies floated in silver bowls of spring water.

The wedding party took pictures by the pond. While at the same time, guests were served an array of hors d'oeuvres. There was blackened bay shrimp salad, pasta primavera, and a concourse of seafood, including oysters on the half shell. These were believed to be a powerful aphrodisiac.

With the photos taken, the wedding party returned, for introductions. Amid clapping and music, gaily, they passed tables laden with china, cutlery, and crystal.

Then the meal, buffet style, was served. The main course included braised brisket, filet of lemon sole, and saffron rice. There was also ambrosia to partake of, and sweet breads, in addition to several Indian dishes created by the caterer; all accompanied by an open bar.

At twilight, the bride and groom danced their traditional first, amid a sea of iridescent bubbles. Gracefully they moved to the strains of the live band seated on a dais, beneath stars that had recently begun to twinkle.

During the father and daughter dance, the tall, imposing-looking Horace stood unmoving. Claiming to be nobody's dancer, he swayed slightly while holding his eldest.

"I'm going to quickly impart the finer points for maintaining a happy union," he divulged. "These things I have to tell you because I know your Ma didn't; even though that was why I slept in the wrong room last night."

"And what makes you so sure she didn't tell me?" Valeria René inquired, chuckling.

Appearing long-suffering, Horace shrugged, "Because *I* happen to be the magic 'n the glue in your mother and my relationship. Therefore only *I* know certain things."

"Is that so?" Chitra appeared, an eyebrow raised.

Surprised by her mother's presence, Valeria René laughed at her father who'd obviously been caught off-guard as well.

With the dance ending, Horace kissed his daughter, and his wife. Then claiming to see someone with whom he needed to speak, he hurried away.

"Yes Mr. Thompson," Chitra teased, "you had better run."

The DJ spun the first up-tempo jam and as the music vibrated throughout the dance tent, LorRen and Beau could be seen gamboling over the whole of the floor. Darting around saner people, Beau led. Laughing hard, LorRen followed, barely able to keep up.

On the next song, Beau allowed the young woman a few moments. Depositing her along the sidelines, quickly he snatched up the bride.

Valeria René, who had been speaking with guests, suddenly felt hands on her waist. She turned, and found herself in a mad whirl. Before she could protest, she was whisked to the middle of the dance floor. There, she and her former roommate dropped it like it was hot, as alongside, others coaxed them on.

The DJ spun into another number, and Valeria René draped herself haplessly around Beau. "Your solo was lovely." She hugged the buff brown man. "Thank you, for sharing, and—" Her face began to crinkle.

"No," Beau advised, "no crying. Fabian won't think I did something to you."

Though her eyes filled, Valeria René smiled.

Smiling back, Beau said, "Don't thank me for singing. You know I'd do anything for you." With his hands at her waist, he also told her, "Make this marriage work. Write down the finer points. Then tell me how to snag my own gorgeous guy."

Valeria René burst out laughing. "Oh Diddley," she eked. "He *is* fine, isn't he—from the inside out."

Feeling someone else's presence, Valeria René turned, and smiled at a handsome ebony-skinned bald man. Taking his hand to pull him close she said, "I was about to tell Diddley that you and I don't have a monopoly on 'happy together.'"

Fabian looked from his bride to the taller Beau. He spoke loudly to be heard over the music. "My wife's right you know." He gave her a sensuous wink. "You like that—'my wife'—don't you?"

Lowering her lashes, she felt desire, all the way to her toes, as Fabian returned his attention to Beau. "Somebody good will come for you too, man." Using his free hand, he clasped one of Beau's as he nearly had to yell over the music. "Hold on to your faith, brotha."

"That sounds so corny," Valeria René laughed, because she could not have been happier. "But we will cheer you on Diddley, just like we did at the club."

"Thaaat's right," Beau called, as recognition dawned. "Y'all met there. Kiss and Lyle met that same night."

Laughing, the three of them made room for Kismet Staar who asked, "What did I miss?"

"Not a thing," Valeria René replied. She stepped back to also include LorRen, her baby sister, as well as Eli, the best man.

"Girlfriend," Kismet Staar called above the music. "This," she gestured to indicate the festivities. "Has been so..." She searched for a word. "It's been so...

"Help me somebody," she pled as her friends grinned.

"Yo, it's just been *love*," Beau called out. "This whole affair has just been so love-filled, until I'll be dreaming about it for weeks. Only, in my dream *I'll* be the star, not Val."

Those gathered guffawed, and stepped back to admit others. Among them was the groom's brother, who yelled, "Looked like the party was going on over here."

As people began speaking, Kismet Staar absently glanced into a far corner. Placing a hand at her chest, she wasn't aware that she gasped.

"What?" Eli and others amid the circle inquired. Fabian's brother craned his neck.

"It couldn't be..." Incredulous, Valeria René turned to Kismet Staar who yet stared off into the dark. "Kiss, that couldn't be Ronni...could it?"

"Where?!" Suddenly indignant, young LorRen intently glowered, trying to see beyond the lighted tents. Fiercely she'd hoped 'that woman' wouldn't show, nevertheless, it appeared she had; to ruin the festivities, LorRen knew.

Distractedly Valeria René and her maid of honor extricated themselves from the now confining circle. As the others drifted, back to the dance floor or elsewhere, the Cohorts, and LorRen stayed put, to find out if Ronni Brown was indeed in attendance.

$\mathcal{I}$F that was Ronni, her two female Cohorts surmised, where had she come from, and why so late? And why was she keeping off in no man's land, they asked, like some type of outcast?

Wondering the same thing, LorRen stayed close. With an eyebrow raised, her reasons for being interested were all her own.

Beau, who had been silent, now stated, "That is Ronni."

Disbelieving, his cousin asked, "How you know?"

"Come on Kiss." He gave her a wry look. "How would I not? I lived with her for three years."

"Well, if that's so much of Ronni Brown," Kismet Staar spoke quickly, "then, go, tell her...come kiss the bride. Yeah, say that."

"No," Beau snapped, because he had never been easily commanded about. "Why don't you do it? You big giving orders person."

Suddenly, his stomach churned because like LorRen, he too had hoped Ronni wouldn't show. Actually, he recalled, the last time he'd seen the ex roommate, circumstances had been less than admirable. Now knowing she was present only reiterated it.

"Go, Diddley," Kismet Staar coaxed, while eagerly Valeria René craned her neck, unaware of what to make of this new twist.

Indeed, the bride had invited Ronni to partake of the festivities, and she had sincerely hoped Ronni would. Many times throughout the day she had even glanced into her gathering of guests, for the one person who would make her day, her celebration, complete. Now it seemed that person had appeared...

"Beau," the bride softly called, pushing a curl from her eye. "Would you please go see if that's Ronni? Ask her to come here, if it is her."

Valeria René, her sister, Kismet Staar, and Beau stood beneath the dance tent, on the edge of a floor that had been erected that morning, on an expanse of lawn. Yet so focused on the little investigation where they, until not one really heard the music that blared all around.

"Why can't one, or all three of you, go to her?" Beau asked, jabbing a finger at the women whose faces were expectantly upturned, like little birds. His gaze lingered on LorRen; who for some reason; appeared angry.

"I can't go to her, bubblehead, because my shoes are satin," Kismet Staar reasoned. "Val's are silk. We can't step off this floor, into that grass; stains, you know."

Beau rolled his eyes, forgetting LorRen as he thought, these clucking old hens.

Unaware of his thoughts, the women—minus LorRen, who stood scowling—continued to whine, mewl, and pester him.

Finally, fully annoyed, he huffed, "Alright! Qui-et! I'll go, but if this shit blows up in your faces, remember. You big babies asked for it."

Beau muttered to himself as he walked. He also sensed this was a soon-to-get-ugly situation. However, to please the two behind him, he headed for the lone figure in the shadows.

"What about *my* shoes?" he growled. The beige suede matched his custom-made beige micro-suede ensemble. His footwear could sustain damage too, but did anyone care about that?

Beau trotted then, because what if that wasn't Ronni, but a groundskeeper? What if the person did a disappear because he approached? Beau knew them ol' hens behind him would never let him forget it. They would incessantly cluck, saying he'd purposely let the person get away. They would also nag him to kingdom come, insisting that the person *had* been Ronni. Therefore, he sprinted.

Approaching the area, his eyes became accustomed to the moonlight, dim after the brighter bevy of candles for ambience beneath the tents.

When acclimated, Beau saw his ex-roommate. "Hey," he called.

Ronni did not respond. She simply stood where she had been, for Heaven only knew how long.

Immediately Beau felt hostility washing off her in waves. Yet since she wouldn't speak, he did. "Val wants to see you."

Still nothing.

Forgetting that, Beau's conscience got the better of him. Before he knew it, he had apologized for all of the wrong he had done Ronni. Despite her antagonistic vibe, he spoke on. He truthfully, told her of his continuing anguish over the acrid situation that never should have been.

He also admitted he'd had *no right* to destroy her property, and though she refused to respond, Beau didn't care.

He was purging him self.

He asked if Ronni had received his apology letter. He said she hadn't cashed the last rent check, or his damage remittance, because his bank statement attested to it.

Yet Ronni refused to reply.

Therefore, Beau revealed that he had initially been angered by the idea that Ronni had been with Vaughn. However, after much thought, Beau realized the man was grown, free to be with whomever he chose; women included; Beau thought but did not say.

He revealed that he'd divested himself of proprietary feelings toward Vaughn Gruskin. Beau then concluded by saying that nothing could excuse the destructive way he'd behaved. Therefore, again he apologized.

Throughout his disclosure, Ronni remained resolute.

Oh well. Beau had said his piece. He would no longer feel guilty. He would move on.

"Just go to Val," he coaxed, forgetting himself. "Say something to her. You don't have to see anybody else if you don't want." Heck, *he* would disappear. He'd be glad to get away from the stoic woman.

Yet Ronni did not respond, so Beau turned, viewing this little foray as a *fait non-accompli*. He tossed over a shoulder, "Val loves you. *She's* never tried to hurt you; but suit yourself, stay over here. Hang out in the dark. Alone."

Hating that last word, Ronni put one foot before the other.

Having begun to walk before she did, Beau heard the woman behind him. Slowly he veered to the right, his pugilistic instincts advising him to keep her in his left peripheral. Yes, just in case he'd need to knock her off balance, because who knew? She could try to jump him, or knife him.

Nearing party people, lights, and music, Beau craved a drink, and a smoke, in the worst way.

Yet he winked at Valeria René whose hands covered her mouth. She was so sweet, and excited. She hadn't seen Ronni in about a month, not since the bride had taken up residence in her new home. Thus with guileless eyes, Mrs. Newly Married greedily drank Ronni in.

Expressionless, as butter yellow approached, Kismet Staar stood aside, while LorRen wore a magnified scowl. Though no one noticed, baby sister inched closer to the oncoming woman.

"This 'ho," LorRen grumbled for only Beau to hear as she folded her arms and tapped a foot.

"Ronneee!" Valeria René called, her face alight with joy; with her knees bent she gushed, "I *knew* you'd come!"

Kismet Staar watched as the bride stepped forward to greet Ronni who remained rigid.

"I wish you could have been at the ceremony," Valeria René confessed, wanting only to hold her friend.

Wearing a tangerine colored ill-fitting sheath, Ronni placed her birthday satchel before her self. Kismet Staar knew Ronni did so to avoid contact, even as the knowing and brash LorRen quietly spat, "This skank."

When she stood close enough to be heard, but not touched, Ronni exacted an air of boredom. "I didn't miss the ceremony," she droned. "How else would I know that Kiss almost bust her butt? Trying to tip— all cutesy—down the aisle."

Kismet Staar eyed Ronni up and down, noting the sallow looking skin, the non-lustrous hair, and those bright salmon shoes. Talk about what *not* to wear! That footwear, Kismet Staar disgustedly thought, would only match that hapless orange-ish frock, in the dark. The pitch dark. Looking away, Kismet Staar dismissed Ronni who could always manage to act up.

"I also sat through *his* song." The mouthy yellow woman jerked a thumb in Beau's direction.

From the platinum case given him by his former neighbors, the Nunleys, Beau tapped out a smoke. Then hungrily inhaling nicotine and tar, he dismissed Ronni and her rudeness.

"I heard that cackling, or whatever he called himself doing while he was up on the mic." Ronni then muttered, "Misogynistic bastard."

Valeria René narrowed her eyes, as she placed her bejeweled hands on her hips. "Ronni…are you *trying*…to be nasty?"

Aware that her sister's ire rose, young impetuous LorRen grew more incensed by the moment, because had she not predicted that Ronni would cause trouble—and on Val's happy day too?

Unaware, Valeria René's usually soft voice hardened. "Veronica. Marie. Brown. Are you *attempting* to be rude?"

Valeria René's eyes became mere slits as she clenched a fist. "I ask because if you're *deliberately* coming across this way, after all the worrying I done over you! Girl, talk about a bridezilla—I will beat you down, to the ground, right here, right now, wedding dress 'n all!"

Ronni, whose face became grotesquely contorted, opened her mouth to speak; but the voice that those assembled heard belonged to another.

"Yo, you betta check yourself," the young gangsta growled at the woman she loathed. "Upsetting my sister…" LorRen then lunged at Ronni, "Or things will jump off right here!"

Wisely Beau stepped in the way, thwarting the impulsive one.

"Chile please," Ronni sucked her teeth. Nevertheless, she backed further away from the baby assassin who flexed bony shoulders. Attempting to maintain her hard edge however, Ronni spared a glance for her former female roommate.

"I was here, for you, Val." She sounded sarcastic, "Since I knew it would kill you if I didn't show. Now," Ronni sighed. "You can't say I've never done anything for you."

She continued. "See Val, when you need me, I appear, and unlike others, I know when to disappear too. I'm out, because I've had enough of the death flowers, the hard chairs, and—"

LorRen suddenly slapped Ronni's face, simultaneously screaming, "I know you done gone crazy, beeitch! Straight cray!"

Beau was stunned, aware that the blow had been so hard that it caused the butter-skinned woman's head to snap backward.

LorRen had also grabbed the sides of Ronni's head with her thumb and forefinger on the perimeter. Using one fluid motion, she quickly forced Ronni backward, causing Ronni to hit the erected dance floor.

Towering over her, LorRen began to stomp Ronni who lay prostrate. She kicked Ronni's chin, neck, and stepped on her torso. LorRen also pranced around Ronni's prone body, so that no one could catch her. As she did, LorRen continued to administer a kick here, and a kick there.

Kismet Staar and Eli became all arms. Both attempted to pull the hothead off the shocked woman who defensively curled her body and rolled onto the grass.

Noticing the commotion, others began to rush over, as Kismet Staar and best man Eli struggled with LorRen, the octopus, who appeared to have sprouted multiple limbs. To them it seemed as though the stunned bride, nor Beau, offered substantial aid.

With her composure gone, Ronni managed to pull herself up, from the grass—but suddenly, she felt pain, in her back. She had been kicked, again!

On her knees, utterly embarrassed and flustered, Ronni flailed away from a would-be savior. Managing to rise, ungracefully she turned.

Stooped in pain, clutching her birthday satchel, quickly she hobbled across the lawn. Losing a salmon shoe, yet she mustered the strength to flee, ungainly disappearing into the dark of the winding drive.

Beau exhaled, releasing a large cloud of smoke. Disgusted, he flicked away his cigarette, because he had warned the women that something might jump off. He turned from the newest batch of excited on-lookers.

Realizing there was nothing more to see, slowly the gawkers dispersed.

Headed for the dinner tent, Beau was aware of being followed. He heard LorRen behind him. Alongside, her and Valeria René's mother irately strode. As Beau, LorRen and Ms. Chitra passed, two females twittered with the laughter that they could not contain.

Beau didn't miss that the heavier of the two bent, covering her mouth. He guessed she was experiencing an uncontrollable fit. "Ooh," she squealed, convulsing on a laugh. "That girl *beat* that woman's butt!"

Passing the laughers, Chitra grabbed LorRen's elbow, and Beau overheard her hiss. "Must you act out Lovey, always, and on *this* of all days, too?" Incensed the mother also inquired, "Why would you fight Ronni like that? And after what I told you?"

Sullen and defiant, LorRen replied. "She provoked me."

Exasperated, Chitra again grabbed her youngster's arm, and jerked the girl to face her. Shaking LorRen, Chitra's accent became more pronounced as she revealed, "*This* is *not* why your father and I sent you to kickboxing! Oh!" Chitra yelped, "*I* should kick, or strangle, *you!*"

Back where the action had taken place, Kismet Staar swung her arms. "Well Mrs. Sinclair," she said, looking sheepishly from Valeria René to Fabian who had appeared. "You wanted her here..."

Feeling horrible, for Ronni, the bride lowered her head. "I know, and look what it got us."

"A blow up," Kismet Staar admitted, "and to think, Diddley warned us."

Sorrowfully Valeria René hung her head. "Kiss, this whole mess could have been avoided..."

"Yep," Kismet Staar eyed the ground where Ronni had fallen, only moments before, "If we had just left Brownie alone."

Chapter 24

$\mathcal{I}$T was Saturday morning, and Valeria René could hardly believe it as she sat on the veranda of the resort where she and Fabian had spent the last week. Sipping coffee she thought, tomorrow…it would be time to go home. Sunday to Sunday, but where had the time gone?

She remembered. Last Saturday she'd gotten married. It had been glorious. Well, all up until the Ronni fiasco. That, Valeria René felt bad about, *and* about LorRen, who'd showed her behind, as Val's nana used to say.

Pushing ugliness from mind, Valeria René remembered that she and her new husband had stayed the night at Canterbury Walk. In the romantic cottage suite, with its high ceilings and enormous stone fireplace, she and Fabian had fallen asleep, she in her wedding gown, and he in his dress shirt and tuxedo pants.

At nearly four a.m. she woke, and heard Fabian's light snores. She hadn't wanted to wake him, but she'd had to. Therefore, she'd tapped him, asking for help.

"Fabe, how'd you let me go to sleep, in my dress?" She asked it while removing her sexy shoes.

When he stood behind her, he undid half a dozen small pearl buttons. "Well baby," he began. "Near the end of our reception you were dog tired. We got here and you wanted to lie down. Just for a minute, you said. Then you were out, like a light."

Yet standing behind her, Fabian told his wife he hadn't had the heart to wake her, so he'd laid down beside her, and that had been that.

Reaching the closure at her nape, his fingers lingered on Valeria René's skin. In the stillness and the cozy lamplight he drew her close, whispering into the hair yet caught atop her head. "I love you, girl." Then wanting to see her face, her front, gently he turned her.

With both her small hands she held to her dress top, and seeing this, Fabian implored her to let it go. For him.

With eyes on his, she did, and Fabian fingered the open lace, the demi cups that showcased her mocha breast tops and her chocolate nipples; all bringing to mind big beautiful cupcakes.

"I like," he said, his voice growing husky with need. He also mentioned that it was cool, the way the garment tipped her breasts up. "So that," he said and bent, "I can do this."

With lips and tongue, he slowly savored an unconcealed nipple. Then he did the same to its mate. He did so again and again, causing desire to pool, molten and liquid, in her belly.

Aware, he faced his wife while walking her backward to the elegantly dressed king sized bed. Easing her down onto it, between her thighs his fingers traced her racy undergarment, and found the slit that was its opening.

Fabian's heart beat faster when he felt moisture, the evidence of her desire, and needing so much more, he felt himself swell, grow larger still.

"Do this," he suggested after his wife had unzipped his pants and discarded them as well as his shirt. "Move your leg." He spread it apart from her other one. "Then let me...ah...slip, right in here."

With Fabian powerfully nude between her thighs, Valeria René felt his weight, his beautifully dark skin, taut over muscles. She felt his restraint too as he teased her, with the knob, the head of his erect penis. She felt him blissfully stroke, from one end of her channel to the other, and she felt herself blossom, unfurl in welcome, as he raised her leg.

So ready, she clasped his shoulders. Raising herself, she gave herself over as he caressed her, ever there. Widening herself for him, for the hand and the rod that pleasured her, but not fully, yet, she whispered. "*Please...*"

Obliging, he pushed, and eased into her silken space.

Inside, he felt warmth and wet.

Gasping, she felt strength and length. "I love your night stick..."

Sliding down the long lean line of his back, her hands were warm, and he groaned. On her, he savored the feel of her buoyant tits, as within her, he enjoyed the feel of her slick sheath, as it tightened, surrounding him. Deeper he burrowed, before slowly he withdrew. Removing his large throbbing cock, he expertly drove back in.

Sensually, Valeria René moved with her man. She attempted to lock her legs around him, as stroking and stirring, he fused his mouth with hers. Within her he created momentum, a storm, as he took her up, and up. Yet just before she thought they would crest and soar, he slowed.

He returned his mouth to her breasts, returned to nibbling the swell and the underside. Then scintillatingly he pinched her nipple, as he employed sweet words, all the while with his dark, hard, good bar, he repeatedly dove deep.

He slid large hands beneath her, cradling her bottom as he murmured and squeezed.

Into her mouth he glided, again and again, using his tongue. With it he copycatted the action that simultaneously took place between her lips below.

In ecstasy she cried out and arched. She did so to meet him, to take more of him, in fact, to receive all that he had to give.

And they rose. She came...up off the bed, and he did too, buried deep inside her.

Afterward, sated and still, she remembered. In a few hours they would head for the airport. So she, lovely, velvet and nude, prepared to bathe.

Wearing no shirt and jeans hastily pulled on, lazily he sprawled. However, he could not get comfortable, thrown across the slipper chair. Although he attempted to watch the flames in the fireplace, the ones he'd coaxed to life, he could not see them. He only saw her. It was always her, and he overheard.

There were the soft sounds she made as she moved, calling to mind a mermaid. Then there were those created, as in warm water she gingerly sloshed. Melodically she hummed too, amid the clinking of the treasured bangles that she'd returned to her arm.

When he could no longer stand it, he rose, and crossed the room. Softly he rapped on the door. Announcing he would enter, both his voice and his man root thickened, with need.

In the jacuzzi tub he saw her, seated, with fragrant bubbles up to her chin. She'd lit candles too.

Sultry and smiling, she held out her sudsy sponge. Dripping wet, she uncoiled, purring, "Wash my back?" *Take me on my back...*she did not say, but the invitation hung there, in the air between them.

Quickly Fabian shed his jeans, elated at the inaugural of many baths with his wife.

And she stood, as crystalline bubbles slid slowly, slowly down her round ripe breasts, then down further still, over her smooth dark body.

Aware that Fabian was besotted and bewitched, with a finger, she beckoned, all while feeling powerful in her womanliness.

"Your seat," she instructed, and pointed to the rear.

In the tub he sat, and raised his large hands. Then he grasped his wife's slim hips, but despite feeling mounting greed as well as need, gently he eased her down, before him, and onto his groin. Snuggling beneath her, he released a ragged sigh.

Wrapping both his arms around her, he buried his face in her hair — like he wanted to bury his manhood in her woman's lair.

But burrowing inside her body would come soon enough. This he reminded himself. Yet the thought did nothing to slow his racing heart.

"You know Fabe..." she spoke softly, after a while. "Ronni said she was at the ceremony, but I can't see how. I know I'd have noticed her there, because I was looking for her." Valeria René sighed. "But then again, if she *wasn't* there, how'd she know Kiss tripped?"

Shaking her head, the bride recalled her former roommate's ugly actions. "And *Lovey...*" the new wife squeezed her sponge, "sometimes she doesn't think things through either. I know she thought she was protecting me, but she was wrong, *so* wrong."

Mournfully, Valeria René confessed that she should have known something would occur. "I should have, the very moment Ronni appeared.

"And now, because of *her* awful actions, Lovey's car and all means of communication have been confiscated, by my dad. And my Ma—boy, was she livid! She snarled that Lovey was hard-headed, and then my dad had to pull her off his child. Now my spoiled rotten little sister will be on lockdown for at least a month. Oh, and baby girl's check, from working in MaMa's office, has to go to Ronni."

Fabian said nothing, and Valeria René mentioned Kismet Staar. "She almost made me laugh, asking under her breath, 'Now why Brownie acting stank—with *us*...when her rusty behind is carrying the satchel that *we* bought, for her birthday."

Fabian smiled, imagining a bewildered Kismet Staar.

Valeria René tried to not to chuckle as she also mentioned that Kiss had been full of clench-mouthed questions. They had been inquiries like

'Val, you think Brownie's drunk? Because who made her wear that get-up? And look at sista girl's hair. Is it not dry as all of Arizona? You see them *shoes*? Where she get them shoes? What color are they? Who forced her into those? Do she think they match, anything—in the world? Don't you just wanna shake her?'

Fabian chuckled, and Valeria René became somber. "I just wish Lovey hadn't taken things so far. You know?"

Savoring the feel of his wife's bottom pressed to his groin Fabian spoke. "I know. I also know that we can't control the actions of others, not even those of our friends and family members."

When Valeria René remained silent, he offered, "Babe, your sister was wrong. She's paying for it. Your friend girl is obviously hurting too." He became insightful. "She's probably upset, about things of which you have no knowledge. So," he shrugged, "call her, when we get back. Apologize. Then let it go."

Valeria René pondered her husband's words, as she thought, to men everything was simple, so cut and dried. She thought it as he asked, "Guess what I'd like to do now, Mrs. Sinclair?"

"What?" she inquired, suddenly feeling excited because she realized that beneath her he had enlarged.

Fabian nibbled on her ear, and her nape. "I'd like to...concentrate only...on us—on *you*, really."

"Ohhh," Valeria René moaned, as Fabian slid his hands up and over her torso. Weighing and fondling her breasts, afterward he used his hands to ease body her up, and then back down again, and onto the shaft that he eagerly buried deep inside her.

She gasped, at the push of him, and the co-joining push of water. Ecstatic to feel him and enjoy the generated sensations, she rode him, until inspired, she turned, and slid wet nipples across his lips.

"Suck," she softly commanded, as with knees outside his thighs she again took him, hard and stiffened, into her body. Then because she was ever emboldened when she was with him she said, "And fu—"

"Shhh-sh." Delectably, his mouth covered hers.

That had been Sunday morning at Canterbury Walk. Valeria René recalled it as she sipped fresh hot coffee. That had been shortly before Drew, Fabian's younger brother arrived, to drive the newlyweds to the airport.

Valeria René remembered rolling along, on the backseat of brother-in-law's car. With Fabian beside her, his hand had been beneath her dress, fingering and fondling her. Enjoying, she had tried not to moan or cry out. She'd bit her lip, and with her pulse pounding in her ears, she'd been unable to hear half of Drew's words. She had only wanted to hear Fabian's ragged breathing, as she tore his clothes off and devoured him, right there in the rear of that vehicle. But the devouring had just been a fantasy.

Yet she believed her brother-in-law had said that he; the best man Eli; and her sister Magi, had carted all of the wedding gifts back to the bride and groom's new home.

Forgetting those things, she'd widened her thighs while they'd whizzed past other cars. Opening her legs, she'd given Fabian easier access, as Drew reported that all monetary gifts would be deposited on Monday. How she'd wanted Fabian right then! Had she been able, she'd have sat on him, and reveled in every moment, every jut, and every sensual thrust.

As she sat on the veranda, watching the majestic aqua blue ocean loll and roll, Valeria René recalled the quickie. Sexy and smooth, her new husband had strolled right into the ladies room at LaGuardia Airport with her. Then in a stall they'd deliciously engaged, just before their flight.

While on the airplane they'd experienced very little turbulence, outside of wanting each other so badly. Yet, beneath a shared blanket they played. When that had only heightened their appetites, they met in the airplane bathroom, just before arriving at their white sand resort. The newlyweds found coupling in the small space nearly impossible, but somehow it had been exhilarating too.

Maybe, she thought when she'd slipped back to her aisle seat, she had indeed become what Kismet Staar had said; a nympho. Perhaps she, Valeria René Sinclair, had become a full blown nymphomaniac, a woman who experienced abnormally excessive and uncontrollable sexual desires. And Fabian was to blame, or thank, for all of it.

Upon arriving at the predetermined airport, the newlyweds took a passenger ferry. Clutching the rails, they watched as it approached the cape island that boasted fifteen miles of beach, and a verdant maritime forest. Although Valeria René had not previously known their honeymoon location, she told Fabian it was a welcome surprise.

Absolution

Looking back, she was glad that she'd packed what her husband had suggested. Mentally patting her own self on the back, she acknowledged that she'd looked fab every day. She had worn long flowing skirts, with sandals. She'd worn orange, fuchsia, lavender, and turquoise; satin camis and palazzo pants. She'd worn an itty-bitty bikini, and glass beads, flowers in her hair, and straw hats to deflect the sun. A few times she'd even poured herself into sexy rev-him-up evening attire and stilettoes.

Seated high above the ocean, she recalled the weather, which had been great, allowing for scuba diving and parasailing. In the air, beneath a colorful balloon—a parachute really—the recently marrieds had been towed behind a fast moving boat. He'd laughed and she'd squealed. In the sunshine she and Fabian had leisurely floated high above the aquamarine ocean, and she couldn't remember ever having so much fun.

At dusk, in one of three pools they'd lounged, as from the tropical landscape the sun's peach rays had slowly faded. Then on foot, when the sun rose again, they traversed sugar sand beaches and nature trails. That evening they partied under the stars, only to browse a colorfully bustling shopping district the following afternoon. They drank too much, at a thatched roof hut, and dined out of doors at a concierge recommended bistro. Yet one lazy evening found them lingering over dessert at their resort's five-star restaurant.

However the eve that she would always hold dear was the one on which the glowing couple dressed. Then on their very own candlelit balcony they were served a gourmet meal. Unobtrusively, musicians played, while below the bowl of the indigo sky, the dark and restless ocean licked and lapped at the beach, making music of its own.

When alone, she and Fabian made love. Come to think of it, she mused, they'd made pure intense amounts of it, and despite the fact that she'd stayed swollen and pleasurably sore, yet she found herself wanting him more.

Valeria René also adored the hotel. Entering, from the sweltering out of doors, refreshing icy cool air would wash over her. She also heard Mozart and Tchaikovsky as she walked the polished marble floors. She saw sun-dappled tropical flora as she visited high-end boutiques. In their many mirrored surfaces she glimpsed those who were on some type of holiday as well. Intrigued, she inspected displayed diamonds, and gems, apparel, watches, and snorkeling gear; but never would she forget the fountain.

Enormous, it sat in the hotel lobby. Its cascades of clear water could be heard from there and all points beyond. Both soothing and invigorating, it was a sound that Valeria René never wanted to forget.

When she was home again, she told herself, and things weren't going particularly right, or her way, she would remember. Then she would momentarily escape. She would do so mentally; she would return, to this glorious week spent away...

With a sigh, again Valeria René realized. This would be her and Fabian's last day. She wondered. What would they do? How would they commemorate their honeymoon's end?

Hearing movement in the spacious Venetian tiled suite behind her, she turned. Perhaps they would go snorkeling, she mused, now that sleepyhead had risen. Or they could—

"Hey babe," barefoot, Fabian stepped out onto the veranda.

Suddenly his wife could no longer think. She could only feel...desire. She licked her lips as she became aware of it, and of her nipples quickly rising.

Fabian noticed. He saw too that his wife held a coffee cup, and that in a vase on the glass tabletop before her a beautiful spray of calla lilies stood tall. He squinted upward, becoming aware of the stunning day, sunny, with cumulus clouds drifting in an azure sky. Below them, he saw that the aquamarine sea was almost calm. Yet it was frothy, where it tumbled and receded from the beach. The breeze was balmy too; but none of it, Fabian thought, was as lovely as the woman who sat taking it all in.

Walking around her wrought iron chair, with its plump striped cushion, he placed a proprietary hand on his wife's neck, beneath her wayward curls. Bending, he took her lips with his own, cradling her face in both his hands.

Valeria René noted the fresh scent of soap, and mouthwash. She liked that her husband's lips were lush, his kiss tender and sweet. But then it quickly changed, becoming ravenous and filled with need.

Thoroughly kissing his wife, whose hair—a sexy unruly mass —blew in the wind, Fabian acted on a thought.

Kneeling before her, he kept his lips just inches from hers, as he eased her silk kimono from her shoulders.

Absolution

When her nakedness became fully apparent, he stared, and her pendulous breasts and her pretty cocoa nipples stared back at him. The sight caused his pulse to race, and his cock to jump.

With her own heart picking up the pace, Valeria René watched her gorgeous dark husband stand; watched him remove his white muslin pants. And her eyes widened as his formidable penis jutted, nearly to his navel. How she wanted him, she thought, and licked her lips.

Majestically nude, and appearing carved like dark granite, again Fabian kneeled, to part her waiting thighs. As the sun crept higher in the sky, the ocean lapped at the sand just beyond their semi-shaded balcony. But no longer aware, or caring, Fabian pulled Valeria René to the edge of her chair.

Breathlessly she reminded him that anyone on the mostly serene beach could see them, if they by chance looked up.

"Then let 'em look," Fabian insisted, as he knelt to suckle.

Holding him tightly, Valeria René pressed her voluptuous breast more into his mouth. Then she could only watch, as with greedy fingertips he parted her. Easing her back, with fingers and his tongue, he teased her labia, before he placed his whole mouth on her, thereby giving her wave after wave of undiluted pleasure.

Enraptured, she cried out, and on his knees, Fabian opened her, wider. Masterfully he massaged her, until rising, just slightly—he slowly slid, into wet and warmth. Arching to receive the whole of his engorged erection, she gasped and began to move with him.

Tightly Fabian held to her hips, but suddenly, he stopped. Gathering her close, ravenously he kissed her. He also ran a hand down a plump breast, and squeezed, before he pulled her up. Then lifting her in his powerful arms, he nibbled her nipples one after the other as he murmured, "Taking this inside."

With her silk kimono slipping away and to the balcony floor, Valeria René clung to her quickly moving man. She excitedly realized, while blossoming, opening again when she was laid among sweetly rumpled sheets, that now she knew. This was how her last honeymoon day would be spent.

Chapter 25

"I'M not going anywhere, to see anybody," Beau articulated, for the last time. He hoped.

Yes, he sat in Valeria René's spacious new, two-storied home. Yes, she had also baked a cheesecake for him. However, he could feel that during this visit he was going to have to upset her.

She wanted him to go see Ronni, and he had already said no. She knew he was through with Ronni, but she kept pestering him, getting on his nerves. Therefore, Beau geared himself to explain, one last time.

"Val, shortly after your wedding, I saw ex roomie. A couple of months ago, I saw her again. Both times, she acted like she didn't know me. So, I'm done. End of story."

Valeria René near-whined, "Diddleee, Ronni's going through something right now. It's taking a toll. Although you saw her, I saw her more recently. That's why I thought it'd be nice if we could go over and patch things up."

"Please," Beau scoffed. "If she wanted that, she'd come to us."

Kismet Staar returned from the bathroom. "What'd I miss?"

Beau waved. "Val's moaning about Ronni, again."

"Well, it *has been* more than a year since everything, starting with your move Diddley." Kismet Staar didn't mention that she'd been thinking, a lot, about her old college dorm mate.

Valeria René turned to Beau. "See? You've been overruled. So now let's let the past be the past."

Beau felt the stir of indignation. "For me, Ronni is the past."

"Fabian said he would go with me, to see her," Valeria René slyly began; "but he's not Ronni's friend. I am. You are Kiss; you were, Beau. So *we* should see about her."

Beau felt disgust. "Val, don't compare me to a man who vowed, before witnesses, to be your slave, in and out of bed."

Kismet Staar ignored her sarcastic first cousin. "Val, why do I sense there's something you're not saying?"

"I don't know, but Beau once claimed love for you, me, *and* Ronni. Now he won't practice what he preached."

With his voice deadly low, Beau warned Valeria René that she was treading on thin ice. "Yo, you and Kiss both think you can fix everything and everyone. News flash, you can't. Learn to let shit go. And Val, go get the cake you baked for me."

She smirked. "I won't, not until you say you'll at least think about visiting Ronni."

Kismet Staar narrowed her eyes. Again, she wondered, why was it so important?

Seated on her plush new earth-toned sofa, Valeria René crossed her ankles. She spoke as though she'd read her former college dorm mate's mind. "You both know life's not promised. So I just feel we should be family, while we can."

Kismet Staar heard something her friend had not said. She just couldn't figure out what it was, yet.

"Ms. Melodramatic," Beau called. "Get my cake. I need almond milk too. And let's talk about something happy."

"How can we? When Ronni's got AID—" Valeria René blurted, and caught herself. Jumping up, she scurried to her kitchen. Lord, she hoped her friends hadn't heard what she wasn't supposed to tell. "Kiss," she called. "I've got soy ice cream."

Dumbfounded, and staring at Beau, Kismet Staar no longer cared about sweets. Forgetting cake, Beau ruminated on what he thought he'd heard, and simultaneously he and his cousin moved. In the lovely, warm-yellow and white kitchen the guests converged on the homeowner, bombarding her with inquiries.

"What did you say out there?" "Brownie's HIV positive?" "How do you know?" "She really has AIDS?" "You sure?" "Did she tell you that?" "How exactly did she say it?" When did you find out?" "Why didn't we know?" "What is she going to do?" "She been to the doctor?"

Valeria René concentrated on cutting the raspberry swirl cheesecake.

Frustrated, Kismet Staar bellowed, "Val, talk! Don't just stand there hacking up that cake. Tell us. How do you know?"

"I d-don't know a th-thing," the mocha-skinned woman stammered.

"You don't know how to l-lie," Beau retorted.

Valeria Rene felt hot, and lifted her kitchen window.

Again she picked up her knife. She further butchered the cake that it had taken her forty minutes to make. Desperately she also tried to recall the soothing sounds of the fountain at her honeymoon resort.

"Gimme that." Kismet Staar snatched the knife, letting it clatter into the sink. "Val, you almost begged us to go see Ronni. Is disease why?"

"I want us to see her because it's right." Valeria René turned away, "And both of you leave me alone, because *before* you weren't trying to hear anything I had to say."

As she stared out of the window, Valeria René felt like a real traitor. Back when Ronni had explained her situation, she'd made one thing clear. She wanted no pity, or sympathy, from anyone, especially not 'the cousins.'

Trying again, Kismet Staar spoke. "Valeria René Thompson-Sinclair, a few minutes ago, you blasted Beau for forgetting that we're family. Now you've shut me and him down. Does family do that?"

Valeria René hugged herself as she peered at the gray beyond her window. Again, she tried to conjure the sounds of the resort fountain.

Watching her, Kismet Staar decided not to press the issue. She rinsed the cake-smeared knife. She laid it aside, announcing she would go. "But remember this Val; fam means nothing, if secrets can keep us apart."

"Secrets haven't kept us apart, Kiss!"

Wow, Valeria René had yelled. Beau and Kismet Staar both appeared stunned, because that they had never before heard.

"We're keeping ourselves apart—all of us, including Ronni..."

Perched on a window seat, Beau calmly offered his two cents. "*You* don't seem to be apart. You seem to be in, and using that knowledge to coerce us to do what you want."

"Go to the devil!" Valeria René spat. "I'm not asking you for anything. Well, not for me, anyway. I want this for us, and for Ronni; even though you two want nothing to do with her."

Valeria René faced Kismet Staar. "Although you didn't say it Kiss, like Beau, you don't want to be bothered either, and that's a shame, because we're all Ronni has."

Anger rose within Kismet Staar and she raised a hand. "You wait one minute, Val. You don't get to speak for me, or guess at what I feel."

Kismet Staar hit the table with a big fist. "I do feel Brownie's acted ugly; but we all have. And just because I haven't shared, doesn't mean I haven't been worried too.

"I pray steadily for that girl. I've also gone by The Quarters, numerous times. I've spoken to Mrs. Nunley. Once she told me that Brownie hadn't been home for days; I found her at the hospital. I call that girl, I leave her messages; I've been sick over her little yellow behind. I've sent cards, wrote notes, and I've left Brownie checks—so don't get on your friggin' high horse with me, just because you broke her down enough that now she's talking to you. Or so help me God; I'll...punch you in the face!"

"Kiss." Beau stepped between the women. "Val's upset."

"Well so am I. Now. Thanks to her!"

"I know, but let's hear her out." Beau faced the curly locked one, "If you'll talk."

"I always talk," Valeria René moaned. "Its how I got us in this hating-on-each-other mess to begin with."

Kismet Staar's eyes narrowed. "What do you mean?"

"Well *I* told you that Beau and Ronni were fighting. *I* opened my pie-hole on the night that began all our separation. When I should have kept my trap shut."

Yes, like Ronni wanted her to do now, Valeria René recalled. "If I'd clammed up, maybe we'd still love each other."

Beau needed clarity. "So, you're saying because you called Kiss, everything that followed became your fault?"

Valeria René nodded. She also vowed within, that she wouldn't tell again. Ronni had let her back in, and she would not betray Ronni by putting her business in the street.

"Val, what happened at The Quarters was inevitable," Beau said. He revealed that he and Ronni had been on slow boil since day one. "And If you hadn't called Kiss that night, I'd be in the pen right now."

Kismet Staar left the room. Teary-eyed, she returned, carrying her purse, her coat, and keys. "Val, you can think or do whatever you want, because like Diddley, I'm through. I'll tell you something else. You ain't gotta say a thing, because I already know things. I see them, and whether or not you believe me, we are all going to cry. More than we have already."

Valeria René reached for her friend. "Kiss, I'm sorry. I didn't mean to hurt you. It's just that Ronni made me promise to stifle, even though we all really need to make peace."

Wearily Valeria René slid onto a chair. As her friends watched, she wiped her sweaty palms on a dishtowel. She also wondered how to say some things, without saying others. "Look," she finally began. "After my honeymoon I kept phoning Ronni, to apologize for Lovey's actions.

"When I finally got the chance, Ronni told me what you guys heard before I messed up your cake Diddley. She told me she doesn't want anybody's pity or anybody's holier than thou attitudes, either."

Beau fingered his dog tags. "Ronni's sick and ashamed..."

"She didn't say that." Valeria René bit her lip, realizing there were many things she could not say. She could not say that she had attempted to explain to Ronni the depth of love that all the Cohorts felt for her, although it sure didn't seem like it, at present.

Valeria René also could not say that finding out that Ronni was infected had been a surprise. She couldn't say she'd been hurt; yet she had told Ronni the truth. When other people found themselves in precarious positions, they didn't shun people. Others didn't push away the very people who would love and care for them.

Valeria René knew too that she couldn't mention how Ronni had exploded... "Cow-crap Val!" the butter-yellow woman had yelled. "I'm telling you what this shit is like! So don't claim to know, not until you've walked a mile in *my* shoes! Oh, and understand this, I only told you because you're a friggin' pest. You won't let me be. I'm not telling Kiss and Diddley though—I don't need them feeling sorry for me."

Valeria René had tried to speak then, but Ronni had interrupted her.

"Face it Val. You don't know anything, not about this, or about what I need. Therefore, I'll tell you. *I don't need you guys.* I don't want you. I don't want any of y'all thinking you can help me. Don't feel you can get me through this, because I'm not coming through. I—am—*dying*!"

Seated at her kitchen table, Valeria René knew her friends watched her. Yet she shivered, because Ronni had been adamant.

"I'm leaving." Kismet Staar jingled her keys, because it made no sense to silently mill around. "Call me, Val. Whenever."

"No, Kiss." Valeria René stood. Internally she wrestled with what she should, and should not, say.

"Val, if this is going to cause a problem..."

"Just listen." Valeria René spoke of Ronni's predicament.

Hurt beyond belief, Kismet Staar pulled out a chair. Slumping, she felt like she'd been punched in the stomach. "But for the grace of God," she gasped, her coat aside.

Valeria René nodded. "Those were my exact words. I told Ronni that without God's grace, anybody could be in her shoes." *But they're not!* Ronni had yelled.

Kismet Staar held her head. "Poor Brownie..."

Now curvaceous knew why her little yellow friend had been aloof. Veronica Marie Brown's ugly actions had been a cover-up! Now Kismet Staar knew that for the longest time Ronni had been trying to force her friends out of her life. She probably thought she was doing it for their good. She'd done it for *their* sakes, knowing that they loved hard.

Valeria René touched Kismet Staar's shoulder. "She thinks we can't continue to love her. She thinks she's been too stupid, for the greater portion of her adult life."

Kismet Staar appeared shell-shocked. "Nooo, that's not the case."

"It's how she feels, Kiss. She couldn't even believe that I would apologize, *to her*, for my reception fiasco. She said she instigated the whole thing."

Well she did, Beau thought.

Unaware of her cousin's thoughts Kismet Staar spoke. "Val, if Brownie doesn't want me 'n Diddley to know..." She felt utterly destroyed, "then how can I go to her? She would know you told."

"Yeah, and now I feel like such a snitch. Although I know this one time I needed to break my vow of silence."

Kismet Staar stood, and pushed back her chair. "Oh Val, you had to tell us. This isn't the type of burden you—or she can carry alone."

"I want to believe that Kiss." Suddenly Valeria René blurted out, "Wait. Ronni's always said I can't hold water. Right? So maybe—"

"She told you because—"

"Yes Kiss; she *wanted* me to tell!"

Standing aside, Beau looked dubious, as he stroked his dog tags.

"Yes Kiss! Maybe Ronni just needs to know that we all still care. What does it matter that she's got full blown AIDS?"

Upon hearing that Kismet Staar and Beau felt stricken.

He turned away, and Kismet Staar held her head. "It's that bad, Val?"

"It is," Valeria René admitted, "but we can make peace, with Ronni and with this."

Valeria René spoke to Beau's back. "Please, let's do this. I ask because you two haven't seen her, lately. Girlfriend is proud but she's also broken. I know because she appears so in public, now. Remember how she would never go anywhere without her face on—her foundation, lip-gloss, and eyelashes? Well now, she doesn't primp. She probably feels like what would it all be for? She just gets up and goes."

Struggling to digest too much information, Beau and Kismet Staar remained quiet.

Mistaking their silence for complacency, Valeria René's voice rose. "Look you two, this thing's eating her alive. At my reception Kiss, you mentioned the way she looked."

Kismet Staar bowed her head, feeling mightily ashamed. She'd made jokes about Brownie, about her clothing and her salmon colored shoes; but *oh God*, Kismet Staar sorrowfully thought. If she had known! She would never have poked fun.

"Hey, we all know Ronni's not good at expressing her feelings," Valeria René pointed out. "However, she loves you two. Don't look like that Beau, because we all need to forgive."

Feeling as though she fought a losing battle, Valeria René asked if her friends remembered the show. "Beau, she cheered madly for you. And remember Cancun? What could have been better than us, Tony, Barry, Mireya, Brett, and others, on the beach drinking, not drowning, and dancing 'til dawn? I'll cherish those memories," Valeria René revealed, "for the rest of my life." Touching Beau's arm she asked, "What about you?"

He stared away, unwilling to be baited.

"Diddley, could you forgive yourself..." Valeria René swallowed, past the lump in her throat, "if she...*left*, before we made peace?"

Valeria René watched the man who appeared nonchalant. She forgot that as an actor, he could give the appearance of feeling any emotion, or none at all.

Mirroring large pools, her eyes threatened to spill over as solemnly she revealed that she laid awake nights. "I worry Diddley. Kiss, I call, just to see if she's okay. I let her know she's got someone. My Ma calls too because God only knows where Cliff, Jr. her brother is, and Calista, her self-centered aunt, doesn't care."

Yeah, Kismet Staar thought, now that Ronni's mother was deceased she really had no one. Other than The Cohorts.

Valeria René softly spoke. "We know how this plague goes Kiss, especially for people who don't have Magic Johnson money."

Turning her eyes on Beau who appeared stoic, the newlywed said she knew him. "Inside you're saying, 'We're all going to die.' But that's the wrong attitude, Diddley."

Yet the cousins remained silent, because never had they dreamed that *this* would be the case.

Finally Kismet Staar found her voice. "I am *so sorry...*" It was all she could manage as tears stung her eyes.

"I am too," Valeria René admitted, "because if I'd kept my mouth shut, at The Quarters, maybe we'd all be okay."

Realizing that Valeria René had always internalized blame, Kismet Staar stepped forward to embrace her. "We'll get through this," she murmured. "And this is not your fault. Not one bit of it."

Hearing Valeria René sniffle, Beau turned away. He also felt around in his pockets for a badly needed smoke. He silently told himself he would go outside; get some air, and a few puffs of nicotine. Then maybe he would be better able to deal with Val and her very soft heart. Maybe then, he wouldn't feel his own heart hardening. Maybe even if given enough time, he would no longer feel like he didn't care for Ronni.

Then again, maybe he wasn't like other people. They hadn't been through what he had. As one who'd suffered loss, he had learned to let go. It was something Val needed to learn too, especially if it was true that Ronni was ill. Looked like she was going to die, sooner rather than later.

With a sigh, Beau turned to leave the kitchen. The space now smelled sickeningly sweet to him, due to the mutilated cheesecake. Squeezing past the embracing women, Beau intended to leave his friend's home. Then later, he would leave the country, to act abroad for a few weeks, *and* he would leave the past in the past.

In Valeria René's front hallway, he opened her vintage, round top, heavy wooden door, and felt an odd chill. Not from outside, but from within. The wintry feeling rose, as a voice pierced the air.

"Where are you going?!" It was Valeria René, yowling. "Didn't you hear anything I said?"

Stopped in his tracks, Beau felt like the normally soft-spoken woman's voice was too loud, too shrill. He also felt she was unreasonably upset. Shoot, the truth was: every day people found out they were diseased. People also knew they were born to die. Death was a part of life.

"You really don't care, do you?" Valeria René asked, because shrugging into his jacket, Beau stepped out of doors. The homeowner glanced at Kismet Staar. "I can't believe he's just going to walk away," she mewled., "He'll forget Ronni...forever."

Beau felt spooked, and like Val had read his mind. He also wondered if he should explain that he *had* to go.

"Not like this," Valeria René said, before he could speak. "Don't leave this way." She knew Beau found it hard to deal with emotions, his own, and those of others.

Yet he walked through the heavy, open, wood front door. He felt the oddest chill as he did, and he felt Valeria René's eyes boring into him.

Glancing back, he saw that she no longer saw him. Her funny colored eyes seemingly lanced right through him, and Beau felt creeped out. Yet, he managed to croak. "Val, I've got to go."

He knew if he didn't leave, curly girl would win him over. Then he would be her puppet. He would do what she wanted, when the truth was he no longer loved Ronni. Sure, he was sorry for Ronni's misfortune, but he couldn't do a thing about it, so maybe one day Val would understand. If she never did...oh well.

To the man who inched closer to his freedom, the homeowner called out, her voice sounding strange "Love doesn't leave. *Love's not supposed to leave.*"

Beau closed the door behind him. Outside, on the top stone step, he cupped his fingers around his lighter. With his much-needed cigarette between his lips, deeply he inhaled. He noticed the sloping lawn with leaves skittering about and the waning chrysanthemums lining the downward slanted path. Exhaling, he tried to forget what Val had called out.

Love wasn't supposed to leave.

Beau descended the winding stone staircase. And he wondered again, what was he supposed to do? What *could he* do?

Absolution

Beneath the gray sky, he tried to forget that when he'd turned to pull Valeria René's front door to, he'd heard her. She'd told Kiss that if he had a heart, he would know certain things, about real love.

Maybe he didn't know anything about love, real or otherwise.

Outside, Beau reminded himself. He was no savior. Upon reaching the street in the Sinclair's picturesque neighborhood, he flicked away the remains of his cigarette. He also hunched closer into his jacket.

Walking under the surly sky, he was unaware that back in the Sinclair's beautiful brick home, Kismet Staar realized why she had envisioned her Cohorts crying. With a horrendous ache, she now knew.

This was only the beginning...

Outside, with only leaves, wind, and every now and again a passing car for company, Beau heard bamboo wind chimes. Hanging outside someone's door, the lonely sound was unsettling.

Suddenly even his bones felt chilled, and the cold quickly crept up, unnaturally inside of him.

Chapter 26

ⒶFTER leaving the Sinclair household, Beau considered Valeria René's words. For weeks, they stuck with him, haunting his days and spilling over into his nights.

Love doesn't leave. Love's not supposed to leave...

Although he'd spoken to Valeria René since what she called her 'episode,' he still could not stop hearing her words.

She had also revealed, during their telephone conversation, that she had no idea why she had experienced such grief. She admitted that since then, she'd felt wasted, and had taken a few days off. "Or people at work will ask, what happened to the optician?"

Beau believed he knew why his former roommate had suffered a bout with grief. Listening, he was also told that Fabian had entered his home shortly after 'the episode.'

Close-mouthed, Kismet Staar had left, and Fabian turned to his bride. Seeing the hollows beneath her eyes, and the pain in them, he'd had to ask. "What the hell happened?" He needed to know why his wife looked like she had seen the living dead.

Seated in his own home, Beau recalled Fabian's question. Beau also wondered if Valeria René had actually had a visit...from someone otherworldly.

Perhaps speaking of Ronni's illness and ultimate demise had caused Valeria Rene to freak out. Maybe that was why she had seemingly seen through him.

Beau sighed, wanting to forget Val and her grief. He didn't want to recall that at the Cohort Quarters, she'd become immobile and anguished anytime she'd been confronted with loss. Wryly, Beau guessed, the old adage 'time heals all wounds' didn't apply to everybody.

Perhaps for some people—like Valeria René—time only suppressed pain. Then when least expected, it would boil up, and bubble over again.

Beau remembered that Valeria René had once told him that she'd never had the chance to grieve for her brother Horace, Jr. with whom she had been quite close. Having a faraway look on her face, she'd said her mother had been barely functioning at the time. The Thompson family had been falling to bits. So as a teenager, she'd stepped up, to keep what was left of her family together. She said God alone had given her the strength.

She also said that some years later, she lost the love of her life, Marc McKennon. Then too, she had wound up a comforter, of sorts, for the McKennon family. Again, at the time, she had not actually grieved.

Suddenly Beau wondered if he was like Val. Perhaps he too felt like losing another someone was too much...

Beau shrugged the thought away, and a different one replaced it. Yeah, he had heard Val's remark about him having no heart, but that wasn't true. He did care for Ronni. However, he just didn't want to be around her anymore. She was ugly, inside. And now she was dying.

He was afraid of sick, dying, and dead people.

Fingering his dog tags, Beau became honest with himself, admitting that he'd never gotten over the loss of his mother. As a child, and then as an adolescent, and later, he'd fought against even thinking of her. He hadn't wanted to grieve, or feel anything. He'd just told himself that she was gone. Yet he couldn't fool his subconscious. It regurgitated everything every so often, in the form of nasty dreams and nightmares.

But what was worse was that he'd lost his uncle, Brantley, Kismet Staar's father. The man had been his champion, his mentor, his friend. Brantley had been a true father, and although Beau hadn't had many years with the man, he still missed his uncle, like crazy. Just thinking about the man made Beau's eyes smart, his throat sting, and his heart ache.

Heck! When would he get over that loss, or others—they were too numerous to think about...

So, Beau guessed, he had loss-of-loved one issues too, like Val. Like her, a few times he'd wondered about lost loved ones. He wondered about his father, Emmett. And too many times to count, he'd wondered as he woke sobbing over Kismet Staar's father. That man, his big brawny uncle, Brantley Moore, had meant all the world to him.

When he told himself the truth, Beau had to admit that he even wondered about Ophelia, his abusive mother. Still.

Was she dead or alive? Part of him hoped she was dead. The other part hoped she was alive. He hoped she had changed. Part of him didn't care. That part never wanted to see her again. Yet part of him hoped that one day they would indeed meet, and start over. The man in him said he didn't need her, or anyone. He knew it was the little boy in him who wished for other things, stupid things, but he couldn't help it.

As an adult, he wanted to believe that Ophelia had tried to find him, because in some strange way he loved her. In that part of him where the truth resided, he felt she should have loved him too; he was her flesh and blood. They were family. He had once been her baby, she'd pushed him into the world. He was her son. Sure he was a big strapping man now, in his twenties, but she had missed all but eight of his years. Those had been fraught with sorrow, fear, running, beatings, and tears; all because of her. Yet he'd missed and needed his mother, every single day.

He wondered about, and also bled inside over a friend of his, one of his first and dearest friends, the little dancer Jervais…He'd soon be dead.

Suddenly it hit Beau! He knew what Valeria René had been saying! Love really was *not* supposed to leave. Real love remained. Look at how he yet loved Uncle Brant, even though the man had been long dead, because it was real love. Beau still loved his first friend Jervais, Jervais, even though Vay had spun out of control because that was real.

Suddenly Beau scrubbed both hands over his face, because he had always said he didn't want to be like Ophelia, selfish and self-centered? Yet for the past year, he'd acted just like her!

Beau *knew* Ronni had no family. He knew she considered—or had previously considered—him, Kismet Staar, and Valeria René, her fam, since her mother's demise. Then, simply because he and she had had a tiff, he'd mentally kicked her to the curb. How shameful, on his part.

He had tried to forget her, to push her very existence from mind.

He had been so wrong, and now he felt ashamed. He actually felt anguish too, and he had to wonder. What if the same had been done to him? What if he'd had no one?

Beau continued to scrub his big hands over his face, while picturing the round brown woman who loved and mothered him, to this day. What if his aunt had left, when his mother had cursed her and told her to go to hell? When Ophelia had punched and spit on her, what if his aunt had never come back? What if lil round Nell Moore had not believed that love remembered? Where would *he* be now?

Absolution

Wearily Beau plunked himself down on his new sofa, as tears stung his eyes. With them clogging his throat, he fingered his dog tags—the ones given him by his aunt, the ones that had belonged to Uncle Brant—and Beau looked around his nice, new, co-op apartment. Immediately he realized. He would have none of what he had, were it not for Love.

If one stocky woman hadn't believed that love remembered, that love didn't forget, *that love wasn't supposed to leave*, Beau would be nowhere. This he knew. If his aunt's husband, his uncle, hadn't believed too, Beau might even be dead. Yeah, I most likely would be, Beau acknowledged, because there had been too much grief, anger, drugs, and life-altering sex—all before he'd turned eighteen.

Taking a deep breath, Beau forgot himself to wonder, what would his A'nt Nell do, if someone needed her? Further still, what would she do if that someone had not yet realized they needed her?

Closing his eyes, Beau suddenly knew! And he felt peace with the answer. His A'nt Nell would do as her *Jesus* would.

Beau heard the laughter. Had that hearty booming sound emanated from him? He guessed it had, because hot dog! That little mocha-skinned, curly haired woman, the one who'd made a raspberry-swirl cheesecake and haplessly ruined it, had caused him to think.

She'd said *Love wasn't supposed to leave*, and she was right. When a person loved another, they weren't supposed to leave, not forever. When love was needed, surely it returned. Love wasn't supposed to go. Or if it did, it returned, when it was real, and when people didn't allow their egos, their Freudian ids, their own needs and wants to get in the way.

Beau repeated the phrase, as quickly he pulled on socks and tennis shoes.

Love is not supposed to leave.

He chanted it, as he snatched up a jacket and let himself out of his chic new home, not far from Manhattan. He chanted, until the phrase became indelibly written on his heart. *Love doesn't leave.*

He ran down the street, because he had to catch the bank.

In his busy multi-cultural New York neighborhood, people hurriedly got out of his way. Yet he skirted a couple entering a Japanese restaurant. He danced around a kid pedaling a colorful big wheel, and he jumped over a dancing boy. *Love doesn't leave.*

Running faster, he smiled, because now he knew that real love could forget, but *real love remembered*, too.

Real Love did not leave, forever.

Chapter 27

$\mathcal{B}$EAU stood with his hands shoved so deep into his jeans pockets that he would have poked holes, had the woman not opened the door when she did.

"What you want?" she warily asked, eyeing him.

Staring at her, he was unable to speak, because she looked so different.

Just like Valeria René had said, Ronni *looked sick*, so utterly ill, gaunt, and thin. There were dark circles beneath her eyes. Her glorious hair that had always been short, thick, wavy, and shiny, was now lackluster and sticking out at odd angles. Even her elbow looked all wrong, with its bone near-poking through her sallow skin, and her skeletal hand appeared too big at the end of her tiny wrist. Unable to help it, Beau wondered when was the last time she'd eaten?

Ronni knew Beau stared, cataloguing her every expression and all of her physical changes, not one of them subtle.

"Well?" she snapped, not about to stand and let him ogle her any more than he already had. "Why are you here?"

Beau blinked and replied, "I'm here..." he swallowed, "because I wanted to see you."

From inside her dimly lit apartment, Ronni glared out. "Well, you see me." She swung the door shut, yelling. "Now you don't."

So she was a magician, huh? Beau was quick, and stopped the door with a tennis shoe. "Ronni. You know what I mean." He stared into the listless eyes. He couldn't believe there wasn't even a spark left, not when before her brown eyes had contained so much fire.

"May I come in?" he asked, his foot yet in the door.

She rolled her eyes. "Would it stop you if I said no?"

Beau didn't reply, and Ronni snorted. "Well, since you'd force your way in, regardless, let me give you my new house rules. Not that you'll abide by them... but nothing gets cut up. There'll be no fighting, and boots stay on the floor."

Beau nearly chuckled because she was still sarcastic; although her head looked like a chick pea, atop her bony neck. That was nothing to laugh or smile about.

When inside the Cohort Quarters, he realized. The large apartment looked nothing like it once had. Most of the furniture was gone. There were no thriving green plants or flowers. The artwork had been removed, and the once familiar homey feel was gone.

Although Valeria René's sheer ivory panels still hung at the windows, now they did nothing for the place. It felt cold, and lonely, but—Beau recalled—he could not dwell on those things. He needed to focus on Ronni, on how she was getting along, and whether or not she needed anything. Knowing however, that she was going to be ornery, he prefaced his task with small talk. From there he could attempt to build up to other things.

"So, how you been?" he asked.

"You're looking at me, dickhead," Ronni spat. She wore a spaghetti-strap dull-colored summer dress, even though it was mid autumn. The dress was too big, the place wasn't warm, and she knew she looked awful. Therefore, she said, "Your eyes don't lie. I've been shitty." Looking away, she picked at her nubby fingernails. She wanted cover, because she felt cold, but she hadn't the strength to trek all the way back to her room to wrestle it from the bed.

Guessing she no longer had her signature French manicured nails professionally adhered, Beau honestly stated, "Ronni, I didn't come to fight."

"Then what ya come for—because if I recall correctly, that's all you and I ever did."

She screwed up her face, like she wanted to cry, but she must have thought better, because instead she quipped, "Oh, my bad. You've probably just come to finish what you started almost two years ago. Well, sorry, no can do, hon. House rules say none of that. No throwing down or stepping on the near invalid. So...I guess you'll be leaving."

"You guess wrong," Beau firmly stated, unwilling to be run off so easily. "I came to apologize, again, and to see how you're doing, and I will leave when I get read—"

"Yo, I don't need apologies," Ronni hissed. "And yo' ass actually did me a favor." She offered as an afterthought, "Yeah cutting up my

Hollywood numbers—during your tantrum was genius, because those things wouldn't fit this piece of shit body now, so thanks. Now I gotta ask: you ready to go yet?"

"I'll say when I'm ready," Beau advised. "And stop talking negatively about yourself." He reminded Ronni that in the past her body had often been referred to as a gift from God.

"Well, soon, it's going to be a gift to a crematorium."

With his eyes misting, Beau hated to hear his former roommate speak ill of her self. She needed to exercise more faith, and so he said. He said she needed to care if she lived or died.

"Yo, you on some new stuff!" Ronni spat. "Heck, caring—one way or another—won't change the fact that my CD4 (T) cell count is low. It won't change the fact that even when I take the recommended protease inhibitor, I suffer side effects that make me sicker. Caring, damn sure won't stop me from dying! So if you think you wanna stay here, even one minute longer, you need to shut up! Talking shit you don't know.

"Okay." Beau nodded. He admitted he *didn't* know much about Ronni's predicament, but he wanted to. In earnest he asked, "Ron, what really happened?"

Shooting up from her ivory sofa, she exploded. "Even with all of your soft talk, I knew! I knew *that* was what your nosey behind was angling at! You say you're sorry, you say you care, but you're like everybody else. You wanna gloat. You want me to tell you how I wound up in this tight spot so you can say I deserve this plague. You think I always was a stank 'ho—a whorelina, and a nasty bitch.

"Well you go on," Ronni hollered, her face becoming a dull red. "Say that, think it, whatever! I don't care, because I know one thing. You are a gay-ass queer boy! You're no better than I am. You remember that!" she screamed, and instantly began to cough.

"Remember this too, fairy," she managed with watering eyes. "*You're next*—If you're not *already* a candidate for this shit. Glitter boy."

Beau was stunned. A few moments ago, he would not have believed Ronni had strength enough for such a tirade.

Nevertheless, watching as she leaned wearily back, he also heard her hoarse plea.

"Just leave, okay? I'm tired, and I don't feel up to answering any more questions, detective. Oh," she added, following another hard bout of coughing, "I wish you'd never come back!"

Beau indeed believed that Ronni was well and truly exhausted, like she said, but it was not because of anything he'd done. It was because she had become so vehemently defensive.

Therefore, he remained seated, on the only chair, a disastrous second-hand print. With his eyes on Ronni, who was sprawled unkempt, quietly he announced that he would stay a while. Then he leaned back, and stretched his long legs, crossing the ankles.

"What's different about this time?" Ronni snarled, like a rabid dog. "You ain't leaving," she spitefully mocked. "You walked out on me so many times, until you had no trouble doing it for real that last time."

Beau stared, and tried to figure out exactly what it was his former roommate was getting at.

"Quit looking at me," Ronni ordered and released a pent breath, "and tell me: why the hell can't you leave now?"

"I can't leave now," Beau tossed back, "because I don't want to. For your information too, I left this apartment, not *you*. I had to. I didn't really want to leave when I did," Beau admitted sitting up, "but it was time. Listen Ronni, I never should have moved up in here to begin with."

He explained that at The Cohort Quarters he had nearly become a child, because of all the love and attention. He'd received it from his roommates, and from the Nunleys, their neighbors; their daughter; and others also freely offered it. "Everybody tried to protect me.

"Here, I couldn't grow" Beau admitted. "I couldn't be the man I was meant to be. Here, like at my aunt's house, it was safe for me to be everybody's baby. Here, I started whining and moaning, about every little thing.

"Women express things, and that's okay, but those same 'expressions' coming from a man, all the time, can grow tiresome. It equates whining. Then that man seems like a pansy.

"See Ronni? I just wanted to grow, find my way. I wanted to really become a man."

Beau did not mention that currently living alone, and working with so many men—most of whom were not homosexual—had proved to be a new and enlightening experience. It proved empowering. In his new surroundings, he'd had to man-up, quickly. He felt he was now becoming accountable and strong—the way he looked. Now his inside was beginning to match his outside. Now he was mirroring his uncle. Those were the reasons why he now also believed he could better befriend her.

"Now, I feel I can be someone that you can lean on. I'm somebody you can turn to, if you need to.

"Ron," Beau spoke softly, "I'm aware that the way I left was uncalled for." He acknowledged it for what felt like the zillionth time. "But I've apologized, and I've requested forgiveness. Even if you don't give it, I've forgiven myself, and I want to be a friend."

He did not mention that it had really hurt when Valeria René divulged that Ronni had said she had no friends.

"Yo, all that chummy stuff is for TV," Ronni scornfully stated, "or for you and Val." Again she coarsely hacked. Before she stopped, she also endured chest-aching, face reddening spasms.

"Ronni," Beau called when there was only silence. "I'm trying here." Therefore, he asked her to cut him some slack.

"What if I don't want to? Maybe I only want you to leave."

Beau shook his head, because here Ronni was, alone. She had even mentioned it while speaking of her illness. But then again, she refused to be a little nicer, so he didn't get it. But he did notice her goose bumps.

"Boo," he called, hoping she would give him a straight answer. "Since you want me to go, I will." He spoke from the hall closet where he hoped he'd find a blanket. "I need to know though; if you need anything, like food. Or money?"

Oh-ho! Ronni almost smiled, she was not going to get caught in that trap. She would not be beholden to any one, well to no one other than Kismet Staar, the woman who had done so much for her. She would definitely not become beholden to a man. She cut her eyes, because men could so easily trap one, with money. They tossed it around, believing they could buy people, especially women, even men who corn-holed other men. They thought money meant everything.

And a man like Beau? Ronni knew he felt like he could treat a woman any old kind of way, as long as he shelled out a few bucks. Well, eff him. He could keep his money, and his soft words. She Ronni Marie Brown was nobody's fool. She was no Minerva Brown. She was not like her mother, who'd believed in a man and had still died alone.

Ronni knew she was going to die, alone, but she would do so because she had chosen to. She would not die alone because she was fool enough waste away, while looking, waiting for, and expecting someone who would never come. And she would never wait on a man—

"Ronni," Beau called, because lost deep in angry thoughts, she hadn't answered him, but she had snuggled into the little lady's throw that he'd found. "Do you need anything?"

Slowly she replied, and her eyes glittered, like little hard stones. "Not from you, and I'm not your 'boo.'"

Beau knew her meanness was deliberate. He knew she had her reasons, yet it stung. However, he would not let her know it, so he turned. "I'll leave now," he said and walked toward the door. "No, don't get up. I'll close it behind me."

"I'm not an invalid," she quipped and struggled up. Pushing aside the throw, she followed Beau. "I can still do things, stupid."

He turned, and looked down at the little yellow woman who knew how to bring out the worst in a person.

"You know Ronni," he said through semi-clenched teeth. "When you're like this, on purpose, it's easy to hate you."

"Well I must have been like this all the time!" She snapped, "Because you've always hated me. The only thing is: now, I no longer care."

Beau ignored the harsh words, to gently nudge Ronni's fallen dress strap back up and onto her shoulder. He also noticed her eyes. Disbelieving they were, and for an instant, something flickered in them. Quickly it was gone, but he knew. His gesture had touched her, inside.

Suddenly Beau realized. All her malevolent words sounded...what? Rehearsed! Yes, because most likely, she was trying to convince herself, more so than others, that she didn't need anyone.

Turning back toward the door, Beau pulled his billfold from his pocket, because it was what his A'nt Nell would have done. It was what her Jesus would have compelled her to do.

He lifted out a hundred-dollar bill, and another. Then recognizing that Ronni might also need to go to the pharmacy, if she bought groceries, he lifted out five twenties.

Seeing Beau place the crisp green bills on her hall table, Veronica Marie Brown experienced a multitude of emotions. Uppermost, she felt like weeping, so she searched for something to say, something that would camouflage the way she truly felt.

"What you paying me for?" she finally inquired. "I didn't do you. In fact, I *wouldn't*, now, not when you could have had me when I was soft and yielding. Yo, you missed your chance buddy. Pick up your money."

With his back to her and his hand on the doorknob, Beau closed his eyes. He breathed deeply, and told himself that she was just trying him. It was what she did. She pushed, until a person acted ugly, then she blamed that person. When the truth was, she *had* to be scared.

Therefore, perhaps, Beau thought, she was just hiding behind an emotional wall. Lord knew he had done it many times. Perhaps Ronni's meanness was just a façade, her way to cope with the miserable hand that had been dealt her.

Slowly Beau turned. Facing the gaunt-cheeked woman, coolly he said, "Everything ain't about sex, girl. And another thing: yo' behind was never yielding, so don't go there." With him, she would no longer get away with being foolish, wrong, or unduly mean.

Quickly, he bent to plant a kiss on her forehead. Rising, he also said, because Valeria René's words still rang within him, "I'll see you again," *because love did not leave, and stay away forever.*

"Don't count on it," Ronni quipped as the tall, beautiful, buff, brown man stepped into the hallway. With him out of her apartment, it had already begun to feel lonely and sad again, without him.

Beau pivoted and serenely smiled down at Ronni.

The gesture was so genuine, and angelic, it nearly broke her heart.

"You know Ron, when I think about it," he divulged, "you're pretty special. You're funny too, so don't change, not ever, little girl."

Then before she could sardonically reply, Beau dashed into the stairwell and was gone.

Just like when he lived here, she thought while closing her door. Leaning against it, she fanned out the money that her friend and former roommate had left behind.

God bless him, she silently prayed as tears cascaded freely down her cheeks, because now she could eat…and buy the rest of her meds.

Chapter 28

$\mathcal{B}$EAU saw Ronni quite a few times, at the Cohort Quarters, before he visited her in the hospital where she lay looking wan and beat.

Leaning over, he kissed her forehead. "So how're you feeling?"

Ronni turned away. She recalled that Beau's cousin had visited, a few days ago. Ronni would just bet Kismet Staar had run and told Beau that 'Brownie' had severe stomach pains. Kiss had probably also blabbed that Ronni had been unable to talk.

Curling into a ball, Ronni hated feeling like people discussed her behind her back. Therefore, she forgot it, and remembered to answer Beau's question. "I feel like I look."

"That bad, huh?"

Ronni managed a thin grin. It however, quickly became a grimace as her body jerked, readying her for a hard bout of coughing. Doubled over, finally, her hacking ceased, and she managed to gasp, "Oh – God! This is awful."

She also said no one should ever have to go through what she had already been through. "And I hear I haven't begun the wretched lap yet..." With eyes widened, she blurted the words, "I'm scared Diddley. I'm *so* scared."

Beau tried to think of something that would sound consoling, but he could not. With a constricting heart, he tried not to think about the pain. He knew that steadily, unmercifully, it coursed through Ronni's already ravaged and disease-weakened little body.

"Well?" she spat, because she hated to be looked at. "Don't you know? To stare is impolite."

Beau did not feel alarm, because in the past few weeks Ronni's outbursts had been many. Therefore, he calmly spoke. "I wasn't staring, at you." He turned his head. "Not much to look at."

Ronni twisted her lips, hating her new existence. She despised not knowing what might happen next. Yet more than anything, she abhorred looking and feeling like moldy leftovers.

Oh, she'd forgotten. She really hated the interns too. When they appeared, she felt violated. They seemed sparkling and clean. When they stood around, gazing at her and her chart, she felt scrutinized, like the squeaky cleans were judging her, for having the disease that was a curse.

Ronni sucked her teeth, and vowed to forget it. Nowadays she had to remember that most of what she felt, she couldn't say.

Although…she *could* tell *Beau* a few more things than she could tell anyone else. Yet, she mused, there were things that even he would never understand. But then again maybe he would. Perhaps he would understand her reason for speaking roughly to those who visited her. Heck, he probably already understood, without her explaining, why she didn't want visitors to gaze at her for too long.

Heck, it was bad enough she had to see herself this way, but being seen the same way by others? Now that hurt.

Swiping a tear, Ronni wished she had no pride. Then she wouldn't care… She wouldn't sometimes bemoan the fact that now she looked nothing like she once had.

"I don't know why I accept any visitors at all," she grumbled. "Visitors only want to see the toll that's being taken. Visitors don't care. They just want to gape, and speculate."

Looking out of Ronni's window, Beau said nothing. He knew that sometimes she was angry, and sad, and that other times she just felt like griping. It was her right.

When she kept on however, he said, "Knock it off."

"I will not!" she snapped. "I'll talk if I want to. Shit. It ain't like I can do anything else. I'm stuck in here. I can't go to the movies, or to the mall. I can't take a trip to Fiji. So I'll talk if I want." She digressed. "I wonder if people think I'm dead yet?"

"Fat chance," Beau chuckled. "If anyone heard you run your mouth, they'd know. You'll be around a while longer."

Ronni smiled, and felt warmed inside, because Beau didn't baby her. He remembered what she'd told him, and Kiss, when they'd first visited. She'd given them the speech she'd given Val, Fabian, and Ms. Chitra, Val's mom. Veronica Marie Brown did not want anyone's pity. "If y'all can't treat me regular, then stay your behinds away."

In the bed that was not nearly as comfortable as her own, Ronni struggled. She managed to turn toward the man in the chair. She recalled he was present so often, until some of the staff believed he was her brother. Where on earth *was* Cliff, Jr. her real brother?

"Diddley, look at me," Ronni ordered. "Get you a good look too."

Not raising his eyes Beau fished around in his leather backpack. "A minute ago, you didn't want me looking at you. Make up your mind. You're starting to seem schizoid."

"Well a minute ago, I'd forgotten that you'll need to know what this is like. I'd forgotten that you'll need to be prepared, for when it's your turn."

"My turn?" Beau's head shot up. "Why say that? What's that about?"

"You're going to wind up here; but unlike me, you'll know what to expect."

Beau sighed. Whenever he visited Ronni, he expected her to raise his pressure. He even expected to sometimes want to strangle her, like now. "Yo, you're way past getting on my nerves. Now you're even treading on what I had reserved."

"I don't care." Lying on her side, she stared at him. "I'm trying to help you."

"Well help me…by shutting up."

"If you want silence, go home."

Beau sighed again, and patiently explained that like Ronni, he had also had a hard day; but instead of heading home, he'd appeared, at the hospital. He had done so because he'd thought she might like some bakery cookies. "So keep your grief."

"Oh just go," Ronni pouted. "Get out. Go to your nice comfortable new home. You're not doing me any favors by being here, because the truth is: I'm alone."

"You are not," Beau argued. "You have friends who're your family. People love you, but you push everybody away, every chance you get."

"Shut up, talking crap," Ronni snapped, "because I didn't see *you* last night."

"I wasn't here," Beau calmly replied, producing a small bakery bag.

"Well *I* was here," Ronni countered, "delirious with pain and fever. I was coughing what little brains I got left, out—and I didn't see you, Val, or Kiss; so, I'll say again, kill that 'you're not alone' crap."

Beau tried to comprehend the magnitude of Ronni's fury.

"Look fairy, I will reiterate," she snapped. "I am in this…*by—my—self*! You don't feel my pain. You don't know what I go through; but you will. Then you will know that of all the asinine things that people can say to you, the most maddening will be," she sing-sang, using the tune from Michael Jackson's mega hit, "*you are not alone.*"

Beau admitted he had offended Ronni, although he hadn't meant to. Therefore, he apologized. "Now, if you'd like to be *left* alone…"

"Do what you want." Dismissing him she waved a frail hand.

Seated on the edge of his chair, Beau used a fingertip to succinctly tap her arm. "Look at me," he ordered. "You and I need to get something straight." He spoke slowly. "You will stop being disrespectful. You will stop calling me names. I don't like it. I don't call you names. No…"

He raised a hand. "Close your mouth." He said he understood that Ronni felt bad, that she was sick, maybe even unto death. "Yet, that doesn't give you the right to be rude. Do it again," he snarled, "and see if I don't use your pillow to smother you. I'll help you out of your misery, so help me Lord."

Ronni's eyes widened. "You wouldn't."

"Okay," Beau confessed, allowing anger to dissipate, "I might not do that, although it would give me pleasure, but I'd stop visiting." He shrugged, "And it ain't like you've got a ton of visitors without me."

Wearily he leaned back. "Now, without offending your very tender sensibilities, why do you insist I'm the 'next candidate?'"

Ronni remained silent, and Beau tapped her again, "Talk to me, little girl."

Without warning, she wailed, and the loud anguished yelp quickly drew a nurse.

When the salt and pepper haired woman was assured that Ronni was as well as could be expected, the nurse retreated.

It was at that moment that Beau saw the tears, and he became sympathetic. "You needed to get that out, didn't you?"

"I did," Ronni blubbered; then because she didn't want Beau to think she was weak, she explained. "I'm not soft, but sometimes I have to cry. I do, because I'm not supposed to be to be here Diddley, laid up. *I'm* heterosexual!

"This," Ronni indicated her ravaged body, "is what happens to homos—to people like you, not to people like me."

Beau felt he'd been slapped backward. He had expected Ronni to say one of many things, but he had *not* been prepared for *that*.

Unaware, her voice caught on a sob as she claimed *she* was supposed to be well. She said sometimes she felt as though she had gotten caught in a dream, a nightmare really, and she wanted out.

"Okay." Feebly Beau patted her arm. He'd meant to be reassuring, like his aunt Nell was when she pap-papped him during times of crises. However, his pats lacked effect.

"Ron, I can understand you wanting this to end. But what does your heterosexuality have to do with anything?"

"I'm straight, Diddley!"

"I know," he dryly acknowledged. "You've said it enough."

"Well then you should know that as a straight person, *I* shouldn't be here. This disease is for deviants—for people like you. No offense."

"Oh, none taken." Beau fingered his dog tags as he thought; well at least she'd had the grace enough to cover her evil-spewing mouth.

"Yo, I'm not really offended," he shrugged. He admitted he was stunned though, to hear that Ronni felt that way. "Now, what I'd like to understand," he revealed, "is why you believe gays and lesbians deserve to be laid up, and not heterosexuals."

"I didn't say that," Ronni groaned, just before she fought through another hard bout of coughing.

"Would you go?" she grumped when she could again speak. "You're making me sicker."

"Nope," Beau shook his head. "You're making your own self sick, with your foolish notions."

Hey, Ronni thought, if she remained silent, maybe Beau would leave. Maybe he would even give her the cookie bag first.

When Beau persisted, asking again what made Ronni more deserving of life than someone like him, she faced him.

"Look." Her voice was nearly gone, and her throat was raw from all the hacking. "I just meant that AIDS is for those who go astray, from the word of the Lord. It's a gay men's disease."

"Oh-kay." Beau had heard it all, now.

Since he seemed not to have gotten her point, to give her statement emphasis, Ronni slowly said, "AIDS is God's punishment for people who are perverse.

"They mention 'the scourge' when you go to church. It's the disease for Sodom and Gomorrah people, those who screw the same sex, Beau. It's not for people like me."

"Oh you mean 'ho's?'" he mock-innocently inquired.

Ronni gave him the finger.

Beau guffawed, and asked, "So now you've found religion?"

Ronni was not amused.

Beau wasn't playing either. He said he knew Ronni had been born in the South, raised in Florida, in the Bible Belt. He said he knew, even if she didn't, that she was simply saying what she had heard someone preach, in some back woods church, where some misguided soul had gotten hold of the microphone.

He also said he knew Ronni was reared in a home where her father—a devil in his own right— had used religion to oppress his family.

"All of that is why I need to tell you something." Beau was calm as he stated, "AIDS is a *disease*. Like cancer or tuberculosis. So don't attempt to make it more, or less."

He also informed Ronni that diseases caused people to be ill at ease. Diseases were debilitating, and, he explained, like other diseases, in *some* cases, HIV was preventable.

"But no disease is God's way of punishing people. Heck, if diseases were punishments," Beau stated, "there would be a whole slew of them. There would be a murderer's disease. Among others, there would be a disease specifically for child pornographers. There'd be one for drunk drivers, baby-killers, rapists, and priests who prey upon parishioners.

"Ronni, if your theory held true, anyone could look at anyone else and know what particular 'sin' they'd committed, because of the disease apparent. However, that is not the case.

"Oh, and another thing," Beau revealed, on a roll, "A'nt Nell showed me, in the bible, where God said he is a healer."

Beau divulged that after seeing that, and after learning that disease and a host of other cruelties entered the world, through sin, never would he forget it. "Don't you forget it either, Ronni."

The woman whose skin had turned the color of butter-about-to-burn sheepishly contemplated her too thin hands. She noticed green veins snaking through the backs. Never before, she thought, had her hands looked so spidery and old. Closing her eyes, she forgot her hands. She also tried not to cry, even as the tears that she wanted to hide fell from her eyes.

Beau noticed Ronni's glistening cheeks. "What's wrong?" Now.

Her voice was barely a whisper. "I deserve this."

Beau finally got his aunt's reassuring pats right, on Ronni's arm. "Don't say that, little girl."

"It's true," Ronni sniffled. She said she had been such a pretty thing, "When I was little, but my father never paid me any attention. My mother didn't have time for Cliff Jr. *or* me. She had to scurry around, doing as my father demanded.

"So when I became a teenager, I realized boys wanted to be with me."

Ronni said she'd also realized that older predatory males wanted her as well. So she used the male ego. She became a trophy, to be passed from one male to the next, because she was getting what she needed. Attention.

However, she admitted, it became harder to keep the attention she attracted, if she wasn't giving it up. So she gave herself away.

"But," she said, unable to look at Beau. "The attention changed. It became proprietary, and I would wind up getting slapped or punched.

"But I wasn't feeling that, because I'd always told myself I wouldn't be like my mother. I wasn't one to be kicked around. So I'd find a bigger, badder guy. He would make the one prior leave me alone. Yet it became a vicious cycle. Then when I got to college, I ran up on the wrong man."

Ronni said Mr. All Wrong had not been a student at her Alma Mater, but that hadn't kept him from preying on the blossoming women there.

In the ensuing silence, Beau spoke, as cognizance dawned. "*He* was the one. You contracted this...from *him*."

Ronni nodded. She said she'd confronted the man some years later, after learning she had the virus. He had been nonchalant.

"Ol' Boy said I should think of the disease as his 'parting gift' to me, and to all the other 'ho's—all the whores he'd messed with." Ronni raised her eyes to meet Beau's. "That bastard wasn't even remorseful."

Sorrowfully Beau shook his head. Such little that it was, he also pressed the cookies he'd bought into her hand.

Grateful, Ronni spoke as she opened the bakery bag. "I should have known though, because when Kiss, Val and I were all in college, stories about that man circulated on campus; but I had to be Ms. Fearless. Now I see I was really just little Ms. Stupid."

"But Ron," Beau had to say, "if you've known about this…since you, Kiss, and Val graduated, why did you mention it only recently? And what about all the people you've been with since college?"

Ronni felt a spark of frisson, because it really was none of Beau's business…but then again, she thought, biting into a pink frosted cookie, she did need to talk to someone.

Therefore, to unburden herself, Ronni told the truth. "Beau, I haven't been with as many people as everyone thinks. I've always used condoms too, simply because I could never do to someone else what was done to me."

Ronni said the man who had infected her, destroyed her life, "The little that I have left."

"But you're always out," Beau mused aloud, "or you used to be."

"You assumed that because I was, I was up in some man's bed." Ronni fought rising indignation, because that would only bring on another hacking fit.

"I don't want to assume," Beau softly remarked. "It's why I'm asking. Like you and Val once wanted clarity from me, about me, I'm asking for the same from you. Whether you give it is up to you; but maybe I'll better understand you, and what you're going through."

"Well," Ronni sighed, as the fight eased out of her, just that fast. "A lot of times when I was out, I was at the *library*, looking up what was going to happen to me. I couldn't read at The Quarters because the books would have given me away…nosey Val would have seen them. You know how she is, like a dog with a bone. She'd never have let me be.

"Anyway, I know you two think I don't read anything but the paper, but Diddley I could tell you so much about this disease until you'd think I was a walking encyclopedia.

"I could tell you," Ronni began, using her fingers to pontificate. "African-American women are one of the fastest growing AIDS populations.

"Diddley, I could tell you that according to statistics from UNAIDS, worldwide, more than half the adults living with this plague are women. According to Centers for Disease Control, in North America, the reported African-American AIDS cases are nine times that of white people."

Ronni sighed. "AIDS is not just a disease, Diddley. It's more like a living thing. It resides where people are poor. It thrives, regardless of race. It runs rampant in communities where there isn't a lot of access to healthcare."

"AIDS also runs amok, Diddley, among people who are misinformed, those who they think they can only get it, or HIV, from someone who obviously *looks* sick."

Shaking her head, Ronni said, "In *my* case, AIDS came about because this little yellow sista just wanted to feel good, about her self."

Beau could hardly breathe, because the truth stung. Heck, Ronni's story sounded eerily similar to his. And he had to whisper, just as his cousin had; *if not for the grace of God...* because he or *anyone* could wind up just like Ronni, with the same plight.

Unaware of her former roommate's thoughts, Ronni said that back in the day she hadn't realized that *reading* made her feel good. "I found out too late; but enough about me, my situation, and what I read."

Beau appeared stunned, and hurt. Through the emotion that clogged his throat he just had to ask, "When you weren't at the library Ron, where were you?"

"Usually at some park, I sat in the one across the street from The Quarters. I went to Bryant Park too, when I was near Forty Deuce," Manhattan's 42nd Street. "If it was warm, I sat on a bench and watched people. I took in the sights and sounds, because I knew this day was coming."

"I've seen you with men." Beau sounded accusatory, "I've seen you by yourself too, and you always seemed to be looking, on the hunt."

"Yes I was with men," Ronni retorted, "because as I said already, I was fine. You know men love a pretty face, firm tits, and a fat ass—you self-righteous sod. If a man approached me I talked. Then if it looked like...we would become intimate, I admitted I had herpes, because that's how this all started.

"I went to the doctor with a case of sores, and bam! I found out. Yep, but before that, following a botched abortion, I was told I would never have children. Yo Beau, don't give me that sad face." Ronni appeared stern. "You betta remember what I said when you 'n Kiss first came up here..."

Beau waved. "I know. You don't want pity."

"Diddley, I 'hunt' as you say," Ronni explained, "because I can't stop; I keep thinking that one day I'll spot the crud that did this to me. I have this insatiable need to know if he's dead or alive. So because I look, everywhere I go, people think I'm looking for sex." She shrugged, defeated. "Now you know; all of you, my 'friends' were wrong."

"I'm sorry Ronni." Beau reached for his former roommate's hand. "Even though you and I have had our fights, I really wish that none of this had ever happened, to you."

Her eyes filled. Feeling exhausted, she pushed her shoulders back into her pillow. Yet she held to her cookie bag. It was a small, but thoughtful gift. She also sounded worn. "Yeah Diddley, I wish that too, all the time. I also wish this would never happen to another soul. So go get tested, okay?"

With closed eyes, she yawned, feeling deflated. "It's wild out there."

Beau was aware that soon Ronni would drift off, so he would go, because she needed to rest. But he would wait until she was fully asleep because she needed strength, much more than she had, to continue to battle this thing that was eating her alive.

Summoned from his thoughts by her soft words, he listened, as sleepily she spoke.

"Don't fall head over heels for anybody, Diddley. Oh, and never neglect, or forget, to protect *you*."

Chapter 29

@T the Sinclair's three-bedroom home, Valeria René and Kismet Staar discussed buying a car.

Valeria René appeared amused. "So you're going to finally break down and spend some money, huh Kiss?" She shook her head. "I don't believe it."

"You will, tomorrow morning when I pick you up. You and I will ride to the hospital, in *my* newbie. Yep, and it sure will be nice—for once—to not have you poking fun at my ride."

Seated in Valeria René's berry-colored boudoir, Kismet Staar inquired. "What are you giggling about?"

Valeria René waved a delicate hand. "I was just wondering if the chuggy buggy gave you the ol' heave-ho."

Kismet Staar feigned interest in the Sinclair's wedding photo. Placing it back atop the bureau, again she thought the Sinclair's two-story home was beautiful, just the right mix of modern with the traditional.

There were creaky, older polished wood floors and banisters, and hand hewn beam ceilings. In the large kitchen, there were limestone countertops. The lady of the house had done a wonderful job too, of decorating and incorporating the whimsical.

Yet stuck on old Betsy, Valeria René laughed and slapped her thigh. "You got stranded, didn't you, Kiss?"

Changing the subject altogether, Kismet Staar confessed that she wanted to know where DaVon was.

Wearing a sexy black dress, Valeria René rummaged through her bureau. In less than an hour, she and her husband would meet friends for dinner and a Broadway play. Ah! She'd found the sheer stockings she'd been seeking. Seating herself at the end of her bed she spoke, crossing one leg over the other, "You mentioning *Vaughn* reminds me..."

Beginning at her foot, Valeria René rolled a stocking upward. "Two weeks ago, I was in the market, near The Quarters, shopping for Ronni.

Anyway, this guy starts toward me, a little too fast. So I got out of his way, because quite frankly, I did not feel like getting mugged that day."

Kismet Staar chuckled and Valeria René continued. "Anyway, I recalled seeing this guy, the one coming towards me. I'd seen him at The Quarters, with Ronni. At the store, he looked different though; I guess because he had his clothes on, but he said hi 'n all. He also said Vaughn got arrested."

"For what?"

"I'm trying to remember," Valeria René crossed her second leg over the first and squinted up at the ceiling. "Now what was that guy's name? Was it—"

"His *name* is of no importance, Val." Leaning forward, Kismet Staar forgot her Vanilla, soy 'ice cream.' "What's pertinent is what DaVon was jailed for."

"Assault and battery; I think, and resisting arrest."

Kismet Staar sucked her teeth, "Figures. I just wonder if DaVon used his whip. You know, the one he used at Ronni's."

"The guy at the market didn't go into details about the arrest," Valeria René admitted. "But he did say that Vaughn—not DaVon, Kiss—is gunning for Ronni. It seems he's heard about her plight. He supposedly said she'd better hope his immune system built up defenses against 'her' virus. Or else, he allegedly said, he'll have to crack her back."

Kismet Staar's eyes involuntarily narrowed and she spoke through clenched teeth. "Now that's ugly, but I would not have expected anything different from that man."

Repositioning her self on the chaise longue that was no longer purple, but now fawn-colored, and occupied the Sinclair's spacious bedroom, Kismet Staar had a thought

"Maybe I should sic my wild-behind cousins on him; talking smack."

"You mean those two that can't stay out of trouble?" Valeria René cut her eyes. "He'd hate to see them coming—Rock 'em & Sock 'em, isn't that what Ronni calls them?"

"Yep, but he should hate to play with people's feelings," Kismet Staar voiced, yet feeling a little salty that the man had not been honest with Beau. Forgetting that, she thought a moment. "Perhaps this little scare with Ronni is just the wake-up call that Vince needs. Perhaps it will aid him to stop his foolishness."

"Maybe not," Valeria René advised. "Sometimes people like *Vaughn* never stop."

Forgetting the man altogether, Kismet Staar asked a question. "Val, you think Brownie uses protection? It's not my business, but..."

Valeria René waved. "I saw a box of condoms, at The Quarters, in her room. The contents depleted over time, so…"

"Well, how did this happen?" Kismet Staar waved, and admitted she was just thinking, aloud.

"I've been thinking a lot lately too Kiss," Valeria René revealed. "I wonder, now more ever, about people's backgrounds. I've realized, again, that women should take protecting themselves very seriously."

"Listen Val…" Kismet Staar cleared her throat, and felt self-conscious about what she would say, so she rushed the words. "I'm thinking about becoming celibate."

Valeria René eyed her friend. "You think you could manage that?"

"I think so. It might be challenging, sometimes, but it might be best, for me—if Lyle and I don't last. For you it would be different because you're married. You don't necessarily have all the risks that single sisters confront."

"I was single too—hello, for a long time. And married people have issues too," Valeria René voiced. "There's infidelity, and the fact that one person could have been infected in the past. Marriage is not a cure-all Kiss. Even I, a newlywed, am aware of that."

"Oh forget all that." Kismet Staar waved, and admitted she was angry. "Every time I think that all this with Brownie could have been prevented, I feel like screaming, and crying. I feel like yelling 'do over!' Like when we were kids."

"I know," Valeria René sagely acknowledged. Spritzing her self with an obscenely sensual scent she rationalized, "But we're adults now, and this thing with Ronni is real. It can't be wished away. However, Ronni *can* have a productive life, if she takes her meds, eats right, exercises, and follows doctor's orders."

Kismet Staar shook her head. "Val, with the way you talk, anyone would know you work in the medical field; oh, and smelling that good, girl…" Kismet Staar changed the subject. "Fabian's going to eat you up."

Valeria René deliciously shivered. "That's the plan."

With a sigh, Kismet Staar reverted to the prior topic. "Val, I mentioned to Brownie the other night, that there are things she can do to re-gain weight and a modicum of health. I also mentioned that 'holistic' might be a way to go; but it was as if she didn't care. After a while, she even told me to shut my fat mouth."

"And I'll bet you threatened her, didn't you?"

"You think I didn't?"

Valeria René chuckled. Somberly then she agreed that sometimes it was almost as if those who loved Ronni were just watching her deteriorate.

"For me," she said, choking up. "The worst part is: knowing that at times she loses all hope."

Valeria René widened her eyes and waved both hands before her face so that gathering tears would not fall. "I hate knowing she used to be so energetic and spontaneous."

"Oh she's still that way, sometimes," Kismet Staar announced. "Have you seen her with Beau? She and he go at it, tit for tat. She gives it to him, he gives it right back. It's funny. Val, I swear, if I turn away while listening, Brownie sounds just like she used to."

"You know," Valeria René sighed. "I never thought I'd say this; but Diddley is good for Ronni. Their sparring has become something she needs."

Valeria René admitted that she'd initially believed Beau was mean, to Ronni. She felt he was too rough, but then he reminded her that Ronni did not want deference. Neither did she want coddling. Ronni simply wanted things to be as close as possible to the way they had once been. "Kiss, with Diddley, she gets that."

"The other day, Brownie threw a glass of water in his face."

Valeria René burst out laughing. "I heard. She called me, asking if I knew what 'that Negro' had done to her."

"Did she tell you she doused him first—dashed water right in his face, like they do on TV—because he said something she didn't like? Then he didn't say anything, he just went in her kitchen," Kismet Staar guffawed. "Diddley said he pilfered around, found a glass, and ran water—"

"Yes!" Valeria René howled with laughter. "Ronni said before she knew anything, Beau was back in the living room. He pulled her up off the sofa, and dashed that water into her face! OMG. She said at least he had the decency to make the water warm."

Kismet Staar and Valeria René squealed, just thinking about the silly scenario that had surely had mouthy Ronni sputtering.

"Oooh, stop Kiss," Valeria René near-whined as she plunked herself down at the vanity in her cozily lit *à coucher*. She examined her face in the gilded mirror, and moaned that re-hashing that stupid story had nearly ruined her makeup. "She said he dried her off..."

Kismet Staar's voice was soft, as she watched the other woman re-touch her face.

"You know, Val, I think I've always known on some level, what I am about to tell you. Now though, it might be painfully obvious, to everyone..."

"What's that?"

"Ronni adores Beau."

Valeria René dusted her face with loose powder. "Yep; it's a good thing too, because studies have shown that the terminally ill need something to live for. I believe Diddley's slowly giving our girl that. He's aiding her to find the will to live."

"You knew?" Kismet Staar appeared stunned.

Valeria René waved as she pulled her evening coat. "Yes. How would I not? I lived with those two for nearly three years. Nobody fights like they did, and nobody teases another person the way Ronni teased Diddley, unless there's more to it."

The mocha-skinned woman laid her coat, folded inside out, on the foot of her bed. She said that previously she'd only speculated on Ronni's feelings, but a particular phone conversation cemented the notion....

"Ronni called and mentioned that Diddley called her, saying he wanted to visit. It was right after you and he left here."

"Oh, after the day you hacked up a perfectly good cake?"

"Don't mention that, but yes, that was when it became most apparent to me that something was up."

Valeria René said that upon mentioning Beau, Ronni became flustered. She said she didn't want him to see her. She said he was too stupid to know that sick people weren't always as glamorous as those who were well.

Valeria René winked. "I concluded that if Ronni was worrying over her looks, for Beau, and nobody else, it was a sign."

Kismet Staar spoke, with incredulity etched on her face. "Val, you're one smart cookie."

"That I am." While placing lipstick, her driver's license, a credit card, and chewing gum in an evening clutch, Valeria René revealed something more; "Ronni's never forgiven Beau for being homosexual. That's because she loves him though, and who wouldn't? He's tall, gorgeous, caring, protective, and if you cook, he'll eat anything."

Kismet Staar frowned. "Sounds like a Great Dane to me."

Picking up her coat, Valeria René motioned for her friend to follow. Teetering on high heels with rhinestone tassels, the homeowner entered her living room. Gesturing toward her new earth-toned sofa, she said it wouldn't be long before the man of the house appeared to pick her up.

Pulling the curtain back for a peek, Valeria René reminisced on the days just before she, Kismet Staar, and Ronni graduated from Georgia's Clark-Atlanta University.

Prior to their commencement exercises, the then very young women had given one another gifts. Each gift was marked with the future time on which it was to be opened.

Valeria René mentioned her gifts, opened only last year.

Kismet Staar appeared wistful. "Val, your gift to me was marked 'your spiritual experience.' That beautiful bottle!"

Again curvaceous saw the carved glass in the eye of her mind. It had been filled with scented oil and exotic flower petals.

Valeria René revealed that the specially blended oils, in Morocco, were believed to protect against negative forces. "Kiss, I never told you this, but I held that bottle on my lap for the duration of the plane ride back to the states. So it would remain unbroken."

"I'm glad you did."

Valeria René again peered out of the front window, because she had seen headlights. "I think I wrote you were to open that gift on the evening before starting your new job, fresh out of our Historically Black College."

"I didn't cheat," Kismet Staar revealed, "and my experience truly was spiritual, as marked. I hadn't seen you or Ronni in what seemed like eons. Then I unwrapped this beautiful tissue-papered bottle, and removed it from a scrolled wooden box…"

"That box was a gift from MaMa to you."

"You told me, and I still store bath beads in it; but Val, when I opened that box and pulled away that fragrant paper...so many memories flooded back.

"I missed you and Brownie so much," Kismet Staar admitted, "until I could only stand in my bathroom and cry. I hadn't realized how much you meant to me, until then. I remembered everything we'd lived...all the studying, the parties, Ronni's mother—Ms. Minerva's death, and even our disagreements."

Dabbing her eyes with a fingertip, Kismet Staar softly spoke. "Val, when I recall what I felt that day, I wonder. Is that what you and I will feel...when...Brownie's gone?"

Valeria René turned from the window. "We just may be relieved. Lil' mama will be out of misery; *or* you never know. One of us may go before she does, but I refuse to think about any of that right now. Not when I might cry and ruin my look.

"So," Valeria René swung her arms. "I'm thinking about the gifts that you and Ronni gave me. They were marked 'for your wedding.' Hey—I always wanted to ask, did you two plan that?"

"Nope," Kismet Staar winked. "But we knew you'd get married, first. It was what you really wanted."

"In that respect, you two had a little more faith than I did," Valeria René divulged. Allowing her eyes to hide a moment behind her long lashes she sounded somewhat subdued. "Kiss, it was like back then we really knew each other, almost better than we do now. So I wonder. Did we lose some intricate part of ourselves, during this trudge that is real adult life?"

"I don't think so," Kismet Staar replied. "Sometimes life's vicissitudes and different time constraints make it seem that way. But we've still got love. We're still all in this together. Look, if we'd lost anything, you and I wouldn't be here right now. We wouldn't visit Brownie tomorrow. We would not have washed her sheets and cleaned for her. You wouldn't shop for her. We wouldn't feed her, and buy her medicine when she can't."

Headlights flashed and a vehicle eased into the driveway, and Valeria René stood, to pull on her coat.

Beneath the chill evening's indigo sky, Fabian tapped his horn.

When both women stepped out and onto the stone staircase that meandered down the sloping lawn, Valeria René locked her heavy wooden door. Then in the lantern lit darkness, she reached for her friend.

Hugging tightly, both women were aware that it was no longer a given that they would again see each other.

"If I never told you before Val," Kismet Staar whispered into her friend's decadently fragrant curls. "I love you, for ever."

Valeria René squeezed curvaceous, and parked behind Kismet Staar's old Betsy, Fabian, seated in his SUV, looked on.

"Oh Kiss, you know I love you, always."

Turning, Kismet Staar ran down the moonlit, flagstone pathway, the one lined by chrysanthemums and small solar-powered lanterns.

Upon reaching her much loved, but old, car, she looked up at the woman who gingerly navigated the stone front steps of her home.

Kismet Staar jubilantly called out, "Val, we love Ronni too!"

Clutching her purse tightly, and tipping on her high heels Valeria René shouted back. "We'll never stop!"

Moments later, with a kiss for her husband, Valeria René strapped herself in.

As Fabian backed down and out of their driveway, the new wife thought as she often did. She and her family of friends would love Ronni forever...because real, good, healthy-for-all-involved love never let go.

It did not leave.

Chapter 30

$\mathcal{B}$EAU stopped walking when he reached the corner. He knew that when the light changed, he would cross the street.

He looked up at the sky. It was a dull gray, when he'd wanted it to be blue and sunny, for Ronni who was being discharged from the hospital.

Beau put his hands in his pockets, because it was cold-ish too, when he'd wanted it to be warmer. Well, he thought, walking briskly along, it *was* November, nearly Thanksgiving in New York, so what did he expect?

His thoughts returned to Ronni. Although his former roommate did not know it yet, he was going to assist her in going home. Of course, she would protest and ask about the play. She'd ask who was doing his part in the off Broadway theatre, and he would tell the truth.

He had feigned sickness. Well, he hadn't actually *said* he was sick, but he had given that general impression. He'd let the director and others know he felt 'a little something' coming on.

They had then agreed that he'd best avert it by resting.

Therefore, he guessed, stardom, as small as his was, was not without merits. Anyway, it wasn't like he was hurting anyone, and he had promised himself, it was his first and last time to do so.

He mused on the fact that he was also aiding his understudy, because now that guy would get in an additional performance.

Beau knew however, that most understudies preferred to go on in the evenings. The crowds were larger and more prestigious then. Also, one never knew what idol-maker sat in the crowd.

Beau forgot his understudy, because come evening *he'd* be done with Ronni, and back on stage.

Entering the hospital's glass doors, Beau thought about the mouthy one. She would most likely try to pick a fight with him. Ornery and independent, she had told each of her Cohorts that she would get home just fine, alone. Well, if she started something, he would tell her to hash it out with her girlfriends. He would say so because at least *he* had showed up; unlike the girls, who'd claimed they had other commitments.

When Beau dashed into her room, Ronni appeared surprised.

"Diddley! What are you doing here?"

He stopped short. He also bent over and placed his hands on his knees. "Downstairs, they told me I'd probably missed you," he huffed, slightly out of breath. He stood, and nodded at the orderly waiting to push Ronni's wheelchair to the elevator. "I'm glad I didn't dally; so if you're all set, I'll accompany you back downstairs."

At ground level, Beau hailed a cab. Then he placed Ronni's overnight bag in the trunk, and made sure she was safely in. Racing around the rear, he got in on the opposite side and made himself comfortable.

Ronni gave her address. After doing so she faced Beau. "Why'd you come?"

He turned from the rapidly passing scenery outside his window. "You mean despite you saying you didn't want anyone 'fussing' over you?"

Not amused, Ronni snapped, "Just answer the question, Diddley. Why are you here?"

Beau opened his window a smidgen. "Well, let's see." He acted as though he had to think about it. "I guess I remembered that you once claimed you had no friends.

"Yes and," he raised a forefinger to silence her. "I also came because I'm a *man*, not some house boy you can easily order around. I go where I want."

"Even where you're not wanted?"

"You know you want me girl," Beau teased and gently touched the shoulder of his brown suede to Ronni's navy pea coat.

When she did not reply, Beau explained that both Kiss and Val were occupied, perhaps working. "Ronni, I chose to come, so you'd have someone with you when you were discharged." He peered out of his window. "Argue though, and I'll shove you from this car."

Ronni bit her tongue. She wondered why Beau cared. It wasn't like she had been a good friend, lately. She hadn't even been all that nice *before* she'd become visibly ill. The truth was she didn't know how.

"Look Ron," Beau began, because he knew she was thinking, too hard. He also knew that the cab driver was most likely listening because he had slowed down, considerably. Therefore, Beau lowered his voice.

"Ron, you've been a real little turd, some of the time, but when somebody loves you, they see about you. People do things for you, even when you say not to. They do it because they want to. Remember that, and just say 'thank you.' Mean it, and be gracious."

When Ronni spoke, her eyes were closed, and her heart hammered harder than it had the other night. The night she'd thought she would surely die. "Beau, what makes you love me?"

"I don't know." He sounded agitated. "I just do."

With her eyes yet closed, and her heart hammering away, Ronni admitted, "Diddley, I've longed to hear those words from you, for so long..."

She scrunched her eyes tighter. "They didn't sound like I imagined, though."

Looking out of his window, Beau slowly swiveled to face his friend. Why had she said that? He wondered. Ohhh... Cognition dawned.

Oh no! Beau's eyes darted hither and yon because how was he to tread lightly? How could he say what he needed to, without shattering the woman who had already been smashed to bits?

Shoot! Suddenly he wished he had gone to work.

Yet his conscience advised him to *man-up*, because he was present; therefore, he had to answer the woman whose eyes were scrunched shut.

Realizing that Ronni was nervous too caused Beau to feel somewhat better, he also recognized that it had taken as much for her to ask her question as it would for him to answer.

Gingerly he spoke. "Ron, the reason my 'I love you' isn't like you imagined, is because...babe, it's not like you imagined. But maybe, this way it's better."

Ronni remained silent, with eyes closed.

"Veronica," Beau continued. "I love you, as you are, for the woman that you are, but my love isn't the sleeping-with-you kind."

Beau prayed she understood, even as he noticed the cabbie.

Although driving, the man attempted to pay rapt attention.

Seeing this, Beau could have Karate-chopped him in the neck, with his nosey self. Instead he forgot the driver, to focus on Ronni. He took her very thin hand. "Please say you understand."

She swallowed, and Beau noticed her wet lashes.

"I didn't want it to be like this," she whined. "I wanted so much more, you know?"

"I know." Beau nodded, and admitted that he felt somewhat flattered, "But you *know* my situation..."

Curious, the cabbie glanced back.

"Yo, mind your business," Beau barked. "Keep your eyes on the road."

Yet with her eyes closed, Ronni opened her mouth, but no words came. She knew what she wanted to say, but then again, maybe she didn't.

Feeling slightly uncomfortable, Beau noted the cars that whizzed past them on the nearly leafless, tree-lined parkway. He told the cabbie to speed up.

'This ain't no soap opera, man,' he wanted to yell, 'so don't drag this ride out.' However, he simply said, "Cabbie...we need to discontinue passing everything in slow motion."

That got the motorist going.

Ronni again closed her eyes. "Driver, please take the North exit. Turn right at the first light." She felt like her heart had been gouged out. She felt like she had, all those times when she'd watched Beau and Valeria René being so chummy. And she hated it.

Ronni felt like a real fool, loving a man who would never love her back, because... he loved *men*. She wondered why *she* had all the rotten luck, when it seemed *other* people got everything. Suddenly, she wished she were by her self, so she could cry her eyes out.

Oh well. Since she wasn't alone, she moved. She made sure that no part of Beau touched any part of her. Since he didn't want her, she didn't want his shoulder, his knee, or any bit of him making contact with her.

"Don't pout," Beau advised. "It's ugly, and childish. Oh, and face that this is our problem." He had spoken quietly, but nevertheless loudly enough to be heard over the angry churn of Ronni's thoughts.

"I," he pounded his chest, "can, and have, accepted you for the multiplicity of things that you are; but you only see one part of me. And you try to make that part the whole."

"For crying out loud," Ronni snapped, her eyes flying open. "Don't beat on your chest like an ape, and don't tell me what I do."

Beau's fingers crept up to find his dog tags, because if he didn't finger them, he would strangle Ronni, *and* the nosey-assed cabbie.

"Look girl," Beau quietly snarled. "I will only say this once! Quit seeing my sexuality. Yes," he growled when Ronni shook her head. "Stop it. Think of me as Beau, or even as a man, or as your friend, but quit allowing my private life to be all you focus on. Don't be so close-minded. Get past stuff, for once."

"How can I?" Ronni cried out because she sincerely wanted to. Then maybe she could finally dislodge Beau from her heart.

"Think about other people," Beau commanded through clenched teeth. "When they tell you their religion is different from yours, you don't keep pondering it. When you interact with people whose political persuasions differ, you don't give them grief. When people think differently than you do, about racial issues, you don't scorn those people as you have scorned me."

Beau also told Ronni that when people's views on drink and drugs differed from hers, she gave those people slack. "But me..." again he pounded his chest, "me you pigeonhole and hurt; me you keep in a box."

Still with the ape crap, Ronni thought and rolled her eyes.

"With me you go ballistic." Beau spoke on, "And you *know* me. You've spent countless hours with me; yet you fail to see *me*, and I'm tired of it."

In silence, Ronni considered Beau's words, before she said, "When we get to my place, you stay in here, okay? Don't follow me upstairs, because I need to be alone. I can't take any more of you today."

"Look, I'll leave when I see that you're safely settled," Beau announced, "after I've carried your bag.

"There," he also pointed out, because he had to make her see. "That's what you do. It's part of your problem. You're too darn bossy."

Beau informed Ronni that she couldn't keep a man—gay or straight— "You wanna know why? Because *no man* wants to be bossed around, all the time! It's friggin' emasculating."

Leaning back, with folded arms, Ronni watched two people in a car in the next lane. They appeared to be in a heated argument. Guess today was the day for it.

Knowing Beau watched her, she grumbled that she did not need a babysitter.

"Yeah, yeah." He spoke to his grouchy friend, in earnest, "Ronni, understand one thing. I came to see you safely home. I took time out of my ever-growing busier schedule for one reason, alone. I know you.

"I take your shi—your *abuse* because I'm finally learning you. I'm beginning to understand you; you're funky and moody, but that's okay."

Seeing the dull gray day, Ronni felt melancholy, and much less like acknowledging that Beau spoke to her.

Regardless, he told his former roommate that although she'd erected an emotional wall of toughness, he knew differently. He knew that inside she felt small sometimes, and afraid. He said that he'd thought about it, and he'd realized something more; that her mother had died alone.

Jerking to face him, Ronni hissed, "You keep Minerva Brown out of your mouth!"

Ignoring the kitten and her little bared claws, Beau spoke on. He said that because Ms. Minerva had died alone, Ronni thought *she* should go the same way. "It *could* be the reason why you act so ugly when anyone tries to care for you. No, just listen," Beau advised. "Since you feel you weren't good, to your mother, or to anyone for that matter, you feel like no one should actually be good to you."

Beau explained that Ronni acted ugly because she didn't want to find herself dependent on anyone. "Somewhere deep inside, you really believe your friends will desert you when you need them most, like you nearly deserted your mother."

Even though Ronni's eyes were shut tightly and her mouth balled into an angry kewpie knot, Beau continued.

He even told the little yellow woman that she wanted to believe she had more than friendship-love for him because he was *safe* to love. Beau said his sexuality made him unavailable, "Sort of like your father was for most of your young life. That's why you've become fixated on me."

Beau explained that studies showed that adults often re-enacted love-patterns similar to those they had seen as children. Therefore, it was natural, Beau stated, for Ronni to seek men who were unable to commit.

"But you've got to quit doing that. Like I've got to stop," Beau said, more to himself, "getting involved with people who are abusive," like his mother Ophelia had been.

"It's a wonder," he also cogitated aloud, "that you aren't into married men."

Remaining quiet, Ronni was not about to let Beau know that she had traveled that road, and had found it a dead end.

Riding along and surveying all they passed, Beau told Ronni to let old hurts go.

"Pray, go to church, see a shrink, or better yet, ask Jesus into your heart. Whatever you do," Beau beseeched, "make peace, with yourself, and your life. Face that it hasn't turned out like you thought it would. Then make the rest of your life the best of your life. Live like you're going to die tomorrow. Live on purpose. That means do all you can, all you want to, today."

Beau leaned forward, noticing that the cabbie was pulling to a stop before the park. Reaching in his pocket, Beau also noted the dry leaves that danced airborne in the chill afternoon air.

Ronni sounded choked as she spoke. "I don't need you to pay."

Peeling off a few bills, Beau ignored her. Speaking to the cabbie, he said, "Here you go, chief. Keep the change." Then to Ronni he said, "Wait for me to open your door." When she put out a hand, he became stern. "Yo, you heard me. Keep yourself in here."

Normally she would have ignored any order from any man, yet Ronni remained. Quickly she also tried to dry her tears. She didn't want Beau, who was outside, to know they'd started when he'd touched the very heart of her with his words.

Looking up, to glance at herself in the rearview mirror, she noticed the cabbie.

Gazing back at her, he sympathetically smiled.

With his curly black hair sticking out at angles beneath his cap, and with his smooth brown face, he reminded her of Valeria René. And Ronni did what to her seemed the strangest thing. She smiled back.

Beneath the tumultuous sky, Beau grabbed Ronni's bag from the trunk. Then he dashed around to hurriedly get her out of the wind. "Upsy daisy," he said, and gently eased her from the car.

She realized then that he really was a good person, and one day he would indeed be the best father, to that child he wanted.

Thumping on the roof, Beau let the driver know that he could safely proceed.

"Don't look at me," Ronni griped, since she wasn't like the ever mothering Kismet Staar who always carried tissues. Having been unable to completely dry her face, she felt semi ashamed.

Noticing that she'd been crying, Beau placed an arm around her and squeezed. Then he allowed her to set the pace as they crossed the street.

He smelled so nice, Ronni thought, cocooned against him. He always did, this warm loving friend of hers.

At the old building, he held the lobby door open and gestured for her to hand over her apartment keys. On worn marble, he started up the steps before her and he thought, man! Something sure smelled good. He called over his shoulder that he would probably stop at his old neighbors' on his way back out. "Yep, because it seems like Mrs. Nunley is in her pots today!"

Ronni nearly smiled, because the man whose voice echoed, would eat anything.

At The Quarters, Beau waited for Ronni to arrive before he unlocked her door. Then standing aside, he pushed it open, and frowned, as did she, because that delicious cooking smell was wafting out of *her* apartment!

Timidly Ronni stepped inside and thought back. She didn't remember leaving any lights on. Then again, she had been rushed to the hospital, so who knew?

She stopped just across her threshold, noticing. The place was warm, and it felt lived in, again, but she never really turned on the heat. She couldn't afford to. She tried to save her money for more pressing things.

Also, Christmas music, with a gospel flavor played. Ronni craned her neck, and saw that in her dining room where there had been no table, there was one. It was set with linen, festive red bows, china, candles, glassware, and cutlery. The whole scene looked like one torn from the pages of one of Val's or Kiss' decorating magazines.

With her eyes darting back and forth, Ronni realized there was something very strange going on...

Entering the apartment, Beau asked who her little elves were.

Ronni's heart hammered as she admitted she did not know.

"Well whoever they are," Beau nodded, and placed her bag by the door. "I love them. Got this place feeling and looking like a home again."

Before Ronni had the chance to feel flustered, women appeared.

"Hey-aay," they merrily sang out. "Welcome home!"

"Hey Diddle Diddle."

Ronni found it easy to smile, through her tears, because there was silly Kismet Staar. She wore a lovely, cashmere turtleneck and slate gray trousers, over which she had tied on a Santa Claus apron.

There was Valeria René too. She'd slung a kitchen towel over the shoulder of her cute pumpkin-colored corduroy dress.

So *this* was why they hadn't appeared at the hospital, Beau mused.

"I guess you didn't go to work Val," Ronni surmised, because the curly-locked one appeared too weekend-ish, with her flat boots on.

"You guessed right. Hello honey." Valeria René approached with a kiss and a hug. "Hi Diddley." She hugged him too; "My beautiful beau."

Curvaceous Kismet Staar took Ronni in her arms. "Hello baby."

Bursting into full-blown tears, the thin sickly woman held tightly to her dear sister-friend.

Crying uncontrollably, Ronni could never have said that seeing her home this way, and just being embraced by the ample-bosomed Kismet Staar felt so right. To Ronni all felt as though she had returned, to some place warm, some place where she was loved and treasured, and the very thought made her cry even harder.

"Ohhh, baybeee..." Kismet Staar cooed, while hugging her friend. "Everything's all right booby." She rubbed Ronni's back. "It's okay Brownie, we're here. We're all here for you."

Standing aside, Beau and Valeria René sympathetically watched. Both were aware that there were a great many things that small Ronni Brown needed to cry out. And what better place to do it, Beau mused, than in the arms of someone who truly cared?

When Ronni no longer cried, Kismet Staar walked her to the ivory sofa. Helping Ronni to be seated, Kismet Staar reached for a pretty fringed throw.

Now where had that come from? Ronni wondered. One of her sister friends must have brought it, she mused, when they'd brought the table, the settings, the homemade food, and who knew what all else.

"I let us in with my key," Valeria René announced, re-entering the living room.

Bending over, she placed a steaming mug of coffee in Ronni's hands. "Its fresh and hot MaMa, and it'll warm you right up, because I know it was chilly outside."

Ronni inhaled, allowing the inviting scent to take her back, to all the Sundays spent together, days when she and her friends had bickered over the paper—*her* Sunday paper. Well really *their shared* paper.

"I love you guys," she admitted, as tears steadily fell from her eyes.

Ronni looked at Beau. "Even you," she said, and smiled—and this new smile didn't feel strange, at all.

"Yeah, yeah," Beau waved, although he felt warmed from the inside out. "I guess I could love you too, a little bit."

Turning to Kismet Staar he said, "I know you cooked, and Val cleaned. If Val knows what's best, she'd better have a new cheesecake for me too; betta have it somewhere—to replace the one she destroyed."

Tickled, Valeria René squealed, "Diddley you must be psychic!"

"More like psych*o*," Kismet Staar mumbled and bustled off to the kitchen.

Curvaceous forgot the other two to inform Ronni that she'd cooked rice, black-eyed peas, fresh turnip greens, cornbread, and succulent roast chicken with gravy. She said she'd started the meat and the greens at her home in Elmont on last evening after leaving the farmers market. "Then I worked half a day, and brought everything over."

"Well, *I* had to take a comp day," Valeria René admitted. "I had to have my new brother-in-law and my sister's husband bring this dining set—Fabian's old set—up, before they went to work."

Curly locks waved at Ronni. "And girl, you needed some living room chairs!" Valeria René turned and saw Kismet Staar carrying laden dishes into the now festive dining room. "Oh-oh. I'd better help."

"I think I'll wash up," Beau said and stood, in the living room that nearly felt like it once had.

Yet warmly wrapped, Ronni eyed him with both her thin hands around her coffee mug. "Did you know about all of this?"

"No, I did not," he truthfully replied, "but I'm happy as heck about it, because now I get to eat, real food, and not my own pitiful attempts at cooking."

"If the buzzer sounds, that'll be Fabian," Valeria René called from the kitchen. "Or it may be Drew. My new hubby and brother-in-law want some of Kiss' cuisine."

When the foursome sat, at Ronni's 'new' dining table, beneath the chandelier—that sparkled, Ronni looked around. It seemed every corner of her home was clean and cozily glowing, when for so long it had been dark, and lonely, like a cave.

Ronni gazed upon the lit tapers in the floral centerpiece, and she heard Val's Christmas music playing softly in the background.

Suddenly Ronni realized, she even felt like eating, when previously she had only felt like wasting away.

"I don't know why you guys did this," she began. Then she remembered; Beau said people did things because they wanted to. Therefore, she took a deep breath, and graciously said, "But thank you."

Surprisingly, she genuinely meant it. Something else he had taught her.

Following the blessing of the food, as her Cohorts passed burdened dishes and platters around, Kismet Staar said she had an announcement to make.

Ronni looked up from tasting the greens and cornbread that were divine. "I have one too."

Kismet Staar deferred, "Okay, you first."

"Well..." Ronni took a deep breath. "I'm going back to work, in Manhattan. I'll be working for the Gay Men's Help Center, the GMHC. I interviewed before I went into the hospital this last time.

"They know my situation, but that didn't deter a man named Curtis Hurst from hiring me, as a consultant. I'm going to travel, to schools, colleges, and other places, to warn people about the dangers of unprotected sex. I will have to speak on prevention, early detection, treatment, and things of that nature.

"The organization gave me lots of literature you guys. So when I'm done studying, I'm gonna need to practice my speeches on you, because I'll be the liaison between Gay Men's and the community.

"They and I have also contacted other AIDS and AIDS prevention foundations and organizations. We've got things in the works."

Ronni looked at the astonished faces of those at the table. "So, what do you guys think?"

They all spoke at once. "I think it's great!"

"You're getting out."

"—Doing something meaningful."

"Good for you, Brownie!"

"You go, lady."

Absolution

"What made you do this?"

Ronni laid her fork down, as she noted the softly playing *O Come All Ye Faithful*.

She sighed, because all of this was overwhelming, her friends, the food, the furniture. Yet she said, "I'll answer one question, before my cornbread gets cold. I'm doing this…because of Diddley."

Beau's head jerked up. "Me? What do I have to do with anything?"

"You're mean," Ronni grinned, "but you keep inspiring me, to be better, not bitter. You even told me not to be so closed-minded. You told me too, a few times, that I should make the best of things. You said I should act like I'ma die tomorrow—"

"Beau!" The others gasped. "That *was* mean."

"Cluck, cluck, you old hens," he waved, and kept on eating.

Wanting to laugh, Ronni continued. "Leave him alone, because I needed what he said. Anyway, now I'd like to keep at least one person a week from going through what I've experienced—if I can."

Touched, Beau looked up, as it became Kismet Staar's turn to speak.

Standing, she announced it was good that Ronni had given her news first, "Because my news may even assist you Brownie, in life and in your new job." Kismet Staar took a deep breath. "You guys know I bought a new car, right?"

"About time," somebody mumbled around a mouth full of food.

"Anyway…" Kismet Staar ignored the snide remark. "You guys thought I traded old Betsy in—"

"Bet you didn't get much for her," someone interjected, followed by the laughter of someone else.

"Listen! Will you?" Kismet Staar pounded on the table, and made silver and china jump. "You clowns ruin everything."

She sat, and turned. "Brownie, forget them. I'll talk to you. I used part of the equity in a piece of property to purchase my new car. The other part I put into investment high-yield vehicles so that I can get that money and more back, but I hung onto old Betsy—for you! That is, if you'll accept her…"

"But Grandma Lacey gave *you* that car," Ronni protested, despite feeling overjoyed.

"Grandma Lacey would love for *you* to now have Betsy," Kismet Staar nodded. "I know it.

"For me," Beau's cousin admitted, "old Bets was a way to stay connected, to someone I loved—my grandmother. So now, I'd like you to have Betsy, so you can stay connected, to me, to us."

Kismet Staar reached in her pocket for the keys. "Take her. Lyle," the sexy dancer, the engineer, "drove her over for me. Brownie, I bought new tires, and I had Betsy's windshield and wipers replaced. I even splurged and had the front seats re-covered. That old girl runs well. She's sturdy. She'll never put you down..."

"Oh Kiss!" Ronni flew out of her chair. Wrapping her twig-like arms around Kismet Staar, she said, "I'd be honored to drive her."

Kismet Staar smiled broadly while rubbing Ronni's back.

"But you could've left the seats alone," Ronni chuckled when she re-took her seat. "I mean my friends will need something to talk about when—in keeping with tradition—I force them to ride with me."

"I never forced one of you to ride with me," Kismet Staar retorted.

"That's a lie—if I ever heard one!"

"Hush up, Diddley."

Valeria René smirked. "I wanna get back to Veronica talking 'bout she got friends. That's news to me."

"She ain't got no friends." Beau waved and guffawed, "But as one of her non-friends, I am going to ride with her, and talk about them seats." This he promised with a wink, "Because we all know: that snagged vinyl is still under that phony cover-up, and we all know something else." Appearing disdainful, he shook his head. "It just tears up a girl's stockings!"

Valeria René squealed with laughter. "That's exactly what Ronni said! Didn't she, Kiss? Many times."

"Yeah, yeah," Ronni buttered her second piece of cornbread, and inside she smiled, because she had just realized something. In life, some things changed, while others remained the same. Those things included her silly friends—and they really were her friends.

But these people were more than that. Her Cohorts were her *family*. They had loved her through thick and thin, in sickness, and in health.

They had also granted her *absolution*. Kiss, Val, and Diddley had truly forgiven her, dismissing her ugly actions. Not one held a thing against her. And surprisingly, *she* too had forgiven them. She held nothing against them.

Sure, previously she'd felt like the ladies had done her wrong by remaining friendly with Beau, after 'the incident.' Ronni recalled severely hating on him for a while... Yet now she remembered what Val had once said.

Love grants *absolution*.

The morning that they'd all shared their inner most feelings, the morning after Beau's show, Val had also said that Love pardons a person who has done wrong. She said Love forgave, and found a way to remain...

Well would you look at that? Ronni thought, as she glanced around her new table. Little Val had been so right. Love really did remember.

"Kiss..." Ronni called, suddenly feeling more jubilant than she had in forever. "Please pass that delicious chicken—and for crying out loud, will somebody get the door?!"

If you enjoyed

Absolution

Book I of **The Cohort Trilogy,**
then find yourself immersed, in

Progression
Book II of **The Cohort Trilogy**.

See how the Cohorts have progressed. See if they've
changed—for better, or for worse…

_____

Then meet them again
in

Iniquities

Book III - The Cohort Trilogy closer.

See if the wild ride that is Beau's life will finally tear his
fragile family of friends apart!

_____

Also...

Meet The Cohorts again in the newest trilogy! Look for it in paperback and e-book.

Photo: Tina Dennis ©

Author, editor,
April Alisa Marquette
Loves penning fiction, as well as non-fiction.
A patron of art and literature, she is committed to writing
beautifully detailed works about people of color and others.
Ever working on something,
she is currently putting the finishing touches on
one of the novels in her *Sea Isles Series*.
Visit her at www.aprilalisamarquette.net

Desire good fiction?

Break up with your significant other, get another.
Go to a little known isle, where all hell breaks loose…
Get through the bayou, but don't sink in the swamp. Do not become
alligator feed. Do it all under a sobbing sky, just before you take refuge
in a cemetery. Then, pray! Cry loud;
spare not in asking for help to come,
and ask for it soon, *or else…*

All in the scintillating mystery

Exodus

by
April Alisa Marquette

Book I of the *Sea Isles Series*, a trilogy

www.ingramcontent.com/pod-product-compliance
Lightning Source LLC
Chambersburg PA
CBHW020443270626
47155CB00022B/1211